DON'T WAKE UP

DON'T WAKE UP

A NOVEL

LIZ LAWLER

HARPER

An Imprint of HarperCollins*Publishers*

HarperCollins books may be purchased for educational, business, or sales promotional use. For information, please email the Special Markets Department at SPsales @harpercollins.com.

Originally published as *Don't Wake Up* in Great Britain in 2017 by Twenty7 Books.

FIRST EDITION

Library of Congress Cataloging-in-Publication Data has been applied for.

ISBN 978-0-06-288622-4 (library edition)
ISBN 978-0-06-287613-3 (pbk.)

19 20 21 22 23   LSC   10 9 8 7 6 5 4 3 2 1

CHAPTER ONE

It was the familiar sounds that awakened her. They were strangely comforting, even though her first instinct was to leap up in panic to see what her colleagues were doing. She heard instruments being placed on a steel tray. Monitors emitted regular beeps, sterile packages were torn open, and in the background there was the ever-present hiss of oxygen.

She could see the scene clearly in her mind and knew she must get up, but the pull of sleep was strong and her limbs felt too heavy to move. She couldn't remember climbing onto one of the unoccupied trolleys, but she must have done it at some time during the night to get an hour or two of sleep. Normally she would have been woken by a call from the red telephone, or the persistent screech of the transceiver. These urgent calls would normally have meant she was up and running even before her eyes were open. But this sleep had made her feel sluggish, and raising her heavy eyelids felt like unfolding thickened skin.

Bright light blinded her, her eyes watered and she had to squint against its glare. It was punishingly harsh and she could barely make out its outline. Confusion mixed with alarm alerted her to her surroundings. She wasn't in a cubicle. They didn't have lights like this in her department; they were small overhead lamps that could be covered with the palm of a hand. *She wasn't in her own department; she was in theatre.* Why on earth was she here? Surely she hadn't wandered up *here* for a kip. *Think.* Had she helped out with a trauma? Had they been short of a pair of hands? It would be highly unlikely, but not inconceivable. She focused her eyes downwards, and then froze. She shivered violently as she saw her body covered in green theatre drapes. The sounds of the theatre were silenced, the rush of blood in her ears too noisy to allow her to hear anything else. Her arms were extended and held down with Velcro on the upholstered armrests. A blood pressure cuff was wrapped around her arm above her right elbow, and a pulse oximeter probe was attached to her middle finger. Yet it was the sight of the two large cannulas inserted in both forearms that scared her most. Orange needles meant aggressive fluid restoration, which in her world spelt shock.

The drip lines snaked up around metal IV poles and out of view to the bags of fluid. She could see the heavy bottoms of clear fluid bags suspended above, but could only guess at the fluid being transfused.

She focused lower, past the green drapes on her chest and abdomen, and then panicked as she saw her painted pink toenails raised in the air. Her thighs, she realised, were spread, her calves supported on knee troughs and her ankles held in stirrups – she was lying on a theatre table with her legs up. From her dry mouth and foggy mind she realised she had just woken not from a natural sleep, but one induced by anaesthesia.

'Hello?' she called to attract the attention of the person handling the instruments. The clatter of steel against steel went on uninterrupted; unnerved, she called louder, 'Hello? I'm awake.'

Given the circumstances, she was amazed how calm she felt. She was frightened and anxious, but beneath this her professional knowledge allowed her to think through what might have happened as she lay waiting for an explanation.

She'd finished her shift for the evening. Her memory retrieved her last conscious thought ... Walking through the staff car park in her new floaty dress and pink shoes, to meet Patrick. This memory reassured her that she must have had an accident. Champagne and roses, she thought. That's what he had promised her after her long day at work. Champagne and roses, and, if she had read him right, a marriage proposal.

Where was he now? Outside pacing a corridor no doubt, anxiously waiting to hear how she was. Ready to pounce on anyone who could give him an answer. Had she been knocked down, she wondered? A car pulling out too quickly, perhaps, that she hadn't noticed in her eagerness to see Patrick's car?

A vague recollection filtered through of tottering along in her impossibly high heels, chest stuck out, tummy pulled in to show off her figure to its best advantage in the new dress. And then a wave of dizziness which buckled her legs and slammed her knees to the ground, a pain to the crook of her neck, a pressure on her mouth, no air, gagging and then ... nothing.

Gut-wrenching fear gripped, and her breathing turned ragged as she fought the panic. How seriously injured was she?

Was she dying? Was that why no one was around her? Had they simply left her here to die?

Her training and instincts kicked in. Primary survey. Do the checks. ABCDE. No, stay with ABC first. Her airway was clear. No oxygen mask or nasal cannula were attached to her. She was breathing spontaneously, and as she breathed in deeply she felt no discomfort. Circulation? Her heart was pounding hard and loud. She could hear it on a monitor close by. But why then were her legs spread? Was she bleeding? Pelvic fractures could be the most serious traumas. Big uncontrollable bleeders. But if that was the case, where were all the worried surgeons? Why hadn't they banded her pelvis and stabilised it?

'Hello, can you hear me?' she now demanded less pleasantly.

The sound of clanking instruments ceased. She moved her head gingerly and was not surprised to find head blocks and a neck collar holding her still. They had yet to rule out the possibility of a cervical spine injury. She began to seethe. Who the fuck was looking after her? She wanted to give him or her a piece of her mind. To allow her to wake up alone was bad enough, but for her to then find her head and arms strapped down and her legs stuck up in the air was an outrage. She could have done untold damage to herself if she'd panicked or ripped off the contraptions that were keeping her safe.

She could hear the sound of clogs moving towards her on the hard floor. Then, floating into her peripheral vision, she saw bluey-green material, someone wearing a surgical gown. She caught a glimpse of a pale neck and the edge of a white facemask, but the rest of the face – the nose and eyes – were above the bright lights, making it impossible for her to see properly.

She felt tears suddenly gather in her eyes and laughed harshly. 'I hate bloody hospitals.' Her visitor stayed still and silent, bringing fresh fear to her overactive mind. 'Sorry about the waterworks. I'm OK now. Look, just give me the facts. Life-threatening? Life-changing? I take it you know I work here, that I'm a doctor, so please don't give me the diluted version. I'd rather know the truth.'

'Nothing's happened to you.'

The voice jolted her, sounding like it came through a speaker system. She blinked in confusion. Was the person beside her speaking to her, or was someone speaking to her from behind an observation screen? Was she in the CT scanner room and not in a theatre? The voice belonged to a man, but not one she recognised. It was none of the surgeons she knew. She squinted up at the masked face. 'Are you the doctor or are they in another room? Are we in the scanner room?'

'I'm the doctor.'

Christ, her hearing was all wrong. He sounded like he was speaking beside her, yet the voice sounded distant, like a telephone voice. Why didn't he turn off the bloody lights and take off his mask and talk to her properly? Hold her hand, even? She sighed agitatedly. 'So you haven't found anything wrong with me?'

'There isn't anything wrong with you.'

Impatiently, her voice rang louder. 'Look, can we rewind here? Why exactly am I lying here and why was I brought in? What does my casualty card say?'

'You know, you really shouldn't get yourself so worked up. Your heart is racing. Your breathing is erratic and your oxygen levels are only ninety-four per cent. Do you smoke?'

Her eyes darted to the cardiac monitor on a trolley beside her. She could see the trailing wires and knew they were attached to electrodes on her chest.

'Look, I don't mean to be rude. You've probably had a long day, but I'm a bit pissed off that I've woken up to find myself alone. Now just so we're clear, I'm not going to make a complaint, but I do want to know who you are. I want your name and I want to know what's going on, right now.'

'Well, Alex,' he said, raising purple-gloved hands in the air which held a surgical stapler. 'Just so we're both clear. Right now, if you don't keep a civil tongue I'll be inclined to staple your lips together. You have a pretty mouth. It will be a shame to ruin it.'

A wave of terror instantly hollowed out her stomach. Muscles rigid, eyes open, her thoughts, her anger and her voice were paralysed.

'Temper isn't going to help you here,' he stated calmly.

Champagne and roses, she thought. Think of that. Patrick. Think of him.

'That's better.' She could hear a smile in his voice. 'I can't work with noise.'

Scenarios played like a film on fast forward in her head. She was in the hospital somewhere. Someone would find her. Someone would hear her scream. This was a madman. A patient on the loose. A doctor? Or someone impersonating one? He had obviously taken control of one of the theatres and she . . . she had somehow stumbled across him. Her mouth, the pressure she had felt. The gagging after she dropped to her knees in the car park . . . He had brought her in here.

He had hit her and then gagged her, with a cloth. He must have anaesthetised her. Chloroform or ether . . .

'Please don't scream,' he said, reading her mind. 'We're quite alone and I really don't want to resort to silencing you. I have a headache as it is. Cold wind always gives me one. Surprised you haven't got one, wearing so little on a cold night like tonight.'

She was instantly aware of her nakedness beneath the green drapes. Her exposed breasts and vagina, her bottom slightly raised in the air and her calf muscles beginning to spasm from the unnatural position they were in.

Patrick. Think of him or anything else apart from being here – Mum, work, the patient who died today. The people who would be looking for her. *Think, Alex.* Rationalise with him. Engage his mind. Say what she was. Who she was. Humanise herself. Isn't that what the textbooks taught? She had practised many times what she'd learned from them. First rule: acknowledge your patient's anger. Second rule: defuse it.

'My name is Alex and I'm a doctor.'

He calmly replied, 'Are you aware you have a retroverted uterus? While removing your coil I had to use a curved speculum.'

Stunned, she could only gape at him. He had already done things to her. While she lay unconscious his hands had been inside her.

Think, she instructed herself. Think this through before it's too late and this is all over. Be nice to him. Make him like you. Try, for fuck's sake, she lectured herself sternly as her tongue lay like a thick slug inside her mouth.

'Th-thank you for doing that. Not everyone would be so considerate.'

'You're welcome.'

His response gave her a tiny glimpse of hope. It was working. They were talking. She hadn't actually seen his face and he probably knew that. She could tell him she didn't know what he looked like and she would forget about whatever he had already done to her. No harm done. He could walk away.

'I wonder,' she said carefully, 'if you would let me up to use the toilet?'

'No need.' His purple-gloved hands disappeared beneath the green drapes and touched her naked skin. She flinched. 'Steady,' he advised as he palpated her lower abdomen. 'Your bladder's empty. I already catheterised you. Output's good.'

'Why have you done that?'

'Major procedure, Alex,' he said, using her name with the familiarity of two colleagues working side by side. 'It will be painful for you to urinate normally for a while.'

Despite herself, a deep sob shuddered from her chest and the sound of her desperate cry filled the room.

'What have you done to me?'

'I already told you. Nothing has happened to you. Yet. The decision is yours. You simply have to answer this question: What does "no" mean?'

Her thoughts scattered as she tried to make sense of the question. Know what? Know him? What the hell was he asking her?

'These, for instance.' He held up her pale pink sandals with their long stemmed heels and delicate straps, which she knew would turn Patrick on, even though they were impossible to walk in. 'Do these mean no? And what of these?' Her stockings were dangled over her face. 'They surely don't mean no. When I undressed you, you weren't wearing a bra and your panties were hardly big enough to make a small handkerchief.'

Her ankles pulled hard against the leather straps, binding them tighter as she tried to draw her knees together. She understood exactly what he was asking. 'Please,' she begged. 'Don't.'

'It's a simple question, Alex. I think we both know what you mean when you say "no", don't we?'

Hatred overrode her fear, and for a moment she felt free and brave. She spluttered as she angrily spat the words. 'I don't understand the question, you fucker. And my oxygen levels are low because of what you gave me. You need to go back to your books. Are you a failed quack? Is that it, fuckhead?'

She heard the intake of breath, the mild tut of annoyance beneath the mask. 'Temper, temper. That isn't going to help you. You've just made me decide.'

He turned to the side and pulled forward a gleaming stainless steel trolley holding an array of instruments, all of which she was familiar with. IUCD hook, uterine scissors, a Cusco vaginal speculum, and beside these an anaesthetic mask. Her body went rigid with fear as she saw him pick it up. A Schimmelbusch. The only time Alex had seen one of these before was in a glass cabinet in the study of a retired anaesthetist. It reminded her of the type of mask worn in fencing, a protective device that covered the nose and mouth. Only this was a cruder version: the size of a grapefruit, it consisted of a cradle of thin wire with gauze woven between so that liquid anaesthetic could be dropped onto it and soaked up before being inhaled by the wearer.

'Open circuit,' he calmly said. 'You can't beat the old-fashioned method. No airway to insert. No anaesthetic machine to monitor. Just gauze and a mask. And gas, of course, leaving your hands free to do other things.'

Her bravery had fled. Her control collapsed. There was no reasoning. There was no escape. He could do what he liked to her and she couldn't stop him. Fleetingly, she wondered if it would be better if she died on the table. She could leave life behind without ever knowing it had ended.

'On the other hand, if I knock you out, it stops you and me from talking. You never know, I may need your help if things get tricky. I could give you a mirror and you can direct me if I have a problem. A vulvectomy can be a tad messy.'

Her breathing was too fast and too shallow. Her head was beginning to tingle as she fixated on the mask in his hand. She couldn't breathe. She couldn't talk . . .

'Last chance, Alex. I can make this easy. A short sleep for you, while I do what we both know you'd rather say yes to, and then afterwards it's home to beddy-byes. So I'll ask once more: What does "no" mean?'

Her entire body began to shake. The big muscles in her chest and buttocks and thighs moved continuously. The head blocks and neck collar, the arm restraints and ankle stirrups visibly shook. Tears streamed down her face along with mucous from her nose and mouth, and through all of it she screamed a silent, 'No' as she made herself say the opposite out loud.

'I'm sorry, I didn't catch that.' Now he was making it difficult for her to be heard. He'd changed his mind, and the mask was now covering half her face and the liquid gas was doing its work.

'I said yes,' she whispered drowsily. 'No means yes.'

CHAPTER TWO

Alex opened her eyes. She was lying on a trolley, a white sheet draped over her, and two of her colleagues calmly stared down at her. Fiona Woods, her best friend and senior nursing sister of the A & E department and Caroline Cowan, senior A & E consultant. Both wore similar expressions – reassuring ones – and warm smiles were quickly offered. She knew exactly where she was, even down to the cubicle she was in: number 9.

She could see on Fiona's fob watch that it was nearly 2 a.m. She had been working here in the department five hours ago, showering quickly in the staff changing room, her dress hanging up, ready to wear, her make-up and perfume on. Such a short time ago, and yet so much had changed. Her life had hung in the balance. If she'd said no . . . if she'd refused . . . if she'd been braver . . .

She screwed her eyes shut, breathed deeply and slowly, and when she was ready she opened them again.

'Hello, sweetie,' Caroline said in her best caring voice. 'Can you tell me what happened? Tell me what day it is, and where you think you are?'

Alex wasn't yet able to speak about the first question. She concentrated on answering the second and third instead. 'It's

Sunday, the thirtieth of October, and I'm in the city of Bath, in my own hospital, and in my own department.'

Caroline smiled again. 'You are indeed, sweetie, only now, it's the thirty-first. You gave us a fright. The storm outside has been horrendous, non-stop rain and wind. You gave us a proper scare.' She nodded reassuringly. 'But you're all right. A couple of grazes to your knees and a bit of a bump on the back of your head, but otherwise you're fine. Good job Patrick insisted the search carry on, otherwise we might be treating you for hypothermia. I'm going to suggest you stay overnight. Do a few neuro obs on you. You were pretty out of it. In a moment I'm going to call in a few others so we can check you over. Stay nice and still, and before you know it we'll have you out of that collar.'

Tears of relief flooded Alex's eyes and she blinked them away. Caroline's fair eyebrows pulled together in a frown. She looked older than she was, her sturdy body and forearms strong and toned, not from clinical work but from the years she'd spent helping her husband on their farm.

'Oh, sweetie, don't cry. We'll have you sitting up with a cup of tea in no time. Fiona, go round up some more bodies. Let's get our favourite doctor sorted out quickly. None of the boys, mind,' she warned Fiona in a friendly tone. 'I'm sure Alex doesn't want that lot to see her cute bum.'

Alex lay perfectly still. She felt deeply tired and was grateful for Caroline's matter-of-fact manner and easy banter. Later she could scream. Later she could howl her head off and crumple in a heap, but for now it was better that she stay calm. She would need to be calm if she was going to be of any help to the police.

Three nurses came back into the cubicle along with Fiona Woods.

'I'll take the head,' Fiona said to Caroline. The other nurses positioned themselves down one side of Alex, and each put their hands on a part of her body. Her shoulder, her hip and her leg were firmly held. Standing at the head of the table, Fiona positioned her hands on either side of Alex's head while Caroline loosened the neck collar and took away the head blocks. The senior consultant then carefully placed her hand behind Alex's neck, and starting at the base of the skull, felt the cervical spine for any sign of tenderness or deformity.

She felt Alex wince. 'That a bit sore?'

Alex started to nod and Fiona commanded her to stay still. 'Hey you, you should know better than that!' Her face was only inches away from Alex's and she smelled of cigarette smoke. Fiona had obviously taken up the habit again. It was a shame, because she had been doing well on the patches.

Over the next few minutes, while rolled onto her side in an in-line immobilisation position with her head supported in Fiona's strong hands, the rest of her spine was checked carefully. Lastly, a moment of humiliation, especially as she knew all these people – Caroline inserted a finger into her rectum to assess sphincter tone. Then it was over and a huge smile covered Caroline's face as Alex was rolled back.

'You're fine, Alex. You're not going to need the collar. I'm going to raise you up a little and then get you that cup of tea.' She looked at Fiona. 'A couple of co-codamol wouldn't do any harm.'

There was no doubt about it, Caroline Cowan was a master at keeping calm in a crisis, the pace and tone of her actions and voice just right for keeping hysteria at bay. She was giving Alex time to adjust to her situation, normalising everything as much as possible so that she would be better able to face the unpleasantness to come. Alex had always admired her, and never more so than now. She was making sure Alex was ready.

As the cubicle emptied of the other helpers, Caroline washed her hands at the sink. A spray of water splashed her green tunic and trousers, and she made light of it as she laughed and pulled paper towels from the dispenser on the wall. Even now, her small laugh was letting Alex know she was behaving naturally. It would be one step at a time. No rush. She was safe, and no one was going to get past Caroline.

'So, sweetie, any questions?'

Alex bit hard on her bottom lip to stem the flood of tears waiting to fall. Afterwards, she promised herself. She would cry afterwards in the arms of Patrick and no one else.

'The police. Have you called the police yet? They need to block all exits. And all theatres need to be checked first. I want the whole works: HIV check, syphilis, gonorrhoea, pregnancy – the lot. I don't care if it takes all night. I need to know what he's done to me.'

The reassuring expression had gone from Caroline's face, replaced by a concerned frown.

'Alex, what are you saying? Why do I need to call the police?'

A thumping sensation started beneath Alex's breastbone. Her breathing came faster and louder, and her shaking limbs caused the sheet to slide off her.

Her voice, she later learned, was heard throughout the entire ward. Above all the other noises – the cries of pain and confusion and fear, the clatter of trolleys carrying treatments to the cubicles, the twenty-odd monitors beeping loudly at different times. Her voice, her words, carried over all of it.

'Because he raped me.'

CHAPTER THREE

A rape case presented in the emergency department has a level of privacy all of its own. A protocol of silence and dignity wraps itself around the situation. The attending nurse, the doctor and the police go about their business without any other person in the department being aware of what has taken place.

In the case of Alex Taylor, there was not a person in the department that night who *didn't* know what had happened, or who hadn't heard what was alleged to have happened. Even before the examination was over there was speculation about what had really happened. The favoured opinion was that she had suffered a head injury; confusion and concussion perhaps.

In the examination room, the forensic medical examiner and the female detective constable didn't disbelieve the distraught woman, or the rape, but they found it more than difficult to believe the rest of what she said. Only Maggie Fielding stayed neutral and objective, keeping to her professional duty of care as she completed the examination and listened to Alex Taylor's lengthy story. She immediately answered every question put to her by Alex.

'The coil's in place, Alex. There's no sign of it having been moved. I can see the strings, everything looks normal.'

Maggie Fielding waited for Alex's next comment. She kept eye contact and seemed in no hurry. Maggie was a striking woman, tall, strong limbed and slim. She had magnificent chocolate-coloured hair that reached her waist when it was down.

The forensic medical examiner, who was also a GP, a New Zealander named Tom Collins, wore a permanent look of sympathy. He'd stepped out of the room while the examination took place.

Raising her bottom for the paper towel to be placed underneath, Alex's pubic hair was combed for evidence. Then the towel, the comb and the hair were dropped in an evidence bag, sealed, signed, dated and handed to the police officer. Her fingernails were clipped and scraped into a separate bag. Hairs were taken from her head. She spat into a sputum pot, and internal swabs from her mouth, anus and vagina were obtained, and blood was drawn. Alex watched as Maggie rubbed a swab on a glass slide, knowing that it would be examined for sperm. Finally, every inch of her was examined for injury. Bruising. Tearing. Bites or teeth marks that could identify her attacker.

Maggie Fielding stepped away and Tom Collins was called back in. Only a few weeks ago, Alex had stood in the same spot as Maggie, beside the same man as he drew blood from a woman who had been attacked by her boyfriend. They had then shared the same status – both professionals, both doing their duty as they documented and photographed the multiple bruises. This time, as far as he was concerned, she was a victim and he was the professional doing his job and trying his hardest to hide the fact that he knew her personally.

'Do you think we could go through this one more time?' the female officer asked.

She had quietly identified herself as Laura Best and told Alex she was sorry this had happened and that it wasn't necessary to address her formally, Laura would do. Except that now Laura didn't look quite so sympathetic. Her freckled face was less open. She looked a bit impatient. All four of them had been in the private exam room for more than an hour, and the heat and stale air were closing in on them.

Laura flicked back several pages of her notebook and began reading. 'You remember walking through the car park, feeling a blow on the back of your neck and then a gag at your mouth and possibly a smell of gas. You then woke up in an operating theatre, found yourself strapped down, your legs up in stirrups, and a pretend surgeon present.'

'I don't know if he was a pretend surgeon,' Alex angrily snapped. 'I said he was dressed as a surgeon.'

Laura briefly pursed her lips before continuing. 'He then threatened to staple your lips together, showed you a tray of instruments, and said he'd removed your coil while he catheterised you and then went on to tell you he was going to do an operation on you, a vulvec— ' She struggled to say the word.

'A vulvectomy,' Alex answered impatiently. 'Yes and yes and yes to all of it.'

'He then asked you a question, which made you think that he intended to rape you. After which you say he anaesthetised you.'

'Yes.'

'The next memory you have is of waking here in your own department.'

'Yes.'

'And you can't describe him or recognise his voice.'

'No. I told you the theatre lights were blinding me. I saw a surgical mask and I could see he was wearing a surgical gown. But his voice . . . it was like he spoke through a speaker system, like he wasn't beside me. English, but then he also sounded a bit American.'

'So this English *and American* doctor did all this to you? Hmm . . . forgive me, Dr Taylor, if I sound dense or perhaps insensitive, but you left here at 9.30 p.m. and you were found in the car park at 1.30 a.m.'

'What difference does that make?'

'These big needles – orange ones you say were inserted in you – they were in both arms. Surely there'd be puncture marks?'

'You're not hearing me. You haven't listened to what I said. They were there. I saw them. That was obviously a part of his plan to fool me into believing I had been injured. To fool me into believing I was incapable of moving. The whole thing was designed to make me think I was defenceless so that I . . . so that I agreed to let him do what he wanted.'

A small smile curved the young officer's lips. She looked at Tom Collins and Maggie Fielding. Alex saw them each make brief eye contact with one another. They were sending messages with their eyes and she was being excluded. This was a private club where only the professionals were allowed – not the victims.

'This would scare me if this was a movie,' Laura Best almost tittered.

Anger drove Alex off the cushioned trolley and she stood in her bare feet and a hospital gown a foot away from Officer Best. 'Well it's not a fucking movie, so take that smirk off your face. I didn't fucking dream this up! I was attacked. I was abducted, and if I hadn't agreed to what he wanted I'd be fucking dead in a morgue right now.'

'I'm sorry if I've upset you. We're not saying this didn't happen,' she said, including Tom Collins and Maggie Fielding in this statement. 'We're just trying to understand. Your underwear and your shoes were in place. Every button on your dress was done up.'

And then she said what she was really thinking, what had obviously been going on in her mind all through this interview. 'Your colleagues tell me you had a difficult day.'

Alex's head whipped up at the careful tone.

'No more than usual. It's always a difficult day in A & E, or haven't you noticed?'

'More so than usual, is my understanding. Unless of course it's every day you lose a baby?'

'I . . . I . . . She was already dead when the ambulance brought her in. There was nothing we could do for that baby!'

'I think Alex has had enough,' Maggie Fielding cut in. 'She needs to rest. And DC Best, next time you have a case such as this I think it would be appropriate to have a more senior officer present, or at least one trained in sexual offences, as I'm sure you'll be told when you report back.'

Maggie Fielding was not Alex's favourite person at the best of times. She was a brilliant gynaecologist, but her manner was usually brusque. Right now Alex was glad of her presence.

'I want Patrick. Where's Patrick? I need him here!'

Maggie Fielding nodded. 'He's here. He's waiting outside.'

'Well I want him! Patrick,' she hollered. 'Patrick!'

In Patrick's arms she finally wept. In between incoherent cries she told him of her night. He was explosive in his shock, demanding that Laura Best find this man. He demanded she get more police in and asked why he hadn't seen a posse of them searching the hospital yet. It was only Alex that managed to keep him from running into the night to search for the man, her grip on his hands unwilling to let go, her need for him to stay finally getting through. In his arms she was finally safe and finally soothed enough to sleep.

CHAPTER FOUR

Laura Best stood next to Patrick Ford. Despite the night he'd spent at his girlfriend's bedside he still looked well-groomed and fresh. He was ready to question her again, judging by the intensity of his gaze. Well he could wait; it was her turn. She didn't get a chance to take a statement from him last night, between him challenging her to find this man dressed as a surgeon and his need to comfort his girlfriend.

They'd just walked around the car park, and he'd shown her where he and a security guard had found the doctor and where he'd been parked. Only a few cars away, and yet he hadn't seen her. His explanation for this was understandable. He'd arrived, waited a short while, then gone into the department to look for her, only to be told she'd left fifteen minutes earlier. He decided she must have got a taxi to his place because he was late to pick her up, so he'd returned home before coming back to the hospital to begin a search.

'Why were you late?' Laura asked him.

Patrick Ford shrugged. 'I wasn't, really. What I mean is I wasn't late considering how long I normally wait for her. She's never on time coming out of the place. I finished surgery – I'm a vet – a bit late, about five or ten minutes, but I wasn't unduly worried because like I said, Alex is always late. I got here about nine forty, maybe nine forty-five.'

'And at what time did you come back again to start looking for her?'

'Probably eleven. It takes me twenty minutes each way to get home and back again. I hung around at home for about a quarter of an hour to see if she'd turn up.'

Laura was surprised. 'So how come it took so long to find her?'

'Ineptness would be a good term to use,' he replied irritably. 'We only initially searched between the cars. We then wasted time searching the hospital, checking wards to see if she was with a patient. Even when we found her, she wasn't obviously visible, lying beneath the trees, because it's pitch black at night over there.'

'How is she this morning? Has she said anything further?'

He shook his head. 'She's sleeping.'

'Do you have any ideas about what happened?'

His head lifted in surprise. 'What do you mean?'

She gave a slight shrug. 'Just any thoughts you might have had about last night?'

'Are you telling me you don't believe her?" His tone was challenging. 'I don't know what to think. I'm shocked by what I've heard. But I haven't for a second doubted what Alex has told me.' He stared at her intently. 'I take it you've searched for this man? You've at least checked out her story?'

Laura nodded her head purposefully. 'Absolutely. Yes. We've searched all the theatres, the grounds, and talked to theatre staff. And now, of course, you and I have just seen where you found her. The branches above her were heavily shaken in the wind. There's debris and bits of branch, some quite heavy, all around where she lay. She had a bump on her head and she was knocked out.'

'So you're saying a tree branch could have knocked her out? ' he said tersely. 'But it's not what she said occurred, is it?'

Laura briefly pressed her lips together. 'What if she'd had a traumatic day? I hear she lost a baby yesterday. Might that have some bearing on her mental state?'

Patrick Ford's eyes narrowed. 'Her mental state! I do hope you're not suggesting Dr Taylor is unbalanced, because I assure you she isn't. I would know. I spend enough time with her. Do not go down that route. If there is another explanation, it will be a physical cause. Concussion, most likely. And yes, possibly from a tree branch hitting her head.' His eyes coolly appraised the detective. 'But until you've exhausted every avenue of searching for this man, I expect you to accept what she said as truth. And if that's all we have to discuss, I'm anxious to see how she is.'

Laura smirked behind his retreating back. A bit pompous for her liking. Good looking and dressed well, though more for the city than the job he did, and bluntly confident, but not someone she would fancy. Still, the meeting had gone well, she had managed to gather a time frame of who was where and when at the time of this so-called abduction. Dr Taylor had certainly been out in the car park a long time. If her boyfriend had arrived on time then none of this would be happening. And Laura Best would not have spent the night searching the hospital. Never let it be said she hadn't taken it seriously; she was nothing less than professional.

When Alex looked into Patrick's eyes the morning after, she worried about what he was thinking. He'd been sitting beside the bed when she woke. He clasped her hand in both of his. In the deep-blue irises she saw his love, his understanding, his concern for what he knew she must be going through, and something else. Separated from all other emotion, standing alone, she saw his doubt.

He didn't say anything when she first looked at him. He simply stared into her eyes, leaned over and kissed her mouth. A gentle pressure, a second of warmth and comfort, and then he sat straighter in his chair and waited for her to talk.

'We didn't have that champagne,' she said.

He smiled briefly. 'It's on ice.'

'The ice will have melted by now. And the label will have soaked off.'

'It'll still taste good. Or I can buy another bottle.'

She entwined her fingers with his and gently squeezed. 'How's my mum?'

'Probably wondering if you and I are coming to lunch. Desperate to talk through the final arrangements for the wedding.'

Alex grimaced. This was the longest-planned wedding in history. Her sister, Pamela, had finally decided on a venue, a dress, a photographer, the flowers and her sole bridesmaid. Alex had left the choice of bridesmaid's dress up to her sister. After trying on more than a dozen, and listening to Pamela's oohing and aahing and indecision because each was so nice, Alex had given up. She could only use so many of her days off for shopping.

'I meant, how is she about this?'

Patrick let go of her hands and steepled his fingers. 'She doesn't know. I thought it best if you talk to her about it. In the cold light of day. Well . . .'

Alex sat up, her eyes watching his every expression. 'Well what, Patrick?'

He shook his head. 'It's just you may feel differently today. Have a different slant on things. You know, darling, you really scared me last night. When we found you I was never more relieved in my life. The weather was appalling. Someone could have driven over you. You could have died out there in the cold.'

The familiar shaking began again. Alex now recognised it for what it was. Panic. Not just because of what had happened, but because of not being believed. She dug her recently cut fingernails into her palms and willed herself to be still.

'Where was I found?'

'In the car park.'

'I mean, where in the car park?'

'Right at the back of it. The security guard and I found you lying on the grass beneath some trees. A couple of tree branches had fallen off close by, and we think one of them may have clocked you on the back of the head.'

'Really. That's what you think, is it?'

He was silent for a moment. 'No. I mean, yes, it's possible you were knocked on the head by a branch, but that doesn't mean to say I don't believe everything else that happened. Look, Caroline Cowan has booked you in for a CT. I think it's a good idea. We don't really know how hard you were hit on the head. By our reckoning you were unconscious more than three hours. It's a long time to be out cold.'

'What's everyone saying, Patrick? What are the police doing?'

'They've looked for him, but no sign as of yet. To be honest, darling, I've seen them talking more to your colleagues than actively searching for this man. I don't think they're giving much credibility to what you say happened. Everyone's worried, of course. But I don't think the police believe you.'

There he stopped, leaving Alex with no doubt of what was being said. She either had brain damage or had lost her mind.

'And you? Do you believe me?'

He rose from his chair to perch on the edge of the mattress so that he could hug her. His words whispered in her ear: 'Of course I do.' He leaned back so that she could see his face, and the doubt she thought she'd seen earlier had gone from his eyes. 'I have no reason to disbelieve you. When have you ever lied to me?'

Alex rested back in his arms. She had grown to feel safe with this man. He intrigued and challenged her in equal measure. His passion for veterinary surgery matched her own for human medicine. He was ambitious and driven, a potent combination in someone who also had the looks of a male model. They'd met because of his passion for rugby. During a game he'd ended up in A & E with a suspected fractured ankle. It wasn't love at first sight. In fact, she'd thought him a pain in the neck. His knowledge of medicine was at the same level as hers and he had dictated the terms of his treatment at length, until she put him in his place and told him she was the doctor and she would decide if he needed crutches or not. A bunch of not overly imaginative flowers arrived in the department the next day, and he had followed it up by asking her out for a drink.

As she hugged him back, she filled with anxiety. She was hurting badly, and never before had she felt so alone. The thought of people disbelieving her was hard to bear. Especially the police. The helium balloon floating beside her said 'Get Well Soon' on a Post-it note taped to the string, and she fondly suspected Fiona had pinched it from a sleeping patient. Get well from what, though? A knock on the head? A hard day at work? Did people honestly think she could make this up?

She eased back from him, looked him straight in the eye and told him bluntly: 'There's a killer on the loose. Not just a rapist. This man is a sadistic sicko. I need you to believe that last night is not a figment of my imagination, or caused by a blow to my head. I lay captured, Patrick, and the only thing that kept me sane was thinking about you. I certainly didn't lie out in a car park for several hours. I lay in the hands of the scariest bastard you could ever imagine. And do you know what gets me most? It's that the police are not prepared to investigate properly. They can't accept that it could have happened. But I'll have the CT and then we can move on with the most obvious conclusion – that I've lost my fucking mind.'

He insisted on being by her side while she had the CT scan. Protected by a lead-lined apron he had smiled at her as she disappeared into the tunnel.

His questions to the radiologist had been endless, his thought being that recent trauma to the brain may not show up so soon after the incident. A cerebral vascular accident doesn't always show unless the haemorrhage has already occurred, he argued. A repeat of the scan in a few days time should surely follow, he suggested. Patiently the radiologist answered all the questions. He pointed out that not only was her scan normal, but that there wasn't even a small bruise to the brain showing on the CT. Alex wanted to laugh as she saw the disappointment on Patrick's face. Patrick clearly wanted there to be a cause other than what had actually happened. And who could blame him? It would be so much easier to accept.

There was tension in Patrick's shoulders and the radiologist was quick to pick up on it. She was fond of Edward Downing and would be sorry when he retired at the end of the year. He was old school, a charming man who was always polite and cheerful and was probably one of the best radiologists in the country. He laughed good-naturedly and winked at Alex. 'Of course, this doesn't rule out nuttiness.'

'Indeed it doesn't,' Patrick replied drily, before seeing Alex's dismay. 'I'm only joking.'

She squeezed his hand gratefully, unable to trust herself to speak. She would get through this. She had Patrick and Fiona and Caroline, of course. She was not alone in this nightmare.

As she and Patrick left the hospital in the early afternoon, he told her his plan. He'd already OK'd it with Caroline Cowan, and he'd cleared his own workload by bringing in a locum. They would have a holiday. A week away. Somewhere hot where they could lie on a beach, drink lethal cocktails and eat lots of delicious food. Where she could recharge her batteries. In her fragile state, Alex could only ponder on why everyone was in such a rush to whisk her away. Surely she should be available if the police wanted to question her further or if they made an arrest and captured this man? Surely in normal circumstances when a crime has been committed the victims don't just up and go on holiday? And that, she suspected, was exactly why everyone was being so accommodating. Because they didn't believe a crime had been committed. They didn't believe she was a victim.

CHAPTER FIVE

Ten days later, they flew into Gatwick airport on the return flight from Barbados with Virgin Atlantic, both lightly tanned, Patrick slightly fatter. He was in a jovial mood but she was a little sombre. He'd kept his in-flight fluorescent yellow socks on even after they landed, and the cabin crew smiled appropriately as he walked past them in his leather-strapped sandals. 'Most comfortable socks I've ever worn,' he said.

He walked several paces ahead of her through the terminal, full of energy, as he scanned the monitors for the conveyer belt from where they could collect their baggage.

Alex knew why he was in a good mood. Last night they'd had sex. She couldn't call it making love, because she hadn't felt loved. He had been generous with his caresses. Every part of her was given attention. He had held off from penetration for far longer than normal and she was on the verge of being ready, her skin and muscles relaxed and her bones melting. She had been ready even as he penetrated, until he whispered: 'This isn't so bad, is it . . .? It's not as if . . .' Then he'd breathed harshly, still holding back. 'Your coil's OK, isn't it? It's safe for me to come?'

So few words, but the hurt went deep. She analysed them over and over. *This isn't so bad.* Did *this* mean in comparison to her imaginary rapist? Each thing he said betrayed his real feelings: *It's not as if . . .*

Finish the sentence, she'd wanted to scream. Finish the fucking sentence. *It's not as if you were actually raped.*

Last night was the only time they had had sex in the seven nights they were away. For the rest of the time she had blamed the shared bottle of wine at dinner time and the several cocktails that followed for her lack of interest and drive. Quickly diving under the sheet of one of the large twin beds, she had feigned drunken sleep each night until she heard his heavy snores. She'd then slipped down the back stairs of the colonial hotel to the private beach reserved for the guests. She'd walked its length, back and forth under the watchful eye of the hotel security guard, wishing the days away so that she could stop pretending that this was an ordinary holiday and that she was an ordinary tourist.

Patrick pushed their cases on a trolley, stopping at WHSmith. 'We need some lemonade or Coke to go with the rum. Finish the holiday properly.'

'We'll buy some en route,' she said tersely, trying hard to hide her annoyance. Even though it was his Land Rover that they'd used to travel to the airport, it obviously wasn't going to be him driving. He'd drunk several glasses of wine on board, and in between meals had asked for lager.

He slept for most of the car journey, his seat in a reclined position and his feet in their yellow socks resting on his side of the dashboard. He roused when she pulled into the Chippenham service station, calling out as she hurried towards the building to use the toilet, 'Don't forget the Coke.'

She stood in the queue, with his Coke and some milk for the morning in her arms, desperately trying to shrug off the wave of depression. He had been easier to cope with in the sunshine, but every mile closer to home increased the sensations of dread. It was all right for him to forget why they had gone on holiday in the first place. It seemed that as far as he was concerned it was over and buried. It may well be that this was his way of coping, but his over-the-top joviality back at the airport and stupid requests like this felt like nails in her head.

She breathed deeply, trying to calm herself. Nearing the counter she scanned the newspapers. The front page of the *Western Daily Press* caught her attention:

Bath Nurse Still Missing

She leaned closer to read the report:

Fears are growing for pregnant 23-year-old Amy Abbott. The staff nurse has been missing for four days. Amy was last seen on Sunday evening in Kingsmead Square. Wearing blue jeans, light green shirt and tan leather jacket, she—

Beeping sounds interrupted her, and then the voice of the shop assistant: 'Two pounds eighty-nine, please.'

After handing over the money she wandered despondently back to the car.

On the last part of their journey she made a decision. She nudged Patrick awake when they pulled up outside his house and told him that she thought it best if they slept at their own places tonight. She needed to lie in because of night duty tomorrow, and he was back at work in the morning, so drinking rum might not be the best idea. She'd drop his car back round to him tomorrow. She said it all in a light tone and was relieved when he didn't put up too much of a fight. Their parting kiss was brief and his wave casual, which suited her fine.

In her apartment she turned on every light, checked the windows were all firmly locked, and double-bolted the front door. She had chosen to live here for security and peace of mind. The entryphone system was linked to the main entrance door, which had been a major plus point.

With a large rum in her hand, she sat with her back against the living-room wall, the telephone beside her, and listened to her messages. Three from her mother, all about the final arrangements for the wedding next week. One from Caroline – cheerful, upbeat – hoping she had a good holiday and looking forward to her return.

The last recorded message had been left at five thirty.

'Hello, this is a message for Dr Taylor. This is Maggie Fielding. I have your results back. I don't normally give them over the telephone, but I'm sure you're anxious to hear them. They're all clear, Dr Taylor, so you can stop taking the antibiotics.' There was a couple of seconds' pause. 'Look, if you want, I'm here to talk . . . Anytime. You have my extension, but here's my home number and mobile just in case.'

Alex didn't write the numbers down. Instead she saved the message. After a third rum she reached up and pulled a cushion from the couch and lay down on the floor. With her head propped on the cushion and her back flush against the living-room wall, she looked out into the brightly lit room with her eyes wide open.

Patrick hadn't said he no longer believed her, yet the mere fact of not bringing up the subject at any time other than last night was beginning to tell. She wondered if he thought she'd experienced some form of psychosis, and whether it would be the easy option to allow him to draw this conclusion. She wondered if her colleagues were thinking something similar. Her mother and sister still didn't even know about it.

And Maggie Fielding was offering her a chance to talk.

Alex knew that a professional counsellor would help her to separate fantasy from fact, dreams from reality – if she'd had some kind of breakdown, or if she'd imagined it.

But she knew she hadn't. Her dress – she remembered how surprised she was to see it back on. When she pulled back the white sheet after Caroline sat her up on the trolley, she had stared at it in disbelief. Laura Best had pointed out that all the buttons were done up. And they were – every one of them. Heart-shaped and fiddly, they were all in their correct buttonholes. Yet not one of them noticed how clean it was. She had supposedly lain for more than three hours out on grass under trees. They had all said how bad the weather was. It had been cold and wet – not one of them had noticed that she was dry.

CHAPTER SIX

Alex reached down and tied the laces on her Nike trainers. She pocketed her stethoscope and tourniquet, pinned on her name badge, clipped a couple of pens to the V-neckline of her shirt, and then went and stood in front of the long mirror. Underneath her green tunic the waistband of the green trousers felt loose. She'd always been slim and toned from the running she did. She'd been second fastest sprinter in the 100 metres for two consecutive years at university, dipping to third when a sixteen-year-old girl took to the track for the first time on a cold summer's day and set a campus record. Alex had read several articles written about her in the newspapers since those days, following the athlete's meteoric rise to world champion after winning gold at the 2016 Olympics.

With her light tan and freshly washed tawny hair held up in a loop at the base of her neck, Alex looked well and full of vitality – at first glance. It was only on closer inspection, beneath the layer of concealer, that the black beneath her eyes was visible. She'd bathed her eyes in Optrex, and they sparkled, but it was only because of the determined look of brightness fixed on her face. Her cheeks ached from practised smiles.

Throughout the day she had fought off the temptation to have a stiff drink, but at the last moment, with her coat on and ready to leave the flat, her resolve weakened and she took a swig of Absolut vodka to wash down 2mg of diazepam. If she wasn't careful, this could easily become a habit. Since the night of her abduction she had drunk every day. A holiday was an excuse to drink, but this nip before work couldn't happen again. She would put it down to Dutch courage. A one-off.

With a deep breath, as ready as she ever would be, she left the changing room and stepped out onto the floor of the department.

It was Friday night and it was heaving. No one gave her a second glance. On the large whiteboard covering 'majors' patients a name was written in every cubicle space. Down the corridor, ambulance crews were waiting to offload their patients. A quick check on the computer showed her that 'minors' was equally busy. She saw Nathan Bell through the long glass partition windows of the doctors' office, eating Doritos and tapping the keyboard, and wandered in to see if he was ready to do a handover.

He was bone thin and overly tall, unable to stay still even when he was sitting. His right foot tapped the ground continuously, causing his knee and thigh to jerk, which was probably how all the junk food he consumed was burned off. He'd been in the department for a year and had proved to be a sound doctor, but patients shied away from him. The port wine stain covering the left side of his face was shocking. Alex had wondered if he had ever explored the possibility of having laser treatment to diminish the deep red colour.

'Be with you in a minute, but there's no rush. I'm staying on until midnight.'

'Why?' she asked. 'Has someone gone off sick?'

He shook his head, his eyes staying on the monitor to read blood results. 'No. Caroline thought that as it's your first day back you could do with some support.'

He said it bluntly, though Caroline, she suspected, wouldn't have wanted her to know this. In truth, she'd probably told Nathan to find a plausible reason for staying the extra hours. He could have said it was Friday night, the place was heaving and he could spare the time. But Nathan Bell didn't do deception well. He was blunt and he was truthful.

She was about to tell him there was no need to stay when a high-pitched screech from the transceiver blasted the air.

'I'm right behind you,' he said. 'Just give me two minutes.'

Fiona Woods was at the control base with the transceiver in one hand and a pen in the other as she prepared to take down the details from the paramedic. Her colleagues around her were hushed so that she could hear her caller more clearly, and some of the patients and visitors stopped in their tracks so that they, too, could listen in.

'Emergency department receiving,' Fiona said calmly and clearly. Her new hairstyle looked torturous; in a French braid too tightly woven, it pulled the skin at her temples. Her naturally frizzy hair was something she constantly battled with, and Alex could bet she'd have a headache at the end of the shift with this new attempt.

'We have a young female, unresponsive at the scene. Glasgow Coma Score, now 12. Systolic pressure 85. Heart rate 110. Resps

26. Sats 99 per cent. She has a bleed through her jeans, either rectal or vaginal. Over.'

Fiona pressed the transmit button. 'Do we know if she's pregnant? Over.'

'Undetermined. We have verbal response, but incoherent. We have no status on history. Over.'

'What's your ETA? Over.'

'Four minutes. We're in the hospital grounds. She made it this far.'

'Thank you crew 534. Emergency department standing by.'

Alex headed straight to 'resus', with Fiona on her tail. As they entered the resuscitation area, Fiona briefed the nurses on what was coming in. Alex was glad she was on duty; Fiona was a brilliant practitioner and, after seven years in this area of nursing, there was very little she didn't know about emergency medicine. Alex automatically gloved up, donned a green plastic apron and went into bay 2 to check the equipment. It was the nearest bay for an ambulance crew and consequently the most used. Therefore it was essential that before and after each patient the stock was checked.

On the wall behind the patient trolley there was a board holding equipment. At a glance she saw everything was in place, but she went through each item anyway. She did the checks in less than a minute and then moved on to other equipment: oxygen supply and resuscitator bag, used to assist ventilation, with a snugly fitted facemask. She pressed buttons and flipped switches, and cardiac monitor screens lit up with alarms beeping as they searched for a source.

Over at the divider unit, which separated the bays, Nathan was pulling out syringes and placing them on the counter; some he filled with saline, others he kept ready for drawing blood. Fiona Woods and another nurse hung two one-litre bags of warmed fluids. On a priority 2 alert, X-ray and path lab were standing by. It was all in the preparation. Be ready, be waiting, and be prepared for the unexpected.

Her blood had seeped through the white blanket, turning a large patch a deep red. It had dripped down the side of the trolley, onto the wheels, and was now wetting the floor. Her face was a stark white beneath the oxygen mask. Her eyelids were flickering and she was making small murmuring cries. In the few minutes it had taken for them to get her here she had seriously deteriorated. She was bleeding out with every passing second.

Even while they were positioning her, Nathan Bell had hold of her left arm, had a tourniquet in place and was inserting a needle. The fluid was attached and a pressure bag put round the litre of fluid to rush it through faster.

'Have we any history at all? A trauma? Anything?' Alex asked quickly, while casting her eyes over the woman's body for immediate assessments. The blood loss was great, and the ashen face and white fingers were alarming.

'It was a 999 call,' the paramedic replied. 'She was found just inside the hospital grounds, clearly trying to find help. The couple who found her said she was groaning and then she slumped on them. Unresponsive initially with us, and then in the back of the ambulance we've had a few moaning sounds.'

'Do we have a name?'

'Haven't checked pockets. She didn't have a bag with her, but there might be something in her jacket.'

The woman was making sounds from the back of her throat, a deep humming, and Alex didn't like it. It was too internal, and her Glasgow Coma Score, the tool for evaluating neurological function and patient's level of consciousness, was dropping.

Fiona Woods pulled out her shears as the other nurse removed the blood-soaked blanket. The woman's blue jeans were drenched at the groin and down to as far as the knees, and more blood was being soaked up by her pale green shirt.

With ease, Fiona cut away the clothing. 'She's flooding,' she said urgently. 'I'm not going to get a catheter in here. And there're clots in her pants.'

Alex moved away from the head end of the trolley and inspected the find. Dark congealed blood was mixed with tendrils of white. 'It looks like foetal matter. Put it in a kidney bowl. Put the trauma call out and state urgent need for obs and gynae.' The call would also bring other doctors – an anaesthetist and a general surgeon. 'We have a Class III moving rapidly to Class IV blood loss. I want more people in here now.'

Over the next twenty minutes fluids and blood were pumped into the young woman, and theatre was standing by. The urgently summoned help had arrived, and in a controlled rush of precise activity, everything possible was done to stabilise and to facilitate aggressive treatment.

The anaesthetist was preparing to put the woman to sleep. Every person attending the scene was tense with the need to get the woman out of A & E quickly so that the bleeding could be explored, vessels clamped, whatever was causing it stopped.

Alex was standing to one side at the head of the trolley getting the respiratory ventilator ready when she saw the woman's lips moving beneath the oxygen mask. She leaned close to her patient's face and, over the hiss of oxygen, she spoke calmly, using similar words to the ones that Caroline had used with her. 'Hello, sweetheart. My name is Alex and I'm a doctor. You're in hospital and you're safe. I'm going to help you now. Can you tell me your name?'

The woman's eyelids fluttered and then her blue eyes stared. Alex saw a natural focus in them, an awareness, and she smiled warmly at the critically ill woman. 'Hi, sweetheart, are you talking to me?'

The voice was weak, the breathing laboured, and Alex sensed in her heart that her patient wasn't going to make it. This moment might be the last that this young woman ever had to speak, and Alex ignored the anaesthetist who was now indicating that she move away so that he could proceed. She was going to give her patient this time.

'Tell Mum I'm sorry. Tell her I love her. I'm so stupid . . . I . . .'

She was panting and Alex quickly replaced the oxygen mask.

Fiona appeared at her side, smiling at the patient, her tone gentle but firm. 'She needs to be out of here now, Alex.'

Alex stroked the woman's forehead.

'I'll tell her, sweetheart, but you're going to get better and you can tell her yourself.'

'Alex!' Fiona commanded through gritted teeth.

'Dr Taylor, you need to let the anaesthetist get to her,' Maggie Fielding stated calmly, her voice finally conveying to Alex the urgency of the situation.

Alex stared at the medical team surrounding her, impatience stamped on all of their faces.

'Dr Taylor, we need to help her!' Maggie spoke for all of them.

The eyelids suddenly lifted higher and the woman's eyes were filled with fear. 'You said you'd help me. You, you . . .' Her eyes rolled back. And then a whisper of final words: 'I should have said yes . . .'

CHAPTER SEVEN

She had yet to be seen by her family, but in a purse in her leather jacket a NatWest debit card and a Barclaycard identified her as Amy Abbott.

She had been declared dead two hours ago and had yet to be moved from resus. Amy Abbott was not going to be wheeled down the corridors to the mortuary. Instead, the coroner's private black ambulance was standing by, ready to take her away. Her clothes had been bagged, her medical notes photocopied, her body briefly inspected. A police officer stood near the trolley guarding her until the time came for her to be collected.

Alex wanted to brush her dark hair, wash her blood-stained hands and remove the hideous airway tube protruding from her mouth, but she didn't. Amy Abbott was no longer her patient. She was now in the care of the coroner. She would be cut open, her organs lifted from her body, each dissected and microscopically examined until an answer to her death was found.

Alex was rooted to the spot she had been standing on for the last hour. She was out of the way of the police, but close enough to see Amy's face. There was no peace written in her features. Her eyes were wide open in fixed surprise and her lips were prised apart with rigid plastic.

A plain-clothes police officer arrived and Alex watched him talking to Nathan Bell, Maggie Fielding and the anaesthetist over in a corner. He looked her way and nodded briefly, suggesting he was aware who she was. The anaesthetist did most of the talking, and from his gesticulating hands, aimed twice in her direction, and the tight expression on his face it looked like he was blaming Alex for the situation.

Immediately following Amy Abbott's final words, the anaesthetist had none too gently pushed Alex aside and taken over. He had tried to resuscitate the woman for a further thirty minutes, with him ventilating and Nathan Bell giving chest compressions. When Alex said they needed to call the coroner, he had quietly agreed. Any sudden death from an unknown cause had to be reported, but when Alex declared she believed Amy had been murdered, his eyebrows rose in astonishment and she distinctly heard him say through gritted teeth, 'Oh God. So *you're* the one.' Leaving Alex little doubt that she had been widely discussed, that he had heard about her abduction, and from his tone, was sceptical.

Fiona Woods and the other nurses had glanced away in embarrassment. Nathan Bell had tapped the floor with his foot and fiddled with the equipment over on the counter. But Maggie Fielding had surprised her. On the pretext of turning off the oxygen behind Alex's back she had squeezed Alex's shoulder comfortingly and offered words of support. 'You did everything you could,' she'd said.

The grey-suited officer walked towards her.

'Dr Taylor? My name's Greg Turner. Detective Inspector. Can we find somewhere quiet to talk?'

Alex noticed a shiny patch staining his dark-patterned tie, and the collar of his white shirt curling up at the ends. He was probably no older than his early thirties, but grey was running through his dark wavy hair and lines fanned his tired green eyes.

Peeling off her rubber gloves and shoving them into her pocket, Alex led the way to the relatives' quiet room. She sank down on one of the low, boxy armchairs and he followed suit, leaving only inches between their knees.

He rested his hands in his lap. 'Why did you decide to call us? Was it because you knew she had gone missing? That she was Amy Abbott? A nurse who worked at this hospital?'

Alex cleared her throat, her mind searching for the right words so that she came across as a professional trying to help. 'I didn't know who she was until after she died. Until after I made the call. I've heard that she worked here, but I've never met her. It was what she said that made me call you.'

Her silence prompted him to ask the obvious. 'Which was?'

'She didn't get to say much. We were getting ready to anaesthetise her when I saw that she was trying to talk. She asked me to tell her mum she was sorry, that she was stupid. And then she said, "I should have said yes".'

Greg Turner's expression was difficult to read. His eyes didn't give away what he thought, nor did his next question. 'And you felt this was reason enough to call us?'

'Yes.'

'Why?'

Alex pressed back against the chair, wishing the room was bigger so she could get up and pace about. It would be easier for her to talk on her feet and not be so close to the man.

'Two weeks ago something happened to me, something that I don't think your officer believed. I was meeting my boyfriend, Patrick, in the car park. I'd just finished a late shift. I got knocked out, and when I came to I found myself in the hands of this man. I was . . . Look, it might be better if you talk to Detective Best. She'll have all the details. I er . . . it's not that it's difficult to talk about. It's just . . . Well, frankly, I'm not sure you'll believe it.'

Unexpectedly, tears rolled down her face.

Greg Turner pulled some tissues from a nearby box and gave them to her. 'Well, it's obvious you believe it. If you don't mind, I'd rather hear about it from you first.'

Over the next half hour Alex told him everything, even down to the CT scan and the holiday in Barbados.

'And this is your first shift back?' was his first response.

'Yes.'

'Do you think perhaps it was too soon?'

Alex shut her eyes in frustration and sighed resignedly.

'Dr Taylor, whether or not this did indeed occur, you're a doctor. Would you recommend anyone else going back to work so soon? You've been through an extremely unsettling experience.'

Alex sat upright, her shoulders pulled back and her chin lifted higher. 'It was what she said. He said the same to me.'

'Her words could have meant anything, Dr Taylor. Her "yes" could have meant any number of things. Her post-mortem is in the morning. At this stage it's best we await the outcome. Amy Abbott's parents will have enough to deal with when they learn about the death of their daughter. Telling them she could have been murdered is out of the question. When I get back to the station I'll go through the statement you gave to DC Best and I'll check on how things are going so far. I'll give you a call when I know. In the meantime I would like to suggest that you don't spread any rumours regarding tonight. It won't do Amy's parents any good, and if I'm being frank, it won't do you any good either.'

'Do you believe me?' Alex felt brave enough to ask.

He stood up. He straightened his suit jacket and did up the second button. 'You've had a stressful time, Dr Taylor. Maybe you've come back to work too soon. I'm sure your colleagues would understand if you needed more time.' He smiled at her politely. 'Yours is a difficult job. I'm sure it takes it out of you, seeing so much pain. Give yourself a little more time, why don't you?'

CHAPTER EIGHT

The skin on her hands had turned red, and her fingers looked heavy and swollen. She had been sitting on the shower tray, knees drawn up, arms wrapped round them, since arriving home. Her work clothes were saturated, clinging to her shaking body, and her eyes were stinging from the tears that still fell.

Over the sound of the heavy spray of water she heard the telephone ring several times and knew it was either Fiona or Caroline, because by now Caroline would indeed know what had happened in her department. She wasn't ready to talk to them yet. They wouldn't believe her, so what was the point? Nathan Bell had tried to stop her rushing off into the night, but Alex had been determined to get out of the place. Everywhere she looked she had seen concern and confusion in the faces of staff. Fiona Woods had given her a hard hug, but even she, after her initial concern, had rolled her eyes in exasperation as Alex tried to explain, and any confidence Alex had left just shrivelled and died.

They were best friends, not just colleagues; each had been there for the other in times of stress, and each had lent a shoulder to cry on when the need arose. They had cried together over the worst cases, particularly young deaths, drowned their sorrows and got drunk. Fiona was one of the few people who were aware of what she had gone through thirteen months ago. But it seemed that Fiona had forgotten all this. And who could blame her?

She had witnessed Alex disrupting an already extremely busy night in the department, causing huge delays for all of them. When Nathan Bell suggested calling in Caroline, Alex had flipped. Her anger had no bounds as she shouted obscenities at the walls in the staff room.

Nathan was shocked, warily backing away from her, while Fiona warded off anyone else trying to enter the room. The beet-root stain on his face, more purple than she'd seen it before, transfixed her until the sight of it repulsed her enough to run for the door.

She knocked over a yucca plant and upended a tea tray during her undignified exit, leaving more mayhem and gasps of disbelief in her wake.

How, she wondered, had her life come to this? She had picked up the scattered pieces, moved on and put that stressful situation behind her. As each new month passed she had gripped her personal alarm less tightly, scanned shadows less frequently. She had met Patrick, and gradually her fear had lessened, and as the year passed she was glad she had made the decision to stay in Bath, and not bottled out and gone back to Queen Mary's. It had become a distant memory, one she thought would never be repeated. Only here she was, thirteen months on, dealing with something a thousand times worse.

This was different. This man wouldn't be satisfied with taking a woman against her will. He wanted the feel and taste of blood on his hands. He was out there, walking around, perhaps even now choosing his next victim, and the police were not prepared to believe he even existed. How could that be possible? Was she such an unbelievable victim? She was being ridiculed behind her back, known throughout the hospital as 'the one', if that anaesthetist's remark was anything to go by. 'The one who had lost her mind,' Alex suspected.

She wished she *had* lost her mind. She wished it was a breakdown, because then there would be some chance of piecing herself back together again, of getting on with her life instead of wondering why he had let her live, why he had left her not knowing if she were raped or not. There were no physical signs found; no internal bruising or marks on her thighs, but then there would have been no resistance from her to cause them. She had been put to sleep, and had no way of stopping or of knowing what he did to her. Or was that his game plan all along? To simply have her think she was going to die, that she was going to be violated? A mind fuck. A sadist getting his kicks.

Whatever his reasons, her normal life had been stolen and replaced with something that could never resemble normality again. Each day she relived the events, reheard her pathetic attempts to reason with him. And all the while she had lain there thinking she was trapped, injured, powerless.

She, more than most women, had imagined how to react if she was ever faced with such a man – the screams she would utter, the scratches and bites she would inflict, how she would fight him off. And in the last scene she was always running, seeing a light, seeing a person ready to help, and then taking comfort, spilling tears of relief as everyone closed in around her, protecting her – and believing her.

She had been brave. A survivor. A woman who could *and would* do anything when faced with the unimaginable.

Not any more.

She reached for the vodka bottle and took another gulp. She was not going back to work tonight, so what was the point in staying sober? This might at least help her forget.

CHAPTER NINE

She wore blue leather clogs and over her tracksuit she wore a surgical gown. She passed the reception area seeing no one, but was not unduly surprised. It was still the middle of the night and there was no receptionist on duty.

She had made the decision to stop drinking and return to the hospital after crawling out of the shower when the water ran cold, before courage failed her and before a decision to never return took complete control.

She made straight for the operating theatres. She wanted to take a look at them at night when there was less traffic in and out of the place, and determine that there *was* a way she could have been transported here that night without anyone noticing.

So far it seemed quite possible.

By each entrance to the building there were wheelchairs ready to use, and on the downstairs corridor below main theatre a few abandoned trolleys were lined up. If she had been put on one of these, covered with a blanket and pushed along by someone wearing theatre clothing, no one would have reason to stop the person and question him.

If anyone caught her walking through here she would have to come up with an explanation. This way, dressed as other theatre staff dressed, if she was stopped and questioned she could claim that she was fetching something.

In theatre 2, the trauma theatre, an operation was ongoing. The light box displaying the warning 'In Use' above the double doors was lit, and guiltily she wondered if the patient in there had been rushed up from A & E, and if Nathan Bell had stayed for the rest of the night or called someone in, possibly Caroline, to relieve him.

There were eighteen theatres in the hospital: eight in the main block, five in day surgery, three in maternity, and two now redundant. The closed theatres were the old day surgery theatres that were now being used as an outpatient assessment area. There were rumours of other closed theatres, Victorian, which she had never seen, below ground level, inaccessible and closed not only to the public, but also staff. Rumour had it they were flooded some hundred years ago, and instead of restoring them, new buildings above ground level had been erected. She briefly wondered whether it was worth exploring them, checking just how inaccessible they really were, and who she would have to ask to get permission. The theatre she had lain in was modern, busy with the sounds of monitors and machinery and the hiss of oxygen. She would search the modern departments first.

Moving down the corridor she nipped quickly and quietly into each theatre, scanning ceilings and surroundings with critical eyes, but didn't see what she was searching for. As she neared theatre 8 she heard the sound of a trolley and quickly hid. Her ears strained to hear where the trolley was going while her eyes stayed fixed on a brass plate on the corridor wall. It was a memorial to the department, and the words seemed to mock her present plight.

The light of all good deeds is eternal.

What about the darkness of evil deeds? Was that also eternal? Or was that something one had to forgive in order to get through the pearly gates? Forgive those who trespasses against you, and you'll get a free pass to heaven.

Taking a chance, she peered down the corridor. Seeing no one, she came out of her hiding place and walked over to theatre 8. She pushed open the double doors and slipped into the anaesthetic room. It was relatively small, with just enough space and equipment for an anaesthetist to do the first part of his or her job. Locked drug cupboards and work counters were on either side of a theatre trolley and a small anaesthetic machine.

She pushed open the second pair of double doors and entered the operating theatre.

Covering one wall was a sheet of steel – a console housing dozens of switches and sockets and embedded glass-plated lights for viewing X-rays. Keeping the lights off, Alex moved over to the operating table. Enough light shone through the frosted panes from the anaesthetic room to guide her, and she was able to see the clear outline of the round overhead lamp suspended above. This was not where she had lain.

This lamp, although round, was much wider in diameter, and it held seven bulbs. A positioning handle on one side protruded like a fixed antenna. When the lights were on, if you were under the influence of drugs you could be forgiven for thinking a giant robotic insect with seven eyes was staring down at you.

Her shoulders drooped as common sense took hold. This was a foolish waste of time. How was she meant to pinpoint exactly what lights she lay under? What had she actually seen? The shape of a large round lamp, maybe smaller than the ones she had just inspected? But it could in fact be any of the ones she had just looked at. She'd been blinded by the glare.

She heard the outer double doors swing open and tensed. Standing still and silent in the near darkness, she saw the shape of someone through the frosted panes. He or she was tall and was wearing blue. A surgeon or an anaesthetist. She could tell by the bright pink headgear. A fashion statement for some, but others wore colour as they recognised the need to be easily identified as the doctor among the caps of blue worn by everyone else.

She waited to be discovered, heart beating wildly. She heard keys jangling and a cupboard door being unlocked. A moment later she heard the metal door banging shut, and then the outer doors leading back onto the corridor being pushed open again. Then silence.

Trembling with relief, she breathed easier. She needed to go home, get away from this place and its memories. Lock her door, drink her vodka and feel less afraid of dark shadows. She was not brave enough to keep searching on her own.

CHAPTER TEN

Greg Turner undid the top button of his shirt and loosened his tie. He smelt a whiff of sweat from his armpit and grimaced. He'd dig out a change of clothing and grab a shower in the staff room shortly. Last night he'd seen Dr Taylor's eyes on the stain on his tie and had wanted to fold his arms. It was rare for him to feel self-conscious, but there was something about her – a freshness, her clean hair or maybe her vulnerable eyes – which made him want to keep a distance until he was washed and shaved and wearing a tie he didn't have to hide.

He sighed. Sleeping in his office chair had not been a good idea, but it had hardly seemed worth going home after his late finish. His workload at the moment was stretching him almost to the limit, and he could have done without the trip to the hospital. It meant more paperwork, and hours he could ill afford to lose on his other cases. And his visit to Amy Abbott's parents had left him with the wretched cries of yet another family ringing in his head.

He couldn't make up his mind about Dr Taylor. She looked sane enough, but her story! That was insane.

The tap on his office door was expected, and Laura Best entered the room. Her blond bobbed hair, cut to jaw length, was sleek and smooth. Her white collarless shirt, tailored to fit, was crisp and clean. Immaculate as always and ready for a new day, Laura Best made a good impression.

She had been with CID eighteen months and Greg knew she was ambitious. She was known as a clock-watcher, but not for the usual reason. Laura Best never minded staying late. She didn't seem to notice the passing hours.

No, the secret nickname was earned because her colleagues were aware she was clock-watching her future. She had let slip that she wanted to make DI before she was twenty-eight, and there was no doubt she was in earnest. She was hell-bent on making her mark in the department. Her cases to date were not only successful, but every bit of paperwork was duplicated and put into the right hands before the cell doors had even banged shut. The fact that she was successful was largely due to her carefully vetting each case. She only coveted sure winners – quick turnovers at that – leaving the time-consuming cases to others.

She was a cool customer and admired by most other officers, but Greg was wary of her. And not because she was making her way to his rank; it had nothing to do with the job. It was personal.

'You look haggard,' was her first remark. 'And you're wearing the same clothes as last night.'

If it wasn't personal, she would not have got away with speaking to him so casually.

'And you, Laura, look as fresh as a daisy, as always.'

'Maybe it's because I work out and don't drink and don't smoke,' she said, pointedly eyeing the empty Coke can on his windowsill where she knew he dropped his cigarette butts.

The police station had a strict no smoking policy, and for the most part Greg honoured the rule, only occasionally lapsing when rain was lashing outside in the early hours of the morning – like it had last night. Or following sex, which had happened on only one occasion in this office. With Laura Best.

'So how was the mad doctor?' she asked. 'Did you read my report yet?'

He nodded. He'd asked for it on his return to the station last night, and he would almost have agreed with Laura's conclusion if he hadn't already met Dr Taylor. She didn't seem mad. Edgy and tearful maybe, but mad? He shrugged off the uncomfortable thought.

'So you don't think there's even the slightest possibility that this abduction could have happened? The search was thorough?'

'It's in my report. Uniform were thorough. Sergeant McIntyre would have had us look under patients' sheets if he'd had his way. The grounds and all floors were combed.' She laughed derisively. 'And sure, there's a possibility, Greg. We see this kind of thing all the time. Why, if you look out your window you may even see an elephant fly.' She mistook his silence as approval and proceeded, without laughing, to shred the doctor's character.

'The woman's deranged. Even her colleagues don't believe it happened. Concussed is their opinion. But if you want mine?' She drew breath, not waiting for a reply. 'She lost a patient that day. A baby, no less. I think Dr Taylor lost the plot. One too many nasty things to deal with and her mind simply flipped. Or . . .' And here she paused. 'She's made the whole thing up for an entirely different reason.'

Greg eyed her sternly. No matter that she made some valid points, it was the way she made them that offended him. 'Laura, don't assassinate the woman. Have a little compassion, why don't you?'

Her eyes and mouth grew round with surprise. 'Compassion! If she's made all this up, she needs locking up. At the very least, she should be struck off. Don't forget there are people's lives in her hands. Would you want her looking after you?'

Greg wished he'd dug out the report himself instead of asking Laura for it. In the confines of his office, when it was just the two of them, her overfamiliarity unnerved him. He could deal with it better out on the floor among other officers, as she was not quite as outspoken, but even then he was on edge in case she opened her mouth and revealed what had taken place in this very office.

He should never have slept with her. But she'd caught him at a vulnerable time. His decree absolute had arrived the morning of that eventful day, and a sense of failure coupled with too much alcohol had made him seek the warmth and reassurance of another woman. Six months ago he had handed her a powerful weapon. One that could easily end his career, if she ever decided to tell anyone.

'She's dealing with stuff that you and I couldn't even begin to understand,' he said, trying to reason with her. 'The nearest you or I get to see what she has to cope with are the ones we find barely hanging on to life. But she's the one who saves them. Or doesn't.'

'Which is exactly my point,' she answered crisply. 'She's dealing with so much bloody trauma that she's imagined some horror happening to herself.' She turned to leave and then slowly turned back. Her eyes raked over his dishevelment – his face in need of a shave, his hair in need of a cut, and the grubby tie hanging loose around his neck. 'And now she's calling us in again for a so-called murder? I'd think about pressing charges for wasting police time, if I were you.'

After she had gone, Greg felt a bitter taste in his mouth. He stood by the window of his office and gazed out at the city where he was born. Bath, a city so beautiful and unique it was designated a World Heritage Site, home to the rich and genteel for two thousand years. Jane Austen, Thomas Gainsborough and Beau Nash had no doubt drunk or relaxed in its curative waters. Waking up to a new day, the outline of the Georgian buildings was as familiar to him as his right hand, but it didn't give him a sense of belonging any more.

Home no longer felt like home. Laura Best's presence was a thorn in his side and, come the New Year, he would have to make some decisions. Either she left or he did.

He was a decade older than she was and he still had ambitions of his own. But this situation was beginning to sap his strength. He should never have slept with her and that was a fact.

He was tired, and thoughts like this were not healthy right now. He had paperwork on the Amy Abbott case to sort out and her post-mortem to attend. Turning away from the window, he set his mind back to work.

Back at her desk, Laura was still smarting from the rebuke Greg had given her; she couldn't help but wonder whether he'd have been as keen to defend Dr Taylor if she'd been old and fat. He made her so angry sometimes she could spit feathers. He had the ability to bring out the best and worst in her, and more often than not, her plain bitchy self. She sighed bitterly. She should never have slept with him. The moment it was over she knew he regretted it. He couldn't even look her in the eye. For her, that had been more than humiliation, as she had really liked him. Over the last six months she had tried to show him that it didn't matter, that she hadn't expected it to go anywhere, and wasn't expecting a Mills & Boon ending; she would have been fine with that if he'd at least had the decency to acknowledge it had happened in the first place.

Laura breathed deeply, trying to calm herself. He'd used her for sexual gratification and that was something she had done her best to forgive. Well, no more. She was done with trying to win him over. Instead she would show him what she was capable of. If nothing else, she would prove Dr Taylor was a madwoman. And then she would move on. She felt a tightening in her throat as she remembered the way he had kissed her and the sickness she had felt when he avoided looking at her afterwards. She was a fool. Well, she had learned her lesson. She would never let her guard down again. A valuable lesson indeed. She just thanked her stars that Greg was completely unaware of how very close she'd been to declaring her feelings, which thankfully were now gone. Her career was all that mattered now.

CHAPTER ELEVEN

The hammering on the front door woke her from her alcohol-induced sleep. She hoisted her heavy head off the cushion and willed her stubborn eyelids to open. It was daylight, but the lamps in her living room were still on. Her sodden clothes lay strewn across the carpet where she'd left them, and an empty bottle of vodka rolled off her stomach as she crawled out of the makeshift bed.

'I'll be there in a sec,' she hollered, grabbing the cushion and duvet off the floor and shoving them behind the sofa.

In the mirror in the hallway she saw her ravaged face. Panda eyes stared back at her from where her mascara had run the night before in the shower. She looked an utter mess and would probably have been unrecognisable even to those who knew her.

She opened the door and peered through a crack.

The police officer from the night before was standing there wearing the same suit with a different shirt and clean tie.

'Can I come in?'

She backed away from the door and let him follow her into the living room. She made no attempt to pick up her wet clothes or hide the evidence of her drinking. Let him think what he liked. Everyone else did, she reasoned. Why should he be any different? 'Would you like some coffee?' she asked.

'Please.'

She left him alone, and while the kettle boiled she washed her face and combed her hair. When she returned he had his back to her, standing at the window, and she saw his brown hair was more like auburn in natural light. Very few men visited her apartment and she wondered if he found it too stark.

'What a fantastic spot,' he said. 'You can literally step outside and row down the Avon. I envy you.'

'I usually run along it, which is pretty special I suppose.'

Her apartment was situated on the south bank of the river Avon, which was the other reason she had chosen to buy it, that and the fact that the grounds were only accessible to other residents, and security was stringent. He had no doubt been able to gain direct access to her front door only because he was a policeman.

A black fur rug and chrome and glass coffee table separated twin brown leather sofas. Silver dome floor lamps stood tall before curving gracefully over each of the sofas, and a third lamp, with a burgundy thread shade, was placed in a corner. There were no ornaments except for two Waterford crystal vases, empty of flowers, on the slim sideboard, and a large piece of driftwood, dried to a silvery grey, set between them.

She had allowed Patrick to guide her in her choice of décor, and had grown to like the room's sparseness until she saw Greg Turner standing next to the clean furnishings. There was an earthiness about him that suggested he would be more at home surrounded by wooden objects and tactile materials. In her mind she saw him with dirty hands, preparing a large coal fire, a dog dozing next to the hearth, which raised its head dopily, in hope of being patted.

She shook her head, despairing of her fanciful notions. He was a policeman in her home, wearing an ordinary suit and tie, and she had put him in different places because of the colour of his hair and the fact that he didn't suit the room. In truth, very few people did, unless they were wearing sharp suits or cocktail dresses. She now saw it as cold – calculatingly chic – somewhere you didn't drop crumbs or throw off your shoes.

'How are you today?' he asked, turning to face her.

'I feel as if my brain has been in a blender. It hurts to move my head.'

He smiled sympathetically. 'Try Resolve – I find that to be the best remedy, but you're the doctor so I'm sure you know what's best.'

'A nice saline drip is what I give to most of my patients. A couple of paracetamol will have to do for me. Have you been working all night?'

'And all morning and afternoon as well,' he replied. He saw the surprise on her face. 'It's a quarter to four.'

Alex was shocked. She had lain in her makeshift bed for nearly ten hours. She'd returned home after touring the theatres just after five, found her way into the living room, and tucked herself against the wall with the remains of a bottle of vodka. She had thought that it was still morning. In another five hours she would be back at work. She would have to face the music; to apologise for leaving Nathan Bell to pick up the pieces, for disrupting the department, for causing a complete fuck-up. Again.

'I've just spoken to the coroner. I have the PM prelims back. Still waiting on toxicology and other results, but he's given me enough to be going on with.'

She inhaled deeply, waiting to hear the outcome.

'He thinks it was self-induced abortion.'

Alex sank down onto her couch. She had been so sure, so convinced that her attacker had been responsible. She took a shaky breath, and tried to get her head around this revelation. 'Why do they think it was self-induced?'

Greg Turner shook his head. 'They're not ruling anything out yet, but the findings are leaning that way. Her fingerprints are on the instrument.'

'What instrument?'

'She tried to keep it medical. There's the possibility that she may have collapsed while doing it to herself, or else she was in too much pain to pull it out.'

'You mean it was still inside her? What did she use?'

'A uterine curette. I'm not entirely sure what that is. It per-forated her uterus and was still embedded post-mortem. The pathologist is writing cause of death as haemorrhagic shock. So what is it?'

'It's a surgical instrument, shaped like a long crochet needle with a teardrop hook. It's used to scrape contents from the uterus. Used during surgical abortion and *always* under anaesthetic. Can you imagine any woman doing that to herself? Inserting a needle through her own vagina? I'm sorry to be so graphic, but that's exactly what this is.'

She saw his grimace and pressed home the point. 'Why would she do that to herself? Not here, not in the UK, not in the twenty-first century. We have the NHS, and an abundance of private clinics all too ready to help. Why would any woman resort to such a risk on her own to get rid of an unwanted pregnancy?'

'According to her GP she had been depressed for a while, more so since she found out she was pregnant. He'd been treating her for gonorrhoea and she was worried it could harm the foetus. She discussed a termination with him two weeks ago. He was waiting on her decision.'

Alex stood back up, waving a hand in despair. 'So why didn't she go back to him? She could have got help easily.'

'We don't know yet why she did this. She was a qualified nurse. Maybe she thought she could handle it by herself. Or maybe depression made her desperate. We're trying to locate the father. Her parents tell us she didn't have a steady boyfriend, but if we can find him, he may be able to shed some light, tell us something we don't know.'

'So everything I told you now sounds ridiculous. You must think me a madwoman for calling you in. I just thought . . .'

Greg Turner perched on the windowsill and crossed his ankles. 'There is no connection that we can find, Dr Taylor. I went through your statement and I checked with DC Best. You are aware that they made a thorough search of both the grounds and the hospital that night. They found nothing. The theatres were all searched. In three of them operations were taking place at the time you say you were in one of them. The entire theatre team for that night have been interviewed and they all agree that there is no way anyone could have occupied one of the others without them being aware of it. The night cleaners were there till gone midnight because there was an MRSA case earlier in one of the theatres, and they had the entire suite to deep clean. Unfortunately, CCTV doesn't reach the part of the car park where you were found, but that area was searched, and there were newly broken tree branches on the ground near to where you were lying.'

Alex struggled to stay calm. She needed a drink; the whisky-laced coffee in her hand was not enough. She wanted the kick of something strong and undiluted slipping straight into her bloodstream. 'My dress, which your officer still has, is something I don't think DC Best noticed that night.'

His eyes narrowed at the tone in her voice when she mentioned the female officer's name, but he sat silently.

'It was dry, bone dry – not a mark on it, from what I could see. They found me in the car park where I lay in the rain, and yet it was dry. How do you explain that, DI Turner?'

'I can't. Maybe the lab can. If it hasn't already been checked, I'll chase it up. I'll also discuss it with DC Best. Though I am sure she would have noticed the state of your dress. She's pretty thorough.'

Alex flushed at the rebuke, but she'd be damned before she apologised. DC Best hadn't even had the decency to ring up and check on how she was doing.

'DC Best came to see you a few days later, but you were away. Your colleagues told her you were having a week off work.'

Alex bit hard on her lower lip to stop it from trembling. She was sick of crying and showing how weak she was. She breathed slowly and steadily until she felt calmer.

'Two weeks ago I had a normal life. I had a job I am good at, colleagues who trusted in my judgement. And now it's in tatters. I can't put it back together again. What would you do if you were me?'

He cradled the coffee mug in his hands and took a moment before replying. 'I've seen many men and women reach a crisis point in their lives. A friend of mine who's a police officer and was on duty during an incident, at this very moment is undergoing therapy for severe stress. He blames himself for the death of a pedestrian who stepped out into the road in front of his speeding vehicle. No matter that he has been exonerated of any blame, he feels he should have known that a man, at that precise moment, was going to appear out of nowhere and walk across that road. The helicopter overhead hadn't spotted the pedestrian, the officer in the passenger seat beside my friend hadn't noticed the man, but my friend blames himself. Talk to someone, Dr Taylor. The mind is a fragile thing. It can deceive us when we least expect it and it can punish us in a way no one can explain. When you're ready you will be able to put yourself back together again. You will have a normal life again.'

CHAPTER TWELVE

In her childhood bedroom, in the house where she grew up, the cream walls still bore the scars of Blu-tacked photos and Sellotaped posters, and in large glass picture frames prints of Andy Warhol's portraits of Jackie Kennedy and Ingrid Bergman still hung. In her childhood bedroom where she had slept and dreamed of her future.

Alex's legs were shaking badly and her grip on the door of the wardrobe was all that prevented her from toppling right in. The dress she was looking at was the same shade of pink she had worn on the night she was attacked. The same style of dress, except longer, and the same type of strappy shoes. Her sister, Pamela, was staring at her with a mixture of anger and resentment. This was not new; Alex felt there had always been resentment from her younger sister. Eighteen months separated them in age, but in terms of maturity, Alex had always felt far older.

Pamela had grown up believing that Alex had achieved her ambitions effortlessly, and that everything she did was accomplished with a snap of her fingers. It never occurred to her to think about the years of studying Alex put in, and the great parties, family holidays and social events that Alex missed so that she could stay focused and disciplined until her exams were passed, her future set, and yes, her ambition achieved.

Pamela went to college instead of university, took a BTEC course instead of a degree, worked part-time jobs instead of getting a student loan and had gone on to be an assistant hotel manager. She had spent the last several years seeming to enjoy life: nice boyfriends, nice girlfriends, nice holidays, nice everything. Nice and safe, with nothing to mar her happiness except for a childish resentment of her older sister. On the few occasions where the sisters met up and Alex was introduced to whoever was with her sister at the time, inevitably the question of 'What do you do?' was asked and Alex would see the admiration in Pamela's friends' eyes and the envious looks her sister gave her. It was the title that peeved her sister most. She was into titles.

Her husband-to-be had a title. He was a laird or lord, a Scottish representative peer, who came from a long line of Scottish landowners in the Highlands. He had been a guest at the hotel where Pamela worked, wealthy, a man beyond Pamela's wildest dreams. He had whisked her away from her job, and on this very day he would be marrying her. Rich, slightly boring Hamish, who Alex was still getting to know, had chosen her little sister when, with a bank balance like his, he could have had his pick of any well-heeled socialite.

It was Pamela who had it all, while Alex was still paying off student loans, struggling with a hefty mortgage and had a life that was falling apart. Yet she persisted in allowing herself to feel like the underachiever, the poor little me that was overshadowed by her older, more academic sister.

'What the hell is wrong with it, Alex?' Pamela shoved her aside to reach inside the wardrobe and pull out the dress. 'It's your colour! If you'd taken the time to come over and see it you could have said then if you didn't like it.'

Alex closed her eyes, determined to pull herself together. 'It's fine, Pamela.'

'Fine! Well, thanks a bunch, Alex. I got you a dress that I thought you'd love. But no, all you can say is, it's fine. You've got yourself a nice tan, found time to have a holiday, and now, on my wedding day, decide you don't like the dress.'

Alex forced a smile. 'I'm sorry. I do like it. It's not the dress. I do like it.'

'I saw your face.'

Alex wondered if now was the time to tell her sister what had happened. 'I promise you it's not the dress. I—'

Pamela's eyes shone with resentment. 'My day, Alex! Not yours! We've done your days. Mum constantly tells us how St Alex has saved yet another life.'

'Pamela, please, it has nothing to do with the dress. I need to tell you something.'

Pamela shook her head, a false smile pinned on her face. 'Not today, Alex. Today is about me, for once.'

The slam of the bedroom door left Alex alone in the room. With trembling hands, she reached into her handbag and pulled out the paper bag she had been carrying with her these last few days. Gathering the neck of the bag, she closed it over her mouth and nose and started to re-breathe in and out of it until her panic attack was over, and her heaving chest and beating heart had both slowed down.

A hysterical laugh burst from her throat as she wondered if there was any point in ever telling Pamela what happened. She didn't think there was. Her sister would think she had made it up. Thirteen months ago, she had seen the scepticism in her sister's eyes when she told her of the other situation, and *that* had been believable, was something many women had experienced. This recent experience, as Laura Best suggested, could have come right out of the movies.

Downstairs the relatives congregated, and her parents were in their room still getting ready. Patrick was in the garden keeping the younger guests amused with stories of 'Animal Hospital', no doubt, and here she was in her childhood bedroom with a paper bag to her mouth, falling apart.

Under crystal chandeliers, dimmed for the evening, the two hundred or so wedding guests gathered in the Assembly Rooms danced to music provided by a six-piece jazz band. A different band had played during the meal – a string quartet, setting the mood. No expense had been spared. At Bath Abbey the choir was outstanding, and when a soloist sang 'Ave Maria', Alex had felt at peace for the first time in ages. The flowers on the altar cascaded in mounds of cream, the air rich with their scent, and as Pamela glided up to the altar she looked every inch a fairytale princess. Here at the reception, matching flowers rose up like fountains before trailing over pale stone columns.

The canapés of scallops, tiger prawns, miniature fish cakes and parcelled salmon were served on banana leaves by an endless parade of immaculately dressed waiters and waitresses. The champagne flutes were refilled time and time again with the best vintage champagne, long before any speeches were made, and the hand-rolled cigars were delivered to every man to try.

It was a wedding to remember, to tell other friends about, and would no doubt make its way into the society column in the *Telegraph* on Monday morning.

Alex watched her sister without envy and truly hoped she would be happy with Hamish, that theirs was a match made in heaven. Judging by the gleam in her sister's eyes, and the flush of happiness on her face, she was having a taste of it now.

They had made their peace as Pamela stepped out of the Rolls-Royce – seeing Alex in the pink bridesmaid's dress, tears had momentarily filled her brown eyes.

'I'm sorry for being such a cow. I'm really glad you're here.'

Alex had kissed her carefully through the veil, and felt better than she had all week.

Across the table, Patrick sat with an audience of small children hanging on his every word. He'd carried on minding the younger guests and was still finding exciting animal stories to amuse them. She stared at him fondly, her recent disappointment in him temporarily forgotten. He was a good man, a kind one; was it really so awful of him to not want to talk about it, be reminded of it all the time? If she'd heard the same story from Fiona, or perhaps Pamela, she imagined she would have a hard time believing it ever happened. He at least was willing to believe her. There was no evidence. There was no logic to it. She had survived a horrific ordeal virtually unscathed, but the police couldn't take it seriously. And neither, she suspected, did Fiona. Not that she had said anything, it's just she seemed to be avoiding her. They talked at work, but it was always about the patient. If last year hadn't happened, Fiona probably would have believed her story, or at least accepted that she'd suffered something more serious than a knock to her head. But last year did happen, and Alex would always wonder if Fiona believed her even then, or thought Alex was in some way to blame?

Maybe there really was no point in dwelling on it. She was alive. Maybe the man who attacked her wasn't a risk to anyone else. Perhaps he was an escaped patient from a psychiatric wing who had got out for one night and in his hours of freedom had targeted her. If this was the case, no one else was in any danger. It was a comforting thought and one that, as the champagne worked at dulling her normally analytical senses, she was willing to accept.

When Patrick raised his glass to her, she saw his eyes caress her, and for the first time since that awful night she looked forward to going to bed with him.

'Penny for your thoughts?' she whispered.

He raised an eyebrow, appearing to give careful consideration. 'Oh, I don't know. Wedding cake, confetti, the "I do" bit – pretty heady stuff when you consider it.' He wiggled an eyebrow. 'Not so sure about the meringue-style wedding dress.'

'Shush,' Alex laughed. 'She looks lovely.'

'I just can't help wonder,' he said, inching closer, his lips grazing her ear, his breath caressing her neck, 'if she has a toilet roll underneath it.'

She laughed out loud and held his gaze until she saw a slight flush rise in his cheekbones. The day had been wonderful. A turning point. A pause on all that had gone before. She would not forget, but she could at least carry on.

CHAPTER THIRTEEN

A multiple pile-up, involving five cars and a coachload of OAPs heading back from a weekend trip to London, had happened at junction 18 on the M4.

In the staff changing room Alex gargled with a strong mouthwash and then blew into her cupped hands to smell her breath. The minty smell reassured her she was OK, but as an added precaution she unwrapped a Wrigley's spearmint gum.

How could she forget she was on call, she berated herself yet again. Fortunately, she'd stopped drinking long before the wedding ended and had in fact limited her intake throughout the long day, not wanting to get drunk. What she couldn't rule out, without a blood test or Breathalyser, was whether she was over the limit. The irony was not lost on her: that for the first time she wasn't drinking out of a need to forget, and she was brought back down to earth with a bump. Such an idiot. So stupid to forget something as important as the fact she had a job to do.

She'd dismissed the thought of ringing round to see if someone else could take over her on-call, not wanting to give any further reason to anyone to shred her reputation even more.

Well, this was her wake-up call. In some ways she was lucky it had happened. She had come very close to the brink with her drinking. She was aware that the man behind the counter in her local off-licence was getting to know her too well. Well, no more. She no longer needed to escape her fear.

Fixing a smile on her face, she stepped out into mayhem. The thirty-minute warning before the arrival of the first casualty had long passed, and injured people could be seen queuing down the length and breadth of the corridor. There was a rush of activity everywhere she looked, and Alex finally relaxed. This was her job; it was what she did best.

It was going well. Even as she struggled with exhaustion, she was pleased with how things were progressing.

In resus all of the bays were occupied. All of the monitors were beeping and sounding alarms. Rubbish bins were over-flowing and discarded equipment cluttered around them. On the work counters, rigid-plastic yellow containers for the disposal of needles were filled to the brim, and used syringes lay abandoned and doctors fought for small spaces to write their notes. A mop and a bucket rested against a wall; there were too many spillages to keep calling in the cleaners. It was quicker for the nearest person to clean up the blood, as the last thing they needed when the place was this busy was a wet floor.

The remaining patients waiting to be seen, although needing urgent attention, were at least more stable than the ones before them. Not counting the walking wounded, so far seven critical and twelve serious cases had been dealt with.

The trauma team was divided up between the patients, and extra doctors and nurses were in attendance to deal with all the injuries. Caroline was in control as always, but Alex saw the sweat stains under her arms, hinting that even she was finding the pace difficult. Maggie Fielding had been called in to attend one of the female patients, and over the cacophony of the horrendous noise of crying and shouting, alarms giving off urgent warning sounds, phones ringing and machinery moving, Alex heard her comfort an injured woman and was surprised at how tender Maggie could be.

The patient in bay 4 was staring at Alex with fear in his eyes, his grip on her wrist desperate. 'You're not going to let me die are you, Doc?'

She freed her hand from his and smiled reassuringly, then made a second attempt to get a cannula into his old veins. 'You're going to be fine, George. Just give me a second to get this thing in and then I can give you the medicine. In next to no time your heart will be beating normally.'

'It feels like it's gonna explode if it goes any faster.'

'You just stay nice and calm and breathe in that oxygen – leave the rest to me.'

The old man was not one of the casualties brought in from the pile-up. He'd been brought in from home and needed to be in resus urgently.

'Damn,' she whispered, and then smiled at him again. 'Your veins don't want to come out to play.' Scooting round to the other side of the trolley, Alex snapped her tourniquet onto his other arm. She let his hand dangle down over the side of the trolley and went down on one knee. She gave a few taps to a vein in his forearm and was rewarded by the sight of it swelling with blood.

Fiona appeared at her side. 'Need any help?' she asked.

Alex felt the gesture to be genuine. The warm smile of welcome Fiona gave her at the beginning of their shift conveyed an unspoken apology. The judgement in her eyes had gone and Alex was grateful.

'You can fetch the adenosine for me. There's no room over here to put anything. It's labelled and drawn up by the drugs cupboard.'

George smiled at them. 'I'm always a nuisance. They can never get the blighters in. I reckon the veins shrivel up at the sight of your needles.'

While Alex got the cannula in, Fiona went to fetch the drug. A moment later she returned. 'Can I have a quick word?'

Alex followed her over to the drug cupboard and Fiona held up an empty ampoule. 'Is this what you got ready?'

Alex stared at it in confusion. The label she had written on was on the syringe. George Bartlett's name was on the label. But this was not the ampoule she had used. If she had given him this drug, George would now be dead. Adrenaline 1:1000 would have caused his already dangerously fast heart to beat even faster.

She stuttered. 'I . . . I don't understand. I didn't get this out. I promise you that. Someone else must have put it there. There's no way I would give him this. No way in a million years.'

Fiona bit her lower lip, her eyes fixed on Alex. 'It was the only ampoule here, Alex. It was right beside the syringe – on this injection tray.' She put the ampoule back on the tray and picked up the syringe.

Alex frantically searched the counter, refusing to accept she could have made such a mistake. The empty ampoule of adenosine had to be around here somewhere. It had to be. She had held it in her hand. She had read the label clearly. She had not made a mistake.

'Someone's binned it,' she cried. 'And dropped this ampoule on my injection tray by accident. Check with the other doc- tors. I'll bet you one of them has used adrenaline in the last five minutes.'

Fiona's eyes glinted with anguish, and Alex felt her chest thump as she became aware that Fiona genuinely believed she had made this terrible error. And then she shuddered when she realised how easily the error could have escalated into a catastrophe.

'Go and have a cup of tea, Alex. I'll get Nathan in here to deal with it. I'll tell him you're taking five minutes.'

Alex felt a heaviness pressing behind her eyes and knew tears were imminent. 'No, I can't do that. I need to deal with it.'

'Everything all right, Dr Taylor?' asked Maggie Fielding. 'Do you mind if I get into the medicine cupboard?'

Alex stepped aside to make room. 'Everything's fine. I, um, I don't suppose you've just drawn up any adrenaline, have you?'

Maggie shook her head. 'No, but I do need some pain relief for my patient.' She stopped searching the contents of the cupboard as the two beside her stayed silent. Her glance took in their still- ness. 'Are you sure everything's OK? Who am I supposed to have drawn up adrenaline for?'

'No one,' Fiona quickly answered.

'What's going on, Alex?' Caroline suddenly barked from behind them. 'What's happening with Mr Bartlett? Why haven't you sorted him out?'

Fiona turned to the drug cupboard and pulled out the adenosine to show to the consultant. 'We're just drawing this up,' she said.

Caroline picked up the injection tray with George Bartlett's name written on it and the empty ampoule. 'What's this, then?' Then she spied the labelled syringe clutched in Fiona's hand. 'Give me that,' she said in a tone that conveyed she was aware something was wrong.

Fiona stared at the ground as she handed it over.

From ingrained practice, the consultant automatically checked the ampoule. 'What—'

'He's not had it. This isn't for him,' Fiona quickly interjected.

'Really!' Caroline replied sarcastically, and her disbelief punctuated her next words: 'It's got his name on it! So clearly he was going to get it!'

Alex chose the wrong moment to let out a shaky breath and saw shock fill Caroline's eyes. Alex knew she could smell the alcohol. She stared at Alex in disbelief before fixing on the syringe she now held in her hand. Finally Caroline raised her eyes again and the disdain Alex saw withered her to the core. Alex wanted to cry; she desperately wanted to explain that this wasn't her fault. But the disgust in Caroline's eyes told her that she would be wasting her time.

'Leave the department,' Caroline Cowan quietly ordered.

Alex was so shocked she could hardly speak. 'I . . . I . . .'

'Hey, there's no need for that!' Maggie Fielding interrupted in her most autocratic consultant's voice. 'There are two of them here, Dr Cowan. Don't you think you should get the facts before you start accusing one of your staff? You haven't even asked who's at fault yet. You've just assumed Dr Taylor has made the error.' Her eyes fixed on Fiona. 'Did Dr Taylor ask you to draw up a drug?'

'No!' Fiona snapped. 'She asked me to fetch a drug.'

A thin smile curved Maggie's lips, her tone offhand. 'Same thing.'

Fiona's eyes blazed and her chin tilted indignantly. 'No! Not the same thing!'

Throughout the exchange Caroline didn't say a word. Her eyes remained steadily fixed on Alex and then she repeated the order:

'Leave now, before I have security escort you.'

Tears stung Alex's eyes as she shook her head.

Caroline's voice was flat, but her eyes glittered with fury.

'I will talk to you later, Dr Taylor. Please don't make it any more difficult than it is already. I want you to leave the department immediately.'

Alex felt dozens of eyes follow her, as, on trembling legs, she moved to the exit, but she knew this was just in her imagination. Everyone else was too busy to even notice that her world had just fallen apart.

CHAPTER FOURTEEN

If disappointment could occupy a physical space, then Caroline's office would be fit to be bursting. Her disappointment was palpable. She was polite and civil, but there was no warmth in her tone as she laid bare Alex's crime.

'To say I'm disappointed is an understatement. I've called this meeting to give you a chance to explain your behaviour before I make a decision on whether to make this formal. As you see I haven't involved HR at this stage; this is an opportunity for you and me to have a frank exchange. If you're in agreement, that is? Do you understand, Dr Taylor?'

Alex swallowed hard and nodded. 'Yes, and thank you for not making it formal.'

'Well that still remains to be seen. So, please explain yourself.'

'I forgot I was on call,' she answered in a small voice.

Caroline stared at her, appalled. 'Forgot? You forgot! That's your excuse?'

'I genuinely forgot,' Alex said earnestly. 'It was my sister's wedding on Saturday and it slipped my mind that I was on call.'

Caroline leaned forward in her chair, her expression stern. 'Well that, Alex, tells me you clearly haven't got your mind on the job. While I understand that this has been a trying time for you, you should have taken more time off to get yourself completely better.'

Alex bridled. 'Better from what?'

'Better from whatever is going on! Do you understand what I'm saying? Do you realise how worried I am about you?'

Alex felt the sting of tears in her eyes. She loved Caroline and respected her more than any other doctor she knew. She didn't want this woman to lose faith in her.

'I'm sorry that I let you down. Yesterday was unforgivable. I know you've lost trust in me, but I truly believe I was capable of carrying out my job.'

'And that, Alex, is exactly why I've lost trust. What you're saying is what every drink driver says after causing an accident: "I thought I was safe to drive." You stupid girl, you're mucking up your life with this nonsense. I want you to be on my team, Alex. I have high hopes for your future. I expect to see you become a consultant here some day, but if you continue like this you're going to ruin it all. You had a bad time last year, and these last few weeks have shown that you haven't recovered from it. Go and see someone and get it properly sorted out. I won't make this formal, but I will have to monitor your behaviour.'

Unchecked, the tears dripped down Alex's cheeks and she quickly brushed them away. Caroline had just revealed that she didn't believe Alex had been abducted, that what happened a month ago was in her mind, imagined because of the 'bad time' Alex had suffered last year.

'Look, take some more time. Go and spend some more time with that handsome boyfriend of yours. He's worried, Alex. He's worried about your drinking.' She smiled to take the sting out of her next words. 'Said you hit the bottle pretty hard while you were away.' She relaxed back in her chair, the sternness now gone from her expression. 'Think about what I've said. Think about your future.'

In her car Alex shook with humiliation. How dare he? How dare he talk behind her back? He had betrayed her. All the hugs and reassurance counted for nothing when he could do this to her. Why didn't he say it to her face? Tell her he was worried. Talk to her about the goddam situation. He was carrying on as if nothing had happened; was it any wonder she was drinking? And when had he had this conversation with Caroline? When had they got so pally that he thought he had that right? Of all the things he could have said, nothing could have been worse than telling her boss she was a drunk.

She picked up her mobile and stabbed the screen till she found his number, and as soon as she heard his voice she shouted, 'Traitor!'

His first words stunned her. 'Caroline had a right to know.'

'To know! You nearly destroyed my career. I'm lucky I'm not suspended!'

'You're lucky that a patient didn't die on you,' he said bluntly.

'It wasn't my fault, Patrick. I didn't cause that drug error.'

'And unfortunately, Alex, you can't prove it. No one's going to take your word if they think you've been drinking.' His voice was bleak and the anger drained from Alex. She had no more fight in her.

'Are you OK?' he now asked.

She sat silent, unable to reply.

'I love you,' he offered.

'But do you still believe me?' she whispered. She heard his sigh and snapped, 'Just tell me!'

'The more I think about it, the more I'm inclined to believe that this was a hallucination, the knock on your head playing havoc with your mind. The police have found no trace of this man, Alex.'

She had nothing to say.

'Are you there, darling? Talk to me. You're not yourself at the moment.'

'Do you remember what I told you about when I woke up on that operating table?' she asked.

'Yes, but—'

'I told you I was blinded by theatre lights.'

'For God's sake, Alex.' His tone was sharp. 'That could have been from me and the security guard. We had torches in our hands. We were shining them into your face.'

'So you no longer believe me,' she stated.

'I didn't say that,' he said softly back.

She pressed the end button and he didn't hear her reply.

'Yes, you did,' she whispered bitterly.

Going to the doctors' party was Fiona's idea.

A bad one, as far as Alex was concerned, but she would go, if only to give Fiona a good night out. She had learned long ago that Fiona had very little else going on in her life outside work and aside from their friendship, and Alex was aware she had paid little attention to her friend these last weeks.

On the last Thursday of every month the doctors' party was held in a different venue, either in the city or on site. Tonight it was being held in the grounds of the hospital, in the social club. The building was sited near the doctors' quarters and meant only a short walk before they reached their beds to sleep off the large quantities of alcohol they usually consumed. When Alex moved back to Bath she had lived in the doctors' quarters until circumstances drove her to search for somewhere more secure to live. She drove to the party with every intention of not drinking.

Fiona clearly intended to fully enjoy herself. Her hair was loose and in its usual form: frizzy and framing her face. She wore slim-fit black jeans and a green silky blouse, to which she'd pinned a novelty flashing Santa Claus broach. Alex stood outside with her as she smoked, her Nicorette patch peeled off her shoulder and stuck to the outside of her cigarette packet. Alex shook her head, bemused, when Fiona returned the sticky patch to her shoulder after stubbing out the cigarette.

'You'll increase your nicotine levels if you keep doing that,' she admonished.

'Oh shut up, Dr Know-it-all,' Fiona laughed. 'You only live once, and I've had a bloody hard day. We're young and one of us is free and single, so let's get this party started. You,' she said, her expression mock serious and her speech beginning to slur, 'need to lighten up. You, more than most, need to start having some fun. You're gorgeous, you cow, and can have your pick. You . . .'

She saw the stricken look Alex gave her. 'Oh bugger, you know I didn't mean . . . Oh look, let's fucking forget about men full stop and just get in there and have a blast. Above all, let's get pissed.'

Alex shrugged resignedly, a half smile on her face. 'Give me a minute and I'll be in. Damned hot in there.'

'Well what d'you expect, wearing a frigging woolly jumper to a party? Can't you take it off?'

Alex shook her head. 'Only a bra. I'll have cooled off in a minute, and then I'll be ready to party.'

The door behind them banged open and Patrick, face flushed and eyes glazed, joined them. 'Hey, you two, the party's in here.'

Alex let out a weary sigh. 'I'm just cooling down, Patrick. I'm overdressed, as you can see.'

His eyes appraised her. 'Darling, surely you have something better to wear than that? You left that little satin jacket in my car. Do you want me to fetch it?'

'Good idea, Pat,' Fiona said, and Alex noted the disapproving look he gave her friend at the shortening of his name. Fiona was aware that Patrick had upset her, without knowing why.

'It's Patrick, Fiona. You know I like to be called Patrick.'

Fiona gave a saccharine smile. 'I do indeed. Which is why I call you Pat.'

'And you can be so nice when you want to be,' he quipped back.

Alex sighed again and Patrick gazed at her. 'Why all the sighs? Is it me? You clearly aren't happy for me to be here, even though you invited me. I saw you arrive an hour ago and yet you didn't seek me out. I clearly can't get anything right at the moment.'

Alex felt a tightness in her chest. She felt trapped and wanted to scream out loud at the top of her voice for everyone to just leave her the hell alone. Instead she gave an honest answer. 'Well, Patrick, at the moment I think it's me who can't get anything right. I can't fabricate or invent a story to suit your version of events. Unless you have concrete proof that I'm not a nutter or a liar there really is nothing more for us to talk about. It's as simple as that, or wouldn't you agree?'

His eyes had taken on a cool glint. 'You're being hysterical, darling, and I really don't think this is the time or the place.'

Alex shook her head in disgust. 'It never is, Patrick. And that's the problem.'

'Perhaps if you drank less, you'd see there needn't be a problem.'

Her eyes rested on Fiona. 'I'll see you at the bar. I need another five minutes to cool down.'

And with that she turned and walked away.

Alex drained her third vodka, wishing she'd worn something lighter, as sweat gathered in the small of her back. Lately she had taken to wearing clothing that hid her shape. She didn't bother to do her hair and used make-up only to disguise her pallor and dark circled eyes. She didn't want to look feminine or sexy any more. She wanted to be invisible.

She caught sight of Nathan Bell at the bar and was surprised. She hadn't seen him at one of these events before. She'd never wondered why, but if she had she would have said he was too introverted to attend. Socially shy. She didn't know anything about his private life except that his mother had recently 'been taken in again'. She didn't know where she had been taken, as Nathan hadn't expanded on his explanation, so she could only assume he meant a hospital. It was by chance that she heard him talking on the telephone, saying to the caller, 'Give her my best, and tell her I'll visit on Tuesday.' When he saw Alex he simply said, 'It's my mother, she's been taken in again.'

Making her way towards him, she gave Patrick a brief glance. He was on the dance floor with Fiona and several other nurses from the department, wearing a gold tinsel garland round his neck and having a whale of a time, judging by his uninhibited dance moves. Caroline looked awkward as she danced more conservatively with a few of the healthcare assistants and orderlies. She'd given Alex a little wave from across the room, but they hadn't spoken. Edward Downing, the radiologist, was gathered in a corner with a fair number of staff from the radiology department, looking separate from the rest of the partygoers, and she wondered if he was having a goodbye party all of his own. Tom Collins and Maggie Fielding, both elegant and tall, were chatting together. She caught their eyes and nodded briefly. She turned her back and spoke to Nathan.

'Hello, Nathan. Don't see you at these dos often.'

He gave a self-conscious shrug. 'Thought I should get out a bit more. Actually, it was Fiona; she said a few of the department were going. So . . . here I am.'

With only the right side of his face showing, Alex noticed he had a beautifully shaped face, with strong flat cheekbones and a long jaw. His lips were pale and not too full.

'How are you?' he asked unexpectedly.

'Fine,' she answered gaily. 'Spiffing.'

'Really? I would have thought things were still difficult for you.'

'Why would you suppose that?'

'The um ... attack a month ago and, um, the situation at work. I'm sorry ... it's not my idea to shadow you. Dr Cowan suggests we work the same shifts for a few weeks. I hope you don't mind?'

Despite the constant presence of Nathan, things at work had been going well the last few days. If anything, two doctors attending one patient at the same time had shortened the waiting time for the other patients. Caroline had used this as the reason for Alex being shadowed. She explained to other staff members that it was a time-and-motion study, and they seemed to accept it, which Alex knew she should be grateful for. If there were gossipy whispers, she wasn't hearing them.

She realised how very lucky she had been over the George Bartlett situation. Any other employer would have demanded a full enquiry over the drug error, but Caroline was giving her a reprieve. She reached over for Nathan's glass and drank a third of his beer. 'Sorry,' she said, not meaning it. She should be grateful to Caroline that she was not pressing for a formal disciplinary process. She should, of course, be grateful that her whole life had been fucked up.

He shrugged, dismissing the matter as minor, and signalled to one of the bar staff. 'Let me buy you one.'

Minutes later, with fresh drinks on the bar and his change back in his pocket, Alex answered him as if there had been no break in the conversation.

'Haven't you heard? I'm a fantasist.'

'Really?'

She gulped her drink. 'Well, it at least lets me call the shots. Brain damaged or nutter doesn't quite cut it. Fantasist. Well, it sounds rather exotic. Alex, the great fantasist.'

She was getting drunk and didn't care if she sounded reckless.

'Would you like to talk about it?'

'No, thank you. I'd rather we had another drink and talked about you for a change, Mr Bell. I want to know why some nice lady isn't with you tonight.'

'I could ask the same about you.'

'Oh, I'm with someone. The good-looking dark-haired man over in that far corner, who thinks I'm a drunk and unable to separate truth from fiction.'

Nathan Bell looked embarrassed. 'I'm sure he doesn't think that.'

'Stop trying to make me feel better, Nathan. It's over. He doesn't fucking believe me! So it's over.'

He winced, and as much as she would like to blame the effects of alcohol for her uncouthness, she couldn't. She had wanted to shock the poor man, but in doing so she had shocked herself. She never spoke this way. Never stepped beyond the boundaries of decent behaviour. She had disgraced herself, and, now embarrassed, she tried to quickly sober up.

'I'm sorry. I've got to go.'

'Go? Oh no you don't,' shrieked Fiona from behind. 'We haven't even had a dance. What's the bloody rush? You've got the lovely Dr Bell here and I'm sure he'd like to have a dance. Wouldn't you, Dr Bell?'

Nathan held up his hands, palms forward defensively, 'No, but thank you anyway. I'm absolutely fine standing here. I was, in fact, thinking I'd make a move myself shortly.'

Fiona stepped back, planting both feet apart. She screwed up her face, squinting at Nathan curiously, and then in near-perfect mimicry, she repeated back his words: 'I'm absolutely fine standing here. I was, in fact, thinking I'd make a move myself shortly.'

Nathan looked startled and smiled gamely, slowly clapping his hands. 'Wow! That's some party trick.'

Fiona gave a come-hither smile, her body becoming fluid as she slinked to the bar, squeezing in between Nathan and Alex, but with her attention solely on Alex. 'Darling, surely you have something better to wear than that?'

The bar lady, having heard Fiona speak, gawped; her voice was full of admiration. 'You're amazing! Can you do any one famous?'

Other people at the bar had stopped talking to listen, and Fiona smiled at her waiting audience. Her eyes trapped Alex. She winked and glanced over Alex's shoulder to where Patrick had suddenly appeared. Alex's voice came out of her mouth, 'Stop trying to make me feel better, Nathan. It's over. He doesn't fucking believe me. So it's over.'

Alex felt as if she'd been slapped. She was shocked by how much Fiona sounded like her, and shocked that her closest friend had been cruel.

'I've got to go,' she mumbled.

As she stumbled through the car park, her face scorched with embarrassment, she was unaware that Nathan was following her.

She came to a halt as she saw her green Mini. Parked earlier with safety in mind, near to the building and lit by the outside lights, the message painted on the windscreen was easy to see.

In yellow spray paint across the entire width of the glass she saw the words: *Alex likes to say yes*.

At the police station, after a brief chat with the officer at the front desk, they were separated. Nathan was shown into an interview room adjacent to the reception area, while another officer pressed numbers on a keypad and escorted her upstairs to DI Turner's office. After being left alone for more than forty minutes, the layout of the room and its contents was imprinted on her brain.

Pale lilac paint on all four walls and an air force blue carpet on the floor. White vertical blinds closed over the only window, shutting out the night and making the room claustrophobic. She was sitting on the visitor's side of the desk, in a chair identical to the one across from her. The *Bath Chronicle*, the *Guardian* and the *Daily Mail* were spread on the desk in various stages of being read. A plastic Tupperware box had its lid off, and a half-eaten chicken and lettuce brown roll looked still fresh. On the radiator beneath the windowsill a battered can of Coke was balanced.

She heard a noise in the corridor, and DI Turner appeared in the doorway carrying a tray with two mugs and a sugar bowl.

'Coffee,' he said by way of greeting, then nodding at a mobile phone on the tray beside the coffees he added, 'Quick thinking by your friend.'

Nathan had snapped several photographs of her car while she had stared at it aghast.

'Sorry about the wait. I sent some officers up to the hospital to hopefully get some CCTV footage from the social club. They shouldn't be too long.'

Alex breathed a sigh of relief. Any time now she would know who had done this to her. And so would everyone else.

'Is he your boyfriend?' Greg Turner asked.

Alex shook her head. 'No. He's a colleague. A friend.'

'And you went to the party with him?'

'No. I was with my boyfriend and another friend, Fiona Woods. Nathan was at the party and he followed me when I . . . Well, I embarrassed myself by getting drunk and Nathan followed me when I rushed out of the club. He was with me when I got to my car.'

'Not planning on driving, were you?' Greg Turner asked with a note of disapproval.

Again she shook her head. 'I just wanted to be alone for a while. I couldn't have driven it anyway. My keys are still in my bag and my bag is back at the party.'

'And your boyfriend?'

'Probably still there. Probably hasn't even noticed I've gone.'

She flushed as she heard the self-pity in her voice, and quickly changed the subject. 'How are Amy Abbott's parents?'

He gave a small shrug. 'Devastated. Unable to come to terms with what has happened.'

'And the boyfriend? Have you found him yet?'

He looked down at his desk and rubbed a restless finger along the bridge of his nose. 'We don't know that she had a boyfriend, only that she was pregnant.'

'You haven't been able to find out anything, have you?' she persisted.

'Dr Taylor, I really cannot discuss the case with you.'

'Nor look at me when you say that?'

He raised his head immediately and she saw he was more than capable of keeping eye contact. She felt foolish. He had honed the skill on criminals, who no doubt tried to avoid this very situation.

'Do her parents believe she did this to herself?' she asked. 'Do they think their daughter died because of what she did to herself?'

He stayed silent, but she knew the answer.

'Of course they don't,' she quietly stated. 'It's unthinkable and hideous that any young woman would do this to herself. And where was she all the time she was missing?'

His lips moved into the semblance of a polite smile. 'We don't know yet. We're still checking. She had lots of friends. As you know she was found on a street. The last sighting we have—'

'Is in Kingsmead Square,' she finished lamely. 'I know. I read it in the paper.'

'Look, Dr Taylor, as far as we're concerned this is not a murder investigation. At the very worst it's suicide, but more likely it's a tragic accident. You really must not think this has anything to do with you. Unless of course you know something different to us?'

Her head was throbbing from too much alcohol and the beat of the too-loud music she had left behind.

'You weren't there when she died. She was telling me something. I know she was telling me something. It was in her eyes . . . She—'

A knock on the door interrupted them. With surprise Alex saw Laura Best enter the room. The woman smiled at her with far more friendliness than Alex recalled. Maybe it was the fact that Alex was now wearing her own clothes and not lying on an examination table that made the female officer regard her as a person rather than as a victim to be questioned. Or maybe she was showing her sunny side for the benefit of Greg Turner?

'Can I help you?' he asked.

'CCTV footage,' she said, holding up a black video case.

'Christ, that was quick – what did you do, fly there?'

Laura Best smiled. 'I was close by, and it was easy enough to pick up. Dr Taylor has had enough to deal with as it is. I'm sure she's eager to see her attacker.'

The stress on the word 'attacker' was subtle, but Alex was sensitive enough to realise it had been a dig.

DI Turner gave the woman a nod and indicated that she should put on the video. From the look and slightly dismissive shrug she gave her boss it was clear Laura Best had already seen the footage and that there was not a lot on the footage. Alex's heart sank, and stayed that way as she watched the action take place on her car.

The vandal wore a dark bulky top with a hood that obscured his head and face entirely, and baggy trousers and gloves that hid the shape of his limbs and skin colour. There was no way of telling who it was.

'I think it's a joke.'

Alex's eyes shot open. 'Pardon?'

She wanted to get up and slap Laura Best's face.

Laura Best glanced at Greg Turner, encouraging him to concur with her opinion. 'A joke.'

'A bit of a *sick* joke,' Greg Turner replied.

'Well, yes, of course, but a joke all the same. Or prank, if you prefer.'

Alex felt sick as the implication of what she was hearing sank in. 'You think someone did this because they know I said yes to him?'

Neither of them answered her.

'You think someone did this because they think I'm an easy lay?'

Greg Turner shook his head firmly. 'Unless you've discussed the intimate details of your case, no one else should know. Do you think it's possible that you may have told someone, who would then do this to your car?'

She shook her head firmly.

'Well, I can only suggest that DC Best could be right about it being a prank. Possibly carried out by someone who heard about your experience and is now being cruel by turning it into a sideshow.'

Alex struggled to her feet. 'I'm tired. I want to go home now.'

'Drink your coffee first. We'll talk a little more and then I'll drive you home,' he offered.

Alex was already walking to the door. 'I don't think so. I'm just a joke. Isn't that right, DI Turner? Well, don't forget to have a good laugh at my expense.'

'Dr Taylor, you might want this?'

Alex turned and saw Laura Best holding out her black shoulder bag. Surprised, she went back across the room to take it.

'The bar lady said you left it behind. Thought you might want it.'

Alex mumbled a thank-you.

Silence followed her as she made her way across the foyer to the exit. Nathan was nowhere to be seen. Silence accompanied her out into the darkness, but she could hear her attacker's voice taunting her beneath his surgical mask. 'What does "no" mean? It's a simple question.'

CHAPTER FIFTEEN

It was six weeks since that horrific night and one week since the doctors' party. Any hope of thinking he no longer was a danger had fled her mind as soon as she'd seen her car. She was terrified that he was still out there and there was nothing she could do to prove it. As far as the police were concerned the message on her car was a prank. She was the butt of someone's cruel joke.

She lifted the paper bag to her mouth and breathed in and out. She had to stop thinking about it, or else she would become a prisoner inside her own home. But it was so hard. Anxiety plagued her all the time. At work she parked as close to her department as possible. She looked at every man she passed keenly. The porters, the nurses and the doctors she came in contact with were now suspects. The male patients she treated, if there for minor ailments, were also considered suspects. And while she stood in their presence studying their features, it was their voices she concentrated on most. But none had his voice. How could they? The pitch of his voice had been distorted. Flattened.

What it reminded her of most was a tracheostomy patient who'd had a voice prosthesis inserted. When he spoke his voice sounded mechanical because air no longer passed through the vocal cords but through a tube instead. Could a man with a tracheostomy have taken her, she now crazily wondered. Someone who blamed her for the loss of his voice? She was going mad with all these wild speculations. He was sending her insane while destroying her life.

Patrick had stopped ringing. The last message, from three days earlier, was still saved. She played it over and over, listening for any insincerity, but his apology for hurting her sounded genuine. He should never have gone behind her back and talked to Caroline. He was out of order. He regretted it entirely, but he felt out of control over the situation surrounding Alex and felt he had let her down. By not believing her. He kept his composure right up until the end where his voice broke: 'I love you, Alex. I want to marry you. Please, please ring me.'

The reason she didn't call back was not because of him confiding in Caroline, though that hurt. It was because he'd admitted he didn't believe her. Without trust and one hundred per cent belief in the person you were supposed to love, there was no foundation to build on. A long-term relationship like a marriage wouldn't stand a chance. As far as she was concerned, their relationship, although not officially ended by either of them, was over.

Standing alone in her kitchen she wished she didn't miss him. She wished a thousand times that everything could go back to those minutes when she first set out to meet him, and that now they were planning what to buy each other for Christmas.

But more than anything she wished she didn't see him as someone different, someone weaker, someone she would never have fallen in love with. It was as if she had lost her Patrick and this new one replaced him, and with sadness she realised he probably felt exactly the same about her. They were lost to each other. Even if they searched really hard they would stay lost because they weren't the same people any more. She had survived a horrific experience, which he believed she had imagined.

Six weeks ago she had a boyfriend she loved, a job she loved, and a life to call her own. In the space of a few hours her sane world had been whipped away. It was now splashed with uncertainty, anxiety and great big splodges of the unknown. If it wasn't for her job and the help of little blue pills, she knew she wouldn't be able to carry on.

Later that afternoon, berating herself for trying to do all her Christmas shopping in one day, she struggled back to the car park under the weight of John Lewis, Marks & Spencer and Thorntons bags. She should have stuck to her original plan and given everyone vouchers instead. It would have saved her time and energy, and she wouldn't now be exhausted and left with the thought that the gifts she'd bought were somehow not quite right. The shirt for her father now seemed too modern, and the dressing gown for her mother was a repeat of what she'd bought her last year. It had been a long day with no festive feeling. She hadn't rung Fiona to remind her they were going shopping, because they hadn't spoken since the party. She had not forgiven her yet.

With carrier bags all over the back seat of her car she joined the lane of slow-moving vehicles making their way to the exit, and hoped the traffic from Bristol back to Bath had eased since the morning. She wanted to stop at a garage and get her car washed; she could still see flecks of yellow paint on the windscreen, even though it had been scrubbed to within an inch of its life. A clean car was one less reminder. When she got home, if she could muster enough energy, she would give her flat a tidy. On the other hand, she had tomorrow off as well and could catch up with any household chores then. It would keep her occupied until she returned to work.

And then she could get back to the business of thinking about other people's lives instead of her own.

Winter darkness had arrived by four o'clock as she drove down the ramp to the basement car park beneath her apartment building, and her mind was free of all these unsettling things. Her thoughts were on what she would have for dinner, the long soak in a bubble bath she was looking forward to, and the TV drama on at nine o'clock.

If she had been driving a fraction faster she would have driven straight over the woman. She slammed her foot on the brake and switched the headlights to full beam. The woman was lying on the ground, flat on her back in Alex's car parking space, completely still. Instinctively Alex opened her glove box and pulled out various pieces of medical equipment that she kept on hand in the event of passing an accident. With a Guedel airway tube and stethoscope in one hand and a handful of bandages in the other she rushed to aid the woman.

Briefly she took in the clothing and make-up: high-heeled black shiny boots, a minuscule red satin skirt barely covering plump bare thighs, and a low-cut black T-shirt under a cream satin jacket. Her initial thought was that the woman had taken a beating, but as Alex examined her closer she could see that she was wrong. Her right elbow was at an impossible angle and her shoulder looked massively swollen. Her finger bones had split through the skin and were bent backwards. Alex ignored the bloody hand; what filled her with most concern was the black mark across the cream jacket, right across the woman's chest. It was the imprint of a tyre. She pulled out her mobile and called for an ambulance.

Placing her ear near the woman's mouth she felt warm breath and at the same time saw some rise in the chest. The vein in her neck was distended and pulsating hard. She was breathing, but how well was another matter. If a car had run over her there was the likelihood of multiple rib fractures and injury to the lungs. She undid the single button holding the cream jacket closed and ripped the thin black T-shirt up the middle. The rib cage was misshapen and there was only a feeble rise on the left side of the chest. Alex was dealing with major chest trauma, and knew that without the presence of a surgical team and the right instruments the woman could die soon.

In the boot of her car there was a chest drain kit, chest tubes, scalpels and other equipment that would inflate a lung, but if there was severe vessel damage only blood or large volumes of fluid replacement would keep her heart pumping. But she must think positively. She needed to focus on keeping the woman alive for as long as possible.

A small choking sound alerted her to the woman stirring and she switched her gaze back to the face. She was astonished to see the woman's eyes open.

'Hello, you've had an accident and I'm helping you,' she calmly said.

The woman tried to answer but no sound passed her moving lips.

'I'm a doctor. An ambulance is on the way.'

Alex felt faint hope. If the woman was conscious, maybe she wasn't internally haemorrhaging. She definitely had a collapsed lung, but Alex could fix that. She needed to keep the woman breathing, that was all that mattered, because if her heart stopped beating Alex would be compressing broken ribs into a possibly damaged heart and lungs.

A small spray of blood was coughed up and some of it showered the woman's face. Using her fingertips Alex carefully wiped it from her eyelids, urgently praying for the ambulance to hurry up. This woman was about to bleed out!

Then the woman spoke. And the low-pitched bubbling sound warned Alex she was drowning: 'Wants to play doctors . . . save me . . .'

She coughed again, and with blood-coated teeth she smiled gruesomely. 'Some doctor . . .'

When the blood flooded the woman's mouth Alex used the bandages, the woman's clothing, and then as much as she could of her own clothing to mop it away. Only when her heart stopped pumping did the blood stop coming.

The ambulance crew arrived to find both women bathed in blood from head to toe, and initially thought them both injured. Later, when interviewed by the police, they described finding Dr Taylor looking like a crazed woman kneeling over the dead body. 'She looked like Carrie in the movie, her hair and face dripping with blood, and her eyes staring,' one of them said. 'Like bloody Carrie.'

CHAPTER SIXTEEN

Four police cars and a transit van surrounded the area where the dead woman lay. The ambulance crew had come and gone, and a dozen police officers had taken their place. The occupants of the apartments, who were beginning to return from work, were told to park elsewhere. The area was a crime scene and no other vehicles would be allowed in for several days at least. Alex shivered in the back seat of one of the police vehicles. She had not been allowed to go up to her flat and change; the blood on her clothes and hands had dried and black crusts were buried beneath her nails.

She had seen Laura Best and another officer walk around her newly washed bottle-green Mini several times. They had gone down on their bellies and inspected it underneath. A female officer had asked her to blow into a mouthpiece, and Alex was grateful for having resisted alcohol for the last few days. She was a suspect in a crime. Not necessarily the prime one, but a suspect all the same. She had given a brief statement to the first officer on the scene and was told that she would be questioned again later. It was more than four hours since she had arrived home from her Christmas shopping trip, and even though the hours were filled with so much going on around her, they were the longest hours she had ever lived.

Maybe if she just got out of the police car and walked across the car park to the lift, she would escape to her apartment unseen. She could have a bath, cook some dinner . . .

The sobs, when they came, robbed her of breath. She was unaware of the car door opening or of hands reaching in to help her out. She was unaware of being escorted up to her apartment, a throw being put around her shoulders and a warm mug being placed in her hands. It was only when the warmth of sweetened tea hit her stomach that she became aware of her surroundings.

Greg Turner stood a few feet away, watching her with troubled eyes. The rain had flattened his wavy hair and the shoulders of his leather jacket were damp, and for the first time he didn't seem so forbidding.

'I'm sorry about this. I'll have words with them later. I think they forgot they'd put you in the back of one of the cars.'

Alex shivered as warmth penetrated her frozen limbs. It was always cold in the underground car park, and sitting there for several hours had made her numb. 'I couldn't save her,' she whispered. 'It was like a war zone. Her blood just kept coming and there was nothing I could do.'

'The ambulance crew said she had massive injuries. I don't think there was much anybody could have done in the circumstances.'

'But I'm a doctor,' she cried. 'That's what I do. I save lives. I should have done more. I should have acted quicker. Got a chest drain in. Got in an airway before she drowned in her own blood!'

'I'm sure you did all you could,' he said soothingly. Then: 'We'll need you to give a full statement. The sooner the better.'

With her hands cradled round the warm mug, Alex saw the dried blood caking her fingernails and could smell its metallic odour as she thawed out.

'Could I have a bath first?'

He hesitated and then relented. 'Sure. But we'll need the clothes you're wearing.'

'I'm a suspect, aren't I? They think I drove over her, don't they?'

He shook his head. 'It's procedure. There might be transferred evidence on your clothes. She was a small-time prostitute. Known as "Lunchtime Lilly".'

Alex stared at him disdainfully.

He raised his hands, suggesting this was not his name for her. 'Lillian Armstrong. Known to her friends and by us as Lilly. She earned the nickname because she usually only worked daytime hours on account of her children being at school and having no husband to mind them at night.'

Alex had guessed what she was, but didn't want to say. She had met many women like Lilly over the years and knew they all had their reasons for doing what they did. She never judged them when they turned up at A & E instead of attending the sexual health clinic for their creams and antibiotics. And often she would be the one to give them tea after they had been patched up from the beatings they often got. It was a sick world, and her job was to treat the sick.

'I'll put my clothes in a bin liner if you want?'

From his jacket pocket he pulled out two large clear plastic bags. 'I'd prefer you to put them in these.'

Alex rose wearily to her feet. 'There's a tyre mark. On her jacket, there's the imprint of a tyre.'

Turner frowned. 'Whereabouts on the jacket?'

'Across her chest. She was crushed.'

'Did you move her when you got to her?'

'Of course I didn't,' she answered sharply. 'She might have had spinal injuries!' She heaved for breath and made a small cry. 'I'm sorry, I didn't mean to snap.'

'It's understandable. You've had a rough day.'

'Why did you ask me that?' she asked. 'Why did you think I might have moved her?'

He shrugged. 'It was just a thought.'

Greg Turner didn't strike her as someone who just had a thought unless there was a reason behind it, but she didn't think he'd tell her what it was. She would have to work it out herself when she was less tired.

It was gone eleven when she finally shut the door on him. She was instructed to present at Bath police station tomorrow to give a full statement. She hoped it wouldn't be Laura Best taking it. While she had been sitting in the back of the police car the woman had given her several appraising looks, her manner remote and cool. Police officers were still examining the car park and outside the perimeter. She heard knocks on several of her neighbours' doors and knew they would all be giving statements, but it gave her no confidence that the police would find anything.

They had a tyre mark, but that, she bet, was all they would have.

Like a domestic animal finding its usual place to sleep, Alex found hers. Her back against her living-room wall, she huddled with a duvet pulled round her shoulders and heard again the woman's final words: 'Wants to play doctors . . .'

Until this moment she had thought the woman was referring to her; her being the doctor and her doing the saving. But suppose that wasn't the case, that in fact the dead woman had been referring to the person who had knocked her down?

Some doctor . . .

Supposing the person who knocked her down was a doctor; why hadn't he or she tried to save her or called an ambulance? Could it be that it was deliberate? Could it be the same person who had targeted Alex? An awful thought consumed her. Had he been on his way to attack her again, only Lillian Armstrong had somehow got in the way? Did he know she lived here?

Wants to play doctors . . .

Lillian Armstrong's words could have been nothing more than the last feeble attempt of a dying woman to make sense of what was happening to her. Alex prayed it was. Otherwise *he* was out there; he was still active and she wasn't a one-off. He was still playing at being a doctor, but now he was killing his victims.

CHAPTER SEVENTEEN

They met at a restaurant that neither of them had been to before. A French bistro on Pulteney Bridge with stone floors, bare wooden tables and plenty of red, dripping candles. It was informal and a bit scruffy, yet expensive, and on weekends almost always full, which was why they hadn't been before. On this Wednesday night, however, there was only one other table occupied and Patrick was seated at one with a panoramic view of the weir.

He was staring at the menu when she arrived, wearing a burgundy shirt she had helped him choose and a smart black jacket. In the candlelight his handsome face looked flushed. A large glass of red wine sat in front of him on the table. His posture was relaxed and she wondered if it was his first drink.

He was surprised when she slipped into the chair opposite him, and she was pleased at placing him so quickly at a disadvantage. He rose to his feet and had to reach awkwardly across the table to kiss her. The lit candle and single flower between them hampered his movements, and her averted face only allowed him to brush his lips against her cheek. If she had turned her head slightly he could have kissed her properly, but she wasn't ready for that.

An awkward silence filled the next few seconds, until he opened the second menu and handed it to her.

'Food looks great. We should have come here before.'

A waiter appeared and poured her a glass of water and enquired what she would like to drink. Alex chose dry white wine. The dryer the better. It would make her sip instead of guzzling it back. Alcohol was her enemy at the moment, and she mustn't forget that. It would be so easy to knock back a couple of glasses of red or a sweeter white before the main course was even served if she allowed herself. Conversation would flow better, awkward moments would be dealt with more easily. But at the end of the evening Alex would want more. She would think of the unopened bottles back at her flat like friends and forget that they were the enemy. Far better to stick to a single glass of white wine.

'I'll have the *moules* followed by the monkfish,' she said to the waiter before even being asked if she was ready to order.

Patrick ordered the same, and asked for another glass of Merlot.

'Thank you for coming,' he said predictably when they were alone again. Then he cleared his throat and moved his hand in an awkward gesture. 'Sorry. That sounded crass. I sound like a host at a party.' He waited for her to look at him. 'I need to explain how sorry I am. Not just for my unforgivable behaviour over Caroline, but for the weeks before when I refused to allow you to talk about what happened. I behaved badly, rushing you off to Barbados like that as if I could simply make it better for you by offering you a bit of sunshine and a pretty beach.'

Alex felt the hold on her insides begin to loosen, and an ache across the bridge of her nose and in her throat as she held back her tears. She wasn't going to forgive him this easily. She needed to hear more.

The waiter arrived with their drinks, and then a few minutes later with warmed bread and bowls of steaming *moules*, and for the next ten minutes there was a peace between them. Il Divo were singing 'O Holy Night' in the background, Christmas tree lights were twinkling, and conversation was limited to the place they were in and the food they were eating as they relaxed and enjoyed each other's company again.

When the main course arrived, she was laughing and Patrick had ordered a bottle of fine Bordeaux. She had forgotten how funny he was, had forgotten that laughter could be an aphrodisiac. She wanted to make love to him so badly she almost asked him if they could get up and leave. She restrained herself by fixing her attention on the décor and then jumped when his fingers caressed the back of her hand.

'Beautiful Alex. Can you ever forgive me? I will never let you down again. I promise you that. I have asked myself why I treated you so badly and the only answer I can come up with is that I thought you were having a breakdown and I couldn't bear to see it.'

She curled her fingers round his and felt her heart soar. They would talk about everything later. She'd tell him about her suspicions over Amy Abbott's death and about the woman who bled to death two days ago in her car park. She had given her statement yesterday along with a DNA sample. Maybe Patrick could help her get the police to believe that there was someone out there making all this happen. He was less emotional than her and might argue her case better.

'Thank you for that, Patrick,' she whispered.

He moved the candle and the single flower to one side and then without restrictions or any resistance from her he leaned over and kissed her. It was a kiss full of tenderness, a balm to heal her pain, and she had never felt more cherished.

'I ask myself if my behaviour helped cause it,' he said quietly. 'Had you been crying out in the months before, needing my help?'

'What—?'

'Let me finish,' he said, gripping her hand. 'I saw you as so strong and perfect that when you said all those things I refused to accept you needed help. Proper help. Not some silly holiday.'

Her body had turned to stone. Her mind was the only thing still working. There were no tremors coursing through her body and no heart racing beneath her breast.

It was worse than she could ever have imagined. He was taking the blame for the things he believed she imagined because he had not seen the signs that she needed help.

It was hopeless. And she was such a fool! He didn't know her at all. None of their deepest thoughts shared over the last year had taught him anything about who she was. He had seen her as someone strong and perfect who didn't succumb to weaknesses. And yet if he truly saw her as such a person, wasn't it reasonable that he would at least want to explore the possibility of another explanation. Didn't he want to stand up and say, 'Well OK, Alex, let's investigate this. You are a sane and normal person. Why on earth would you say this happened if it didn't?'

But of course, as far as he was concerned there was no need to say this, because as far as he was concerned it didn't happen. None of it. She had simply lost her mind and needed proper help.

She managed to stand. And through stone-like lips she managed to speak. 'Goodbye, Patrick. Thank you for asking me out tonight.'

CHAPTER EIGHTEEN

'You got another call from your admirer,' Laura told Greg as soon as he arrived at work. She had been on the night shift, but looked as if she was just beginning her day. Her perfume smelled fresh as he stopped by her desk, and her pale blue shirt was crease free.

He didn't need to ask who the admirer was; he already knew who Laura was referring to. Alex Taylor had called the station several times in the last two days wanting an update on Lillian Armstrong's death, and because she always asked for him Laura was reading more into it than there was. But he had nothing to tell her yet; he was still waiting for the post-mortem results.

'What did she want?'

'To know if we have any news on Lillian Armstrong. For one of us to blue-light it over and hold her hand, probably.'

Greg set down his briefcase, now giving Laura his full attention. 'Did she have another incident happen?'

Laura stared open eyed, her eyebrows raised high. 'You mean like another murder, or an imaginary surgeon wanting to operate on her? Have you asked yourself why Lillian Armstrong was in that car park, in that building in the first place? It's not her usual hunting ground. She would have been way out of her league looking for a client there. She had to have been invited, that's for sure. Access to the car park can only be gained either internally by the residents or by a key fob. That sound an alarm bell, Greg? Like the fact that Dr Taylor lives there? Like the fact we have no witnesses to a car fleeing the scene? That conveniently there's no CCTV to capture the moment?'

He gritted his teeth. 'I meant like someone leaving a message on her car again.'

'Oh, that.' There was something in her voice that told him she had a different opinion.

'We both saw someone at her car.'

Laura shrugged. 'She could have done it herself. Donned baggy clothes and nipped away from the party for a few minutes to do it. Then have a witness with her when it gets discovered.'

'She couldn't have known Nathan Bell would follow her.'

'Couldn't she? He doesn't look to have that many admirers, with his face.' She grimaced. 'She might have given him reason to follow her, and in the dark she may not have minded.'

Greg felt his back teeth begin to grind. Laura's way of thinking sometimes nauseated him. 'So a leg over in the back of her car is what you think enticed him to follow her?' He picked up his briefcase, seeming to consider what she said. Then he lowered his voice and made it sound sincere. 'Good job you have the experience to think that way. We need women like you to know how other women behave. I'll give it some thought, Laura. You get on home; you look tired.'

Laura stayed at her desk for several moments after he left, thinking on that comment, and an hour later as she settled into bed she was still wondering if an insult had been intended.

It was despair and desperation that drove Alex to Maggie Fielding's house. She had no one else to turn to. Maggie Fielding didn't ask questions over the phone, or show surprise that her offer of several weeks ago was only now being taken up. She simply gave a time that she would be in and directions on how to get to her home.

And now, standing in the dark on the pavement outside Maggie's house, Alex strongly regretted making the call. She hardly knew the woman, and what little she did know gave her no comfort. Maggie didn't strike her as someone who would be happy handing out tea and sympathy. She looked more suited to lecturing. But it was too late to back out of the meeting. A curtain had moved and she had been seen.

There were three steps up to the dark blue front door, and as she raised the brass knocker, the door opened.

'I saw you arrive,' Maggie Fielding said by way of greeting. 'Did you walk or drive?'

'Walked,' Alex answered as she stepped into a vast hallway. 'Couldn't find my key fob to open the gates of the car park where I live.'

'Good. You can have a drink, then.'

The hallway was magnificent, the walls rising to fifteen feet or more painted aubergine and the archway and picture rails a muted gold. Large flagstones, like old pavement slabs, gave off a wonderful echo as her boots clip-clopped over them. The large gilded mirror over a gold-lacquered hall table should have looked too ornate, but didn't. It spoke of great confidence.

'How old is the house?' she asked.

'Built in 1730. My father's great-great-grandfather, or I think even one further back, was the first person to own it, and it's stayed in the family ever since.'

The sitting room was even more spectacular. From floor to ceiling, bookcases were filled on every shelf with serious-looking literature. Between two of them an arched alcove painted in a deep, ruby red housed a writing table with turned baluster legs and a tier of narrow drawers on each side of the central recess. A black and gold lamp base topped with a black lampshade gave out a muted light, and along with an Apple Mac, was the only item on the desk.

Heavy gold curtains hung over the Georgian windows, and high-backed red brocade settees faced each other in front of a grey stone fireplace.

The splendour of her surroundings and the obvious wealth of this woman whom she didn't really know awed Alex. She had grown up in an early-Edwardian semi with a downstairs that would probably fit into this room. Her parents had provided both their daughters with enough luxuries in life. They certainly hadn't gone short of anything, but this wealth was a wealth backed up by old money. There had to be at least a dozen more rooms in this house.

She again regretted making the call. It was like visiting royalty.

'Look, I have to make a quick call,' Maggie Fielding said. 'Make yourself at home. Have a wander. The kitchen is on the left at the end of the hallway. There's some white wine in the fridge that you can pour for us. I'll only be a few minutes and then we can talk.'

Alex was pleased to have a moment alone. If they had started talking straight away she would have probably gone into patient mode and drivelled on about lack of sleep, weight loss and night-mares until the woman politely but determinedly rushed her back out of the house. She needed to calm down and think like a sane woman before she said anything about how she was feeling.

Maggie held up her mobile phone to indicate she was now going to make her call, and Alex slipped out of the room, giving the woman privacy, and went in search of the kitchen. She had to walk along a second hallway as she turned left to get there.

Another room to take her breath away. White wooden cup-boards surrounded an island made of rich dark wood where at least a dozen people could stand and prepare food. A round copper sink was set into the wood, presumably for washing vegetables. Two more sinks, deep and wide, were set beneath a window looking out onto a high stone-walled garden, large and private enough to hold grand garden parties.

Determined not to be further fazed by such blatant affluence, she went in search of the fridge, which she found in a prep room just off the kitchen. The silver fridge provided cool water, cubed ice, crushed ice and probably even a vodka and Coke if you pressed the right button.

She pulled out the bottle of wine without even glancing at the label. She didn't want to know how expensive it was. She didn't even want to be drinking it. She wanted to be at home in her mod-erate luxury surrounded by her own things and drinking vodka.

Out of politeness, she would stay for one drink and tell Maggie Fielding everything was fine. And—

A fleeting movement caught her attention and the fine hairs on the back of her neck sprang up. She couldn't move; instinct held her rigidly still as whatever it was on the shelf above the fridge was close enough to jump on her head. Petrified, she made herself raise her eyes and saw eyes staring back. Then its fat brown body moved and she saw its long repulsive tail.

The bottle slipped from her hands, smashing to smithereens as it hit the stone floor, and the scream she unleashed almost ripped her tonsils out.

Maggie Fielding tore round the corner and saw her guest rooted to the spot in complete terror. Shaking uncontrollably, Alex was guided to the nearest chair. It took several attempts before she finally understood what Maggie Fielding was telling her.

'It's Dylan. I'm so sorry. I forgot he was out. I'm so sorry, Alex. I just completely forgot.'

Alex stared at her stunned. 'You mean . . .'

'He's a pet rat. Terribly tame and now probably cowering in fear.'

'Aren't you worried he'll pee and poo everywhere?' It was the only thing she could think to say.

Maggie Fielding smiled. 'He doesn't. He's house trained. Or rather, I know his habits. He doesn't poop out of his cage.'

Like a professional waiter she uncorked a second bottle of white wine and poured Alex a large glass. After the first few gulps on an empty stomach Alex felt herself calming.

She wasn't prepared to meet the rat formally, but Maggie Fielding was determined that Dylan would make a better impression on second introduction. When she returned she had a box of Cheerios in her hand and Dylan perched on her shoulder.

As she set the rat down on the worktop, Alex stood up and backed into a corner. 'Does he jump at you?' she asked nervously.

'No. He's a friendly little chap if you give him a chance.'

The rat hadn't moved from its place. Maggie gave the box a slight shake; his large head lifted, and his pointed nose and whiskers moved. His eyes were fixed on his owner. Maggie took out a single Cheerio and held it between her fingers. Without hesitation the rat scurried towards her. He sat up on hind legs, long bony feet splayed, and claws that looked far too naked and small stuck out in front waiting for food. Maggie placed the Cheerio into the bald claws and the rat – very delicately, with its two long teeth – began to chomp away.

'You want to try?'

Alex shook her head and Maggie chuckled.

'Maybe next time.'

Alex didn't think so. Not in this lifetime. She would rather deal with the fear of buildings collapsing around her as she helped trapped people than put one single finger anywhere near that rat's teeth and claws.

When the prep room floor was cleaned, and Dylan was safely back in his cage, the two women finally sat down to talk. It had taken time for her to warm to this woman, but Alex had to admit she was beginning to like Maggie Fielding, and in her mess of a world right now she needed new friends. 'Tell me, where did you get all the wonderful art?' Alex asked Maggie.

'From my grandparents, mainly. They spent a lot of time living in France and Italy. Many of the paintings were brought back by them. I'm not really an art collector myself. I haven't the time.'

'What about the one above the writing desk?'

It had caught Alex's attention when she'd arrived, as soon as she stepped into the sitting room, and during their conversation her eyes were drawn to it time and again.

A woman was lying on a bed, her breasts bared as she stretched her arm towards the retreating man. In her hand she held out a garment, as if gesturing for him to come back. But he was walking away, already dressed.

'It's called *Joseph and Potiphar's Wife*. The artist is Orazio Gentileschi. Many artists, including Rembrandt, have painted the lovely lady.'

Alex had never heard of Potiphar's wife, but she wished she had so she could discuss the painting. Her father's passion was art, but she had taken little notice of the large and expensive books he borrowed from the library.

'She seems so sad. Her lover is leaving her, isn't he?'

Maggie, as Alex was now calling her, winked and gave a sly smile. 'Read up on it, Alex. It will educate you.'

She poured them both more wine, and for the first time in ages Alex enjoyed the pleasure of sipping instead of guzzling, not needing the quick fix of alcohol to settle her nerves. She was wonderfully relaxed and no longer wished to discuss her troubles, but Maggie was expecting her to; this was why she was here, to talk to this woman, still a relative stranger, about stuff she could share with no one else. Alex would rather they just got to know each other more and forget for a while about the man who attacked her and who was still terrorising her.

'Can I ask something personal?'

Maggie's dark eyebrows rose in amusement. Her chocolate-coloured hair was down and nearly touched her waist. She was dressed in a cream sleeveless polo neck made of fine wool, and brown tailored trousers. She was attractive, and that combined with her mind and confidence would make her a very desirable companion for someone.

'Are you married?'

Maggie burst out laughing. 'Honestly, Alex, for a minute there I thought you were going to ask if I was gay. And no I'm not, to both. I was nearly engaged . . .' Her eyes dimmed briefly and her voice lowered. 'Nearly. But he had a bit of a problem with commitment. I think in the end he only liked being here so he could use my parents' recording studio. Loved to hear the sound of his own voice. Still,' she said more briskly, 'better to learn sooner than later.'

'What do your parents do?'

Maggie's eyes showed sadness. 'Did. My mother was a concert pianist and my father played cello. They were both killed on tour in a coach crash. We weren't very close, I'm afraid. I think they were disappointed that I didn't follow in their footsteps and instead chose medicine. My mother thought it an inelegant choice of career.' She flexed her slim hands and studied them. 'Having said that,' she continued, 'I like what I do, and in the end I suppose that's what matters.

'And now,' Maggie raised her wine glass, 'I have an occasional lover, boyfriend, but not a permanent fixture.' She gave a small sigh. 'This is my first consultant's post. It will be my first Christmas back in the city since I left home to go to medical school. I have this big beautiful house waiting to be filled with a family, but I just haven't got the time. I turned thirty-two last week and being what I am, and doing what I do for a living, I did briefly think about my biological clock, and then I thought, hey . . . I haven't got time for a husband, let alone a child.' She sipped her wine. 'And you? Or did you think I was going to let you get away without asking?'

'No boyfriend, no lover and no suitors standing by.'

'What about the one I met? He looked very beddable.'

It was Alex's turn to laugh. 'He was! Is! It's just a shame he's such a prick. He still loves me; in fact he wants to marry me. The only tiny hitch is that we have a slight difference of opinion – he thinks I've lost my mind.'

When Maggie didn't answer straight away Alex felt embarrassed. From the heat in her face she knew she had turned a fiery red.

'Listen, I've got to go soon. I'm on an early tomorrow and I need to do a few things tonight. It's been really nice chatting to you, though, I appreciate it.'

'Alex, there's no need to be embarrassed. I don't think for one minute that you've lost your mind. I'll be honest, I'm more inclined to think you suffered some sort of post-traumatic episode. Something that manifested itself as real, maybe something in your past or something to do with the type of work you do.' She paused, and a wry smile curved her lips. 'I wondered why you let *me* carry out the examination on you that night. I thought perhaps it might have been because I was still quite new to the hospital – a relative stranger, so to speak. But you didn't like me, so I still thought it odd. You could have refused.'

Alex felt her face grow warmer. 'Why would I? You were the best. I was lucky you were there to deal with that wretched policewoman. But it is true . . . I didn't like you. Every time I met you, you were so dismissive.'

Maggie sighed. 'It's true, but I can't help it, Alex. When I'm focused on a job everything else becomes irrelevant, including my manners.'

Alex raised a mocking eyebrow. 'You're not so bad, I suppose, when you're not in work.'

'I'm glad to hear it,' Maggie said, equally mocking. She chewed her lip for a second, her eyes considering Alex. 'I think you owe it to yourself to explore this further, and if you think it would help, I can put you in touch with someone I know. He's very good. He's a psychoanalyst and has a lot of experience dealing with post-traumatic stress. He also practises hypnosis, retrieves memories, that kind of thing.' She gazed at Alex expectantly. 'You've gone quiet. Have I said too much?'

Alex shook her head. And strangely, instead of feeling disappointed by what Maggie had said, she felt some relief. Maybe, just maybe, she should explore the possibility of this being in her mind. Not the message left on her Mini; that was real enough, but perhaps it had been carried out, as suggested by Laura Best, by a joker.

Maybe she should undergo hypnosis, even though she was highly sceptical. For all she knew, this expert might uncover stuff she had blocked. It was a chance worth taking to know one way or another, if only to stop her looking at every dying woman as a victim of her attacker.

'Will you put me in touch with him?' she asked.

'Of course,' Maggie Fielding said. 'I'll ring him soon. Now, forget all about rushing off home. You're staying to dinner and that's final.'

CHAPTER NINETEEN

Greg crouched down, staring at the ground around the parking space where Lillian Armstrong was found. Her spilled blood was still on the floor. It had spurted onto the wall by her head and now looked like dry brown paint. Dr Taylor's footprints showed where she was led away, gradually petering out until eventually they became invisible to the naked eye.

His immediate thought, when Dr Taylor told him about the tyre mark across the woman's chest, was that she had been moved. And now of course it was obvious. The cars either side of her had been parked there all day. She had lain with her head facing into the wall, and yet the tyre mark indicated that a car had driven across her chest. So unless she positioned herself this way, someone else had.

Lillian Armstrong had to have been invited to this place. Laura was right about that.

She had been a small-time prostitute, working under the guise of a masseuse. If she was serious about her profession she had certainly picked the wrong city to work in. Despite its ancient history of debauchery, Bath had no red light area, so unfortunately, for the likes of people like Lillian Armstrong, when you came to the notice of the police you were remembered. She had been arrested and cautioned several times for loitering – once in Monmouth Street toilets on suspicion of soliciting, but the charge was dropped. And once, in a restaurant, where Greg and his then wife had been dining. His wife had just told him that she'd filed for divorce, and Greg had sat stunned until the raucous voice of Lillian Armstrong had penetrated his skull. Greg had gone to the aid of the restaurant manager as Lillian was disturbing one of the diners, a man sitting alone, trying to hide his face behind the menu. Greg had ended up accompanying Lillian to the police station, because while dealing with her, his wife had taken the opportunity to leave.

Back at the police station she had the audacity to claim that her business cards, printed on cheap pink card with her name and phone number, offered a legitimate service.

Unwind with Lillian. Spend your lunchtime with a relaxing massage.

Hence the nickname.

The pathologist had called Greg earlier and said there had been little chance of her surviving; she had injuries to her trachea and bronchus. Most patients die at the scene with this type of injury, coughing and drowning in blood. Even those who reach hospital alive have a high mortality rate. Greg would tell this to Dr Taylor when he next spoke to her, give her some peace of mind. He would give her his mobile number as well, save her calling the station and being on the receiving end of Laura's wrath.

Poor Lilly, he thought. Beneath the make-up and the tarty clothes she was really just someone doing a job to earn money and look after her kids.

The communal area of Lillian Armstrong's building was a stone stairwell with paint-sprayed graffiti, and other crap thrown by the residents, covering the walls. The block of flats, six storeys high, was an eyesore in an area where riding stolen mopeds and motorbikes was a hobby. Jola Bakowski, Lillian's neighbour, didn't look like she belonged there.

She had been living in the UK for four years and been a neighbour of Lillian Armstrong for three of them. She was single and shared the two-bedroom flat with another Polish girl. They both worked at the same hotel. The flatmate was working a double shift and was still at work. The small square living room with its low ceiling and bland beige walls was an uninspiring box, but was also immaculate.

It was the home of someone who prided herself on cleanliness. Jola placed a tray set with teapot, china crockery, and a plate of very moist looking cake on the table, and then proceeded to serve Greg as if he were an honoured guest.

'Thank you, Jola,' he said, taking the cup with every intention of drinking the tea, which was not something he chanced in most other homes he visited in the course of his job. He was parched and famished, but he'd talk first and then have a piece of cake.

'Was Lillian a good neighbour?'

Jola gave a ghost of a smile. Her age was difficult to judge; anywhere between twenty and thirty, he guessed. She was small and wore her clean brown hair back in a short pony-tail. She had a pretty, natural face, free of make-up, and shy brown eyes.

'She was a friend. I liked Lillian very much. She was very kind. She show me the way when I move in – where to put rubbish, to catch buses, to say English words properly. She always say, "I went, not I go, to shops. I am. Not I is." I am very sad she is dead. Her children will now be orphanages.'

'Orphans,' Greg corrected gently.

'Thank you. Yes, orphans. Do you know where they go now?'

He nodded. 'Temporary fostering. They're with a family who look after children in these circumstances until such time as a permanent home can be found for them. Did you ever see their father?'

Jola shook her head. 'Lillian never marry him. She say, he is bastard and better off without him. I never see him.'

'Would you know what he looked like if he did visit?'

'Lillian show me a photo when they are young. He is black man, but I never see him and Lillian say she never see him. She never have money from him for children. She say he hide from responsibility.'

Greg sipped at the tea and awarded it ten out of ten. A perfect cup of tea, and so much better for being in a china cup. A mug of tea never quite tasted the same. 'Can I ask you about Lillian's work?'

Jola shrugged. 'Of course. She not hide what she do. But she very discreet and she change job this last year. She no longer give the sex.'

Greg was surprised at her directness and found it refreshing. 'And why do you think she stopped? Did she not have men come to her flat?'

'Of course,' she replied with another shrug, which could only be described as Gallic – head tilted, and shoulders and hands rising. 'But they not come for the sex. Lillian stopped the sex. She had problem with her . . . how you say . . . she say it to me. I erm . . . I get "the clap", Jola. She not wear a Johnny one time cos she get more money, and she get the clap. So she no do it any more.'

'Surely that would give her more reason to wear a condom in her business if she carried on?'

Her head slowly shook from side to side, and she stood up as if to reinforce her argument. 'She no longer do the sex, cos she get a fright when that happen to her.'

'OK, OK. I believe you,' Greg calmly replied. 'Can you tell me why she was dressed in clothes that looked like she *was* working in her old job when we found her?'

'I no idea,' Jola said, looking a little distressed. 'She dress nicely when she do her job – black trousers and black top. She give very good massage and she dress nicely when she not do job – jeans, top, nice coat. Even in old job she dress not too sexy. She look after her children and she always a happy mother, never shout at children, never hit them. And they happy, you can tell.'

After few more questions Greg stood up to take his leave. The last time Jola had seen Lillian was the day before her death, and she was happy and normal and had booked a Haven holiday for the February half-term. Weymouth, she'd told Jola, a seaside holiday for her and the kids. Even though it would be in the winter they'd build snow castles if need be.

As he made his way down the steps and away from the concrete building the image of Lillian Armstrong's last choice of clothing filled his mind. She had been as obvious as a red light. Despite Jola's protest that she had stopped selling sex, Lillian Armstrong had been dressed for business. But with whom, that was the question.

CHAPTER TWENTY

Heavy rain pelted the windowpanes in the CID suite and thick clouds darkened the sky. The lights were on in the department, even though it was only ten o'clock in the morning. The sound of the rain and the darkness outside made the office feel oppressive, and the noise of the tapping of keyboards, ringing of mobiles and a dozen different voices were giving Greg a headache. Laura Best was back on day shift and her mere presence, even though she had yet to say or do anything annoying, irritated him.

She was minding her own business and had been at her desk for an hour, working. At what, though? he wondered.

He looked over her shoulder at her computer screen. 'What are you looking at this stuff for?' he asked.

She turned her head and stared at him. 'I want you to read this, and then I want to talk to you about something. It's a thought I've been having over the last few days.'

'And what about the stuff you're meant to be doing? Checking with Lillian Armstrong's friends about punters that are more dubious than most. Checking to see if they know any of her regulars. We need her mobile contacts, if she has a Facebook page, or Twitter. We know nothing about what she was doing in the hours that led up to her death, or what she was doing in that car park in the first place. These are the things you should be working on, Laura, not looking up some illness. Get with the programme, why don't you?'

She smiled, unfazed by his annoyance with her. 'Take a chill pill, why don't you?' she retaliated. 'This stuff I'm looking at might be the answer to your prayers. I've been doing a little checking on Dr Taylor and she's not as pure as she makes out.

'I've talked to some of the staff in A & E and rumour has it she made some almighty cock-up a couple of weeks back and it's been covered up. The nurse I spoke to reckons she was going to administer the wrong drug – she made some hoo-ha about someone mixing them up. Apparently it would have killed the man if he had been given it.

'And another piece of information I gathered from one of her close friends – Fiona Woods. She said something that got me thinking. She said something along the lines of "it shouldn't have happened to her again". I tried to get her to talk, let her think I was being sympathetic.'

Greg raised an eyebrow at this. He had seen Laura Best's sympathy in action. He had been on the receiving end.

'And then she said, "I don't mean literally happen again. It's just, I thought she'd moved on." Now what could she have meant by that, I wonder?'

He could almost see her licking the cream from her lips as she smiled smugly. 'So I'm going to do a little more digging on our Dr Taylor.'

'And in the meantime, why have you got this stuff up on your screen, about Munchausen syndrome, of all things?' he answered, no less curtly. He shouldn't feel protective towards Alex Taylor, but he did. He felt bound to protect her. Laura Best was gunning for the doctor and he had seen her annihilate people before, whether they were innocent or guilty. It didn't matter to her as long as she got a result.

'Well, let me read it to you, Greg, and then you might not be so snotty.'

Greg nudged aside Laura's office chair and lent closer to the monitor screen. 'No, let's not. I'll read it myself.' Greg quickly scanned the document, which stated that Munchausen syndrome was a psychological disorder, where someone pretends to be ill or deliberately produces symptoms of illness in themselves.

Greg stared at her in disbelief. This was way below the belt, even for her. 'Are you seriously suggesting Dr Taylor has Munchausen's syndrome?'

'I saved the best for last, Greg,' she said, wearing another smug smile. She clicked the mouse and a new document appeared on the screen. 'Munchausen by proxy makes for a far more interesting read. I—'

'That's where the mother makes the child sick,' he interrupted coldly and sarcastically. 'You're barking up the wrong illness.'

She sighed as if trying to keep calm with a naughty child. 'Patience, Greg, and all will be revealed. This isn't just about mothers who make their children sick. It's about people in caring roles: nurses, doctors, medical professionals who deliberately make their patients sick with the sole purpose to then save them so that they can be praised and revered. It's also referred to as "playing God".'

Greg felt a rush of coldness. He didn't like the fact that Laura had dug this up. But there was stuff here that could apply . . .

'This is bollocks,' he snapped. 'And you'll be up on a charge for defamation of character if you're not careful.'

'Is it? I don't think so, Greg.'

'It was Alex Taylor who told us about the tyre mark on Lillian Armstrong's jacket. You think she'd do that if she's just run over the woman? Use her car and then point us in the direction of the weapon?'

'Who said anything about her using *her* car? She could have used someone else's, for all we know. Don't you think it's a little interesting that she keeps popping up? She's abducted, attacked. Then her patient, Amy Abbott, is murdered, according to her. Then a message is left on her car. Next she makes a serious drug error where someone nearly dies. And to top it all, now she's first on the scene at a hit and run. It would tie in nicely to her theory of a mad doctor being on the loose. For someone who is supposed to be innocent, there's a lot of stuff going on around her. But, if she has got some mental illness like I think she has, this would then all make sense. You could even expect bodies to start mounting up.'

She swung the chair round and stood up. 'I intend to investigate her and then we'll find out if I'm right or wrong. Oh, and for the record,' she said in a tone that bordered on insolence, 'Lillian Armstrong had a Facebook account, full of drivel: what the kids had for dinner, what the kids did at school, what the kids were doing tomorrow. Nothing whatsoever about what she did for a living. Her phone records are presently being checked and her ex, or rather the father of her children, has an alibi for the time of her death. He's a taxi driver in Southampton and is logged as working that day.'

Greg stared at the screen long after she'd gone. He felt as if a savage dog had just been unleashed, snapping and snarling and baying for blood, and he couldn't stop it. Neither could he warn Dr Taylor that it was coming her way.

CHAPTER TWENTY-ONE

Nathan broke off a piece of Galaxy and handed it to her. He had taken to sharing his junk food with her as a matter of habit, and Alex had stopped thanking him after the first half a dozen times, as it was becoming annoying to them both.

'I'll have no teeth left if you keep buying this stuff. And my father the dentist would kill me, seeing as he kept my teeth nigh on perfect till I left home. Can't you bring in healthier options? Dried fruit, perhaps? A sandwich, maybe. Nuts would be nice.'

She saw his lips twitch as he carried on writing up his notes. 'Alex, if you want healthy options you can bring them in. I haven't got time to make sandwiches or shop for dried fruit. The vending machine in the corridor supplies me with everything I need, and I can get fish and chips or a Chinese on my way home.'

'You'll end up diabetic if you're not careful. Or you'll have a heart attack or kidney problems. You'll be a food junkie when you're ninety, with no teeth.'

She realised he'd stopped writing and wasn't replying to her after a few silent seconds.

'What?' she asked as she raised her head and saw him staring at her. 'What's with the look? Why are you staring?'

The doctors' office was empty except for the two of them, but he still lowered his voice. 'I recognise the signs. You're taking something, Alex. And it's not alcohol. Something is giving you a level of calmness that I don't think you get by doing yoga or some other kind of torture. Occasionally I hear it in your voice. A little too relaxed, you might say.'

She was shocked that he could so easily recognise her careful cover-up. She was still only taking diazepam, but had increased the strength to 5mg. Still not enough to space her out, but it just took the edge off the panic. She was nervous about her visit to the psychoanalyst tomorrow, and was more than half afraid that he would tell her it was all in her mind.

'Relax, no one else has noticed. It's only because I'm working with you that I can tell. Caroline hasn't noticed because she's too busy trying to smell your breath. But Alex, you need to stop. It will affect how you work, and I would hate to see you make a mistake.' He turned back to his notes. 'Maybe yoga or something like that isn't such a bad idea.'

Hiding her burning face, she pretended she was OK with what he said. But of course she wasn't. Nathan was becoming a good friend. He was kind and undemanding, and she valued his confident and capable mind. He never let on that he minded chaperoning her, never let on to the patient that this wasn't completely normal.

She trusted him. She had also realised, since the night of the doctors' party, that she liked him. She no longer averted her gaze from his face when he was looking at her full on. The birthmark was becoming less noticeable as she saw the man beneath the blemished skin.

Blushing now for a different reason, she wondered what on earth was the matter with her. Nathan Bell was a colleague, for goodness' sake. Just because she recognised he was attractive didn't mean to say she had to get all hot and bothered.

She jumped when his hand touched her.

'You want the last piece?' he asked, holding up a square of chocolate. Still feeling the heat in her skin, she took the chocolate and ate it.

A short while later, after cooling her flushed face with cold water, she stared in the mirror and groaned. Her hair needed cutting, her eyebrows plucking and her skin was pale and washed out.

She wondered what Nathan thought of her. What he'd say if she asked him out for a drink? No, scratch that. Definitely a bad idea. A walk in the park, maybe, or they could go to see a show or an exhibition. That was a better idea. She could have a spare ticket because a friend had let her down.

Feeling like a silly teenager, she stared at her reflection again. There was no harm in wanting to look attractive again. Her shoulders were straighter and her head held higher as she walked back to the department, and on her lips there was a hint of gloss.

CHAPTER TWENTY-TWO

It had been a good night so far and the hurt she felt had melted away. Fiona had hugged her as if her life depended on it and repeatedly said sorry for being stupid and callous, just to get attention. She had never meant to mimic those actual words, but they were fresh in her mind and just fell out of her mouth. 'I'm a jealous cow, sometimes,' she said. They met up at nine and had several cocktails before making their way to the city centre. They were now in a nightclub with a load of wasted people.

A tall young man with his upper body and face painted a *Braveheart* blue was jumping up and down on the spot as high as he could. He looked like he was off his head. Beside him, his partner was dressed in a red tutu, a red top with black spots, and had black mesh wings attached to her back. On her head she wore black wired fluffy antennae and on her feet a pair of white trainers.

The ladybird and the warrior were not the only ones to stand out. The place was crammed with them. Everywhere Alex looked she saw strange clothing and wondered if it was a fancy dress night. She felt old.

'Nathan Bell!' Fiona yelped in a strangled screech. She had a bottle of Peroni in one hand and a Nicorette inhaler in the other. Her brown frizzy hair had been straightened for the evening, narrowing her already thin face. 'Nathan Bell? Are you kidding?'

'Shush, will you? Don't let the whole world know,' Alex shouted back, equally loudly. It was impossible to talk quietly. The music, or rather the noise, was louder than a train passing through a small room, and in truth nobody, unless they had their ears against Fiona's or Alex's mouth, could hear their conversation.

'I can't believe you're going to ask him out,' Fiona yelled some more.

'Oh shut up, will you? I wish I hadn't said anything,' Alex answered crossly.

'It's just he's so . . .'

'What!' Alex challenged, feeling a sting of resentment for what she felt was coming. 'Ugly? Unattractive? Embarrassing to be seen with?'

'Boring! I don't give a flying fuck what he looks like. You've seen my exes. None of them were beauties. No, he's fucking boring, that's why I can't believe you're asking him out. Jesus! Think again before you get yourself into a situation. He's gonna fancy the hell out of you and then you're going to have to dump him.'

Alex really wished she hadn't said anything, but this was the first time in ages they'd gone out. So tonight, after making up and catching up on normal work stuff and skirting around her recent experiences, they naturally chatted about men. Fiona had no current boyfriend, and now, neither did Alex. Only a potential one, and she had told Fiona about him.

Her expression must have shown how she was feeling, because Fiona lunged at her and Alex was suddenly buried against her breast. 'Come here, you silly cow. You know I love you, babe, and I'm only concerned about you, but if you fancy him, go for it.' She eased back, letting Alex breathe again. 'At least he's not a dickhead like Patrick.'

At the mention of Patrick, Alex felt a small knot of pain in her stomach. It was hard to believe it was over. Maybe it was too soon to be thinking about someone else.

'You fancy him, go for it,' Fiona hollered. 'At least you can be sure he'll fancy you back!'

Alex stared at her and then got as close as she could to avoid shouting. 'What do you mean by that?'

Fiona waved the plastic cigarette casually. 'Nothing.'

Alex knew she was lying. 'Fiona, did you think what happened last year was my fault, that I asked for it?'

Fiona's mouth dropped open, her eyes widened. 'Babe, don't be stupid. You weren't to know that would happen, even if you did fancy him.'

Alex looked away. It was clear Fiona believed that some of it was her fault, implying that she was so besotted she had walked into the situation blindly.

'And what about what's happened to me recently? My car? And the night I was found in the car park? Do you think this is all in my head, Fiona?'

Fiona sighed. 'Look, babe, a lot's going on in your life at the moment. You know you're a sensitive soul, don't you? That brain of yours has a capacity to overthink things sometimes. None of us knows how we'll react when we're stressed.'

'Like making a drug error?'

Fiona shook her head. 'You said you didn't do it. I believe you. And so did Dr bloody Fielding. Cheeky cow. Talk about doctors sticking together.'

'They don't,' Alex protested. 'I'm sorry she said that to you. She . . . she probably just knows I've been having a rough time.'

'OK,' Fiona conceded. 'I believe you, and she's right of course. Like I said, none of us knows how we'll react in times of . . . and I don't mean you caused that drug error.'

'But perhaps I painted the car myself?' Alex asked sharply.

Fiona shook her head. 'Alex, there's no way you could have done that. You were at a party, for God's sake.'

Alex felt like crying. Why couldn't Fiona have just said, what are the police doing about it? Or, we need to find out who did that? Or, you need to be careful because someone is stalking you, doesn't like you, is trying to scare you. Instead she had given a lame reason to explain why Alex couldn't have done the actual deed. Leaving gaps large enough for Alex to fall through.

'Hey, Miss Moneypenny, you want me to whisk you away from all these bad men?'

Alex stared in amusement. Fiona really should have gone on the stage. She was a born entertainer.

'You fancy a kebab?' Fiona yelled in her own voice.

Alex didn't, but she would agree to anything to get out of this place. She was rattled by what Fiona had said. Their friendship was important to her, but at this moment it felt a little false, and it left her with a bad taste in her mouth.

'Why don't we get a takeaway and go back to mine instead?'

Fiona grinned. 'Now you're talking. But on one condition . . . I get the bed.'

Alex yawned as she settled under her spare duvet on her couch. She was comforted by the thought of Fiona sleeping in the next room. The night had ended earlier than expected; it was only just gone one and she was pleased at the thought of not waking up tomorrow hung-over.

Conversations from the present and past played on her mind, and she squeezed her eyes shut to banish Fiona's voice from her head. She loved Fiona and didn't want these negative thoughts. Regrettably she had a good memory and she would always remember what Fiona said a year ago, *Are you sure that it was as bad as you say it was, babe? Are you sure you didn't lead him on, give out the wrong signals?*

Turning sharply onto her side she thumped her pillow, willing away these dark memories. She would not give into self-pity. Fiona had been brilliant to her after it happened, had insisted Alex stay at her place until she was mentally strong enough, had helped her find this apartment. Without Fiona she would not have coped. She focused her mind on pleasant thoughts, sunny days, beach scenes, blue skies, silky sand, Nathan's eyes . . .

The shrill of the telephone jerked her wide awake.

Her mind grappled with several thoughts. What day was it? Was it the hospital, or Patrick, or her mother? She grabbed the receiver to shut off the noise and mumbled hello.

'Soon . . .' the voice said, and her breath caught in her throat. His one word seared her brain and took over her entire being.

She unclenched her jaw and stuttered her plea. 'P-Please.' His silence stretched, then he spoke again.

'I'm coming back for you soon.'

Shaking uncontrollably, the receiver fell from her hand, and when Fiona touched her, she jerked as if electrocuted. 'Christ, don't tell me you're on call again?' she pleaded with Alex.

Alex couldn't talk. Small whimpers struggled from her throat. She stood rooted with fear.

'Christ alive . . . I'll say it's my fault. Or better still, I'll say you're ill. Let me—'

Her scream silenced Fiona. Then neat vodka, forced on her by Fiona, burned her throat before words formed and she told Fiona that *he'd* called.

'I'm calling the police!'

Alex shook her head. 'They won't believe me.'

Her chin lifted determinedly 'They'll believe me! They'll trace the call!'

Alex laughed, a hysterical sound. 'They will *never* trace him! And what can you tell them? That you heard a phone ringing? That you found me shaking in my shoes? They won't believe me, Fiona. They think this is in my head.'

CHAPTER TWENTY-THREE

Laura Best dug her elbow sharply into the ribs of the young man sleeping beside her. He called out resentfully and wriggled further away. Not giving up, she shook his shoulder hard and spoke loudly in his ear. 'Oi, sleepy head. Time to go home.'

Bleary eyed, Dennis Morgan raised his head off the pillow. 'I can't drive. I've been drinking.'

'Get a taxi, then,' she said.

'But my car?'

'I'll bring it to work in the morning.'

'But then I'll have to get a taxi to work as well.'

'Not my fault, Dennis. You shouldn't have assumed you could sleep over.'

'Well you shouldn't have opened the wine,' he snapped, now wide awake and looking at her with disbelief. 'Are you serious? You really want me to leave?'

With her head raised higher than his, because she was half propped up in bed, he saw her nod.

'I don't believe this!' he said, sounding completely astounded. 'What did I do?'

'We finished, Dennis,' she stated calmly.

He flushed, angrily. The meaning of her words doused any notion that she was only half serious. They'd had sex, and now she wanted him gone. Scrambling out of the bed, he scurried around looking for his clothes.

'What's your problem? I wasn't going to walk out of here and let the neighbours see me. I would have been discreet!'

'The neighbours don't worry me, Dennis. Sharing my bed does.'

He stopped in the process of buckling his belt. 'Thank you very fucking much. I thought making love usually led to sharing a bed.'

She gave an amused smile. 'Don't take it personally. It really isn't.'

He was angrily throwing on his jacket now. 'Sure. Nothing personal in sex, right? I'll take my car tonight, thank you very much. Not sure I want you in it any more.'

She sighed theatrically, impervious to his distress. 'Keep to the back lanes then, there'll be less chance of you being seen.'

He had his back towards her and was walking out the bedroom door when she called sweetly, 'Dennis, want to do it again sometime?'

'No, I don't,' he shouted back. 'You're not that good, Laura.'

She laughed softly, but ceased as he shut the front door, triggering feelings of guilt and shame. She had done it again. Pushed someone close to her away. Punishing them for what she had experienced. Despite the degradation she had felt at the hands of Greg, she was willing to make someone else feel the same pain. Dennis was nice and he really liked her. But a bitterness had grown in her this last six months, a bitterness that had set a hardness around her heart, and she was not prepared to allow it to crack.

She had thought Greg liked her. What a foolish notion.

Her mobile pinged, and with resignation she reached for it, but the text wasn't from Dennis, it was from her friend Mandy, a call handler. Dr Taylor had received a threatening phone call from her abductor. Laura smirked. Of course she had. It was only a matter of time. Sending back a text, she asked her friend to keep her informed.

With her mind now on her job, she got out of bed and went downstairs. In the kitchen she turned the lights on and closed the blinds properly. Her neighbour, Gus Bird, liked watching her when his wife wasn't home.

She poured herself a glass of milk and then took the beige envelope out of her briefcase and sat at the kitchen table.

It had been easy to get hold of this information; she was the police after all, and it was only a photocopy she required. The fact that she knew the woman from personnel made it just that little bit easier. There was no need for a search warrant, or for anyone else to be involved. There was one proviso – that she shred the document afterwards and tell no one where she got her information.

Dr Alexandra Taylor's professional résumé was now in her hands. She scanned the first couple of pages. Even without reading it in detail it was impressive, and Laura felt a livid jealousy. The doctor was only two years older than herself, twenty-nine next month, and there were far too many letters after her name: Cambridge University – MBChB. Intercalated BSc. FCEM (Fellow of the College of Emergency Medicine). ALS/ATLS Trainer (Adult Life Support/Adult Trauma Life Support).

Some of the places where she'd worked jumped off the page: the Royal London; St Bartholomew's; St Mary's; Paddington. The Royal Victoria, Belfast.

With a tight lump in her throat she turned several more pages and saw interests and hobbies. Running was listed first, climbing next. Wilderness medicine third, whatever that was. And then she read her special interest: 'Helicopter flying (holds commercial helicopter licence). Spent six months with HEMS (Helicopter Emergency Medical Service).'

Laura's jealousy ballooned. Alex Taylor was not only a highly qualified doctor, she could fly a fucking helicopter! She had taken a dislike to the woman within ten minutes of meeting her, and the dislike had grown every hour thereafter. The deferential and reverent way in which she was spoken about was evident as soon as Laura walked into the hospital. There had been a hush as colleagues' eyes followed her across the floor to the private exam room, a message in those eyes saying, 'Look after her; she's special.' The immense respect Tom Collins had for the woman was obvious. The Kiwi forensic medical examiner could hardly find the time to say good morning to Laura when he was at the police station, yet he had sat outside the examination room for well over half an hour looking every bit as upset as any relative. And this was a man who never showed his feelings.

Dr Taylor certainly seemed to have it all – brains, career and respect – and she had worked in London, where Laura had wanted to work. She had applied to the Met, but had been flatly turned down. She had fared little better with the Thames Valley Police and the other constabularies where she applied. The rejection letters were all the same – sugar-coated and dangling the carrot that she might be considered if she reapplied when they were recruiting again.

She was finally accepted by Avon and Somerset Police and had worked in every provincial town in the area, where the possibility of getting involved in anything exciting was almost non-existent, before being given the 'prize' of Bath city.

Laura was stuck in a city where serious crime rarely happened, and when it did, especially a murder, it stayed in the public's minds for years to come. It was famous for its architecture, its Georgian buildings, Jane Austen and the fucking Romans. She now wanted it to be famous for the next big serial killer – another Dr Harold Shipman would do – so that she at last could have a bite of the cherry and make her name by catching him . . . or her. Not a thought she would share with anyone, of course. She wasn't that stupid. She didn't want to be labelled, like the good Dr Taylor.

She could spend the next five years stuck here and still end up without a promotion – unless she got her teeth into something big. And Dr Alex Taylor could well be it. Mulling over the last few weeks, there was certainly some interesting stuff mounting up: her supposed abduction; the death of Amy Abbott, which

Taylor declared a murder; the death of Lillian Armstrong, who Taylor just happened to find; and the talk of that near-fatal drug error, which again Taylor was involved in. Maybe it was only by chance that she never had the opportunity to make her patient sicker before she saved him. Did she, in fact, intend to just kill him? Laura was aware this contradicted her theory about Munchausen's by proxy.

Alex Taylor could well be a serial killer. It wasn't beyond the realms of possibility. She certainly had the medical expertise to go undetected. Now all Laura had to work out was the motive, and the comment Fiona Woods let slip could be the answer. What was it that shouldn't have happened again? That was what Laura needed to know. Then she might have a case.

CHAPTER TWENTY-FOUR

Alex glanced at her wristwatch and saw she had an hour and ten minutes until she finished her shift and then another forty minutes' wait before her appointment. She would have enough time for a quick shower, a bit of make-up, and to grab a cup of tea if the place stayed quiet like it was now.

It was unheard of to be so quiet in mid-December. Emergency departments at this time of year were usually chocker, and in many of them the trolleys were taken up by the elderly. Falls, chest infections and hypothermia were the most common reasons for bringing them in, and sadly, sometimes, they became ill from sheer loneliness, from living alone in the long dark days of winter. They became unnerved and sometimes forgot what day it was, whether they had eaten or drunk enough fluids, or taken their medication.

With Christmas Day only two weeks away, some of them would be thinking about the loneliness, of sitting alone with their hand-delivered Christmas dinner, hoping the meals-on-wheels lady wouldn't rush away.

Being in a hospital bed on Christmas Day where there were others to talk to was a good reason for being admitted in mid-December.

She folded her arms and tried to shake off these depressing thoughts; she had enough worry of her own. Her insides ached with anxiety. She was tired of being disbelieved, ridiculed and pitied. She was tired of her own endless thoughts and burning questions. Was she going crazy? Had she somehow hallucinated that night? That what she heard and what she saw was not real. That she had imagined everything. Was she no longer in control of her own mind? Was the phone call Saturday night even real? She and Fiona had given statements to a young PC, but so far had heard nothing back. This appointment with a psychoanalyst might be the only solution.

She was fretful about meeting him, and she recalled Fiona's parting words as they'd hugged each other goodbye on Sunday morning.

'That was a shitty experience for you last year. And you got over it pretty quickly, babe. Maybe you weren't really over it. Perhaps if we'd reported it properly, got the fucker into some trouble, it would have been better for you. Would have let you move on properly.'

Alex had listened carefully, and was only interested in one thing: had Fiona told anyone else?

'No, of course not. Only you, me and Caroline know, and the agent who put the bastard onto us of course. Caroline had to let them know so that we could get rid of him. But I haven't told anyone else, babe. We decided on that.'

Alex had decided on that. There had been no witness and no evidence. It would have been her word against his and she hadn't wanted to take that risk. She had made a conscious career choice when she decided to work in Bath. This was her city, where she had grown up and where she had returned and wanted to stay, and where one day, *if* she ever met the right man, she would be happy to raise a family. She had decided last year that she wouldn't go to the police, because she had a future to risk.

Fiona may not have discussed her past with anyone else, but her words revealed what she thought of this present situation. What Alex had suspected all along. Her best friend didn't believe it had happened.

The psychoanalyst's name was Richard Sickert. She had googled his name and had been alarmed to read that a man named Walter Richard Sickert was reputed to be the real Jack the Ripper. Walter Richard Sickert, an artist, had painted four pictures based on the real-life murder of a prostitute, which took place in Camden Town, London, in 1907 He died in Bath in the 1940s. She wondered if they were related.

He was dressed casually in a blue checked shirt, black cords and black and tan golfing-type shoes. His dark hair was damp, as if from a recent shower.

His glasses were fashionably framed, black rimmed and oblong, and his age was hard to judge, possibly late forties or early fifties, but he could be younger, judging by the litheness with which he moved.

The porch and the entrance of the terraced property looked unremarkable, giving Alex the impression that this was his home. There was no brass plate on the outside wall announcing his business, and she wondered if it was deliberate so that the people who walked through the door felt under less pressure to hurry in and avoid scrutiny.

The office, apart from a desk with telephone and files, resembled a very cosy sitting room. Two armchairs, in rich brown suede, were placed at a comfortable distance from each other and separated further by a sturdy wooden coffee table. A lamp on a sideboard was switched on, and over in a corner of the room extra light came from a standard lamp with a large cream tasselled shade.

It was a relaxing room, created with comfort in mind, but it was the silence of the place that was most noticeable. Blissful silence and peace. She sank into one of the armchairs, and would have been quite happy to sit there for a long time without speaking a word.

He gave a small smile as if reading her mind and sat quietly in the other chair, leaving her to her reflections.

Minutes passed, and prompted by the thought that she should say something, she said the most natural thing. 'Thank you for seeing me.'

'You don't need to talk if you don't want to. I'm quite happy for you to sit here and relax. There is no rush, and if you want to spend the next hour simply sitting quietly, please do so. Dr Fielding has, with your permission, I believe, brought me up to date with what's been happening to you, so as I say, there's no rush.'

She rested her head back against the softness of the chair. 'I thought you'd be full of questions.'

'No. That's not how I work. For the mind to give up information or to sort stored information it needs time to compose itself. Just sitting quietly with no pressure to think is often what the mind needs most. A space to just be.'

'My mind doesn't seem to want to shut down, it seems to go into overdrive as soon as I stand still or try to sleep.'

'Would you like to tell me a little about yourself? And, just as a formality, do you mind if I take a medical history?'

She shrugged agreeably. 'Fine.'

From the table he picked up a clipboard with a sheet of typewritten paper already clipped to it. Then, clicking his biro, he held his pen ready.

'We'll start with something simple. Any childhood illness other than colds and cough and such like?'

'No. Exceptionally healthy right through to fourteen, when I contracted glandular fever. Left me a bit debilitated for several months, but after that I grew strong again.'

'Any history of depression?'

She shook her head. 'Nothing diagnosed. But I was depressed for a while last year, and of course the last few weeks haven't exactly been joyful.'

'So you didn't seek a medical opinion or receive any prescribed treatment?'

Alex felt her neck redden. 'Err no. I just . . . muddled through or blanked it out, I suppose.'

He scribbled something on the paper and she wondered if he could tell she had not told the complete truth. The diazepam she was taking was certainly a prescription drug. She wondered if he was writing the word 'liar'.

'So apart from glandular fever and a bout of possible depression, no other medical history? No head injury?'

Again she shook her head. 'No.' She paused. 'Well, that is until a few weeks ago. The hospital said I suffered a mild concussion possibly from a fallen tree branch.'

'This was the night you believe you were abducted, I take it?'

'Yes.'

'And you disagree with their diagnosis?'

She shook her head in despair. 'I don't know. I just don't know any more. It definitely felt real. It happened. This can't be in my mind. It . . . it . . .' She breathed faster and could feel the thud of her heart under her breast.

'OK,' he said calmly. 'You're doing fine. Slow your breathing down and try and relax.'

Alex took a few deep breaths and felt the tightness in her chest ease.

'Better?' he said after a moment.

She nodded.

'Last few questions and then we can move on.

'Any history of hallucinations, sleepwalking or nightmares?'

'Nightmares? Yes. And poor sleep, particularly at the moment.'

'What about alcohol or use of drugs?'

'No,' she said firmly. 'No to drugs. Alcohol? I've drunk possibly a bit more in the last few weeks, but nothing excessive.'

He again scribbled on the sheet of paper and Alex wondered if he was now underlining the word 'liar'.

'OK. Well, that's the last of those questions.' He put the clipboard back on the table and laid his pen down. He smiled. 'So now tell me a little bit more about yourself.'

Alex shrugged. 'I'm a doctor – it's what I am, what I do.'

'And?'

'It's what I wanted to do my whole life. It is my life.'

She sighed tiredly and closed her eyes. She heard water being poured into a glass and then heard it being placed down in front of her.

'Thank you,' she said after taking a sip.

'How are you feeling generally?'

Alex heaved a sigh. 'Exhausted. Terrified. My mind won't shut down. Every man I look at, I see as a potential abductor. I have nightmares of walking through the hospital and I hear him walking behind me. I start running, thinking if I can get to the end of the corridor, I can hide. But the corridors keep changing. The doors and the exits disappear. The signs pointing to the entrance to the wards have nothing but blank walls beneath them. I'm trapped. Every time I go round the corner at the end of a corridor, there's another corridor. And he keeps coming . . .'

'Can you see him?'

His words were spoken softly and his voice soothed her.

'No. But I can hear him! His footsteps are getting closer!' she cried.

'Turn around and face him. Ask him what he wants.'

'He's invisible. He's invisible to everyone. No one believes he exists. But he's real . . . He touched me!'

'When did he touch you?'

'When I was unconscious, he undressed me. He saw me naked and he touched me inside.'

'With?'

'I don't know if he . . .' She faltered, and then her voice, just above a whisper, was full of despair. 'He wanted to . . . he said he was going to, but I don't know if he did, but he wanted to . . . and I said yes.'

'And you're convinced this was real?'

'Yes!' she said screwing her eyes tightly shut. 'It was real! I was there. I saw him.'

'Are you afraid he will come after you again?'

'Yes,' she said firmly. 'He told me he's coming for me.'

Richard Sickert sat silently, but his eyes rested on her, and she felt reassured. Then he spoke: 'I want you to do something. I want you to keep your eyes closed and imagine yourself in that corridor. It is long, and the walls are high. You are on your own. You begin to walk down the corridor and then you hear him. Now slowly start to count with each step you take. You can still hear him, but his steps are not getting any faster. They match your steps. When you get to ten, you see a glass door. There is a handle you can open. The sun is shining through the glass. The light is bright . . .'

'It's in my eyes. I can't see his face, but I can hear him.'

'What does he say?'

'He's telling me nothing's happened to me. I get angry and tell him I want to know what's going on and he holds up his purple hands. The stapler. He threatens to staple my lips together and he says . . . he says . . .'

She suddenly sat bolt upright. Her eyes opened wide, staring into space, as the memory of what she heard became clear. 'Alex!'

Her eyes then fixed on Richard Sickert. 'He called me Alex before I mentioned my name. This man knows me! I wasn't just a random victim.'

CHAPTER TWENTY-FIVE

'He knew who I was, Maggie,' Alex said firmly for the second time.

Maggie raised an eyebrow, her lips pressed together, making no comment. She carried on lightly toasting pine nuts in a dry pan. On the island worktop she had prepared rocket salad with diced red onion and halved cherry tomatoes, before mixing the contents in a large shallow dish and drizzling on some balsamic vinegar and olive oil. The pine nuts were the last ingredient to go in.

In the Aga two marinated lamb cutlets were ready to serve and on top of the stove two large white plates were warming.

Alex had gone straight to Maggie's house after her appointment with Richard Sickert, unable to face going home to be alone with her thoughts. Maggie was gracious enough to invite her in for supper. She regretted not stopping on the way to buy a bottle of wine to at least replace the one she had broken, and was now feeling a little embarrassed for having intruded on the woman's time again.

She might have had a prior engagement, for all Alex knew. She might be standing there at the Aga right now thinking that her uninvited guest was becoming a nuisance.

Maggie felt the dinner plates with the back of her hand and then used an oven cloth to take out the succulent lamb. Still silent, she finished preparing the meal, laid cutlery on the worktop, and then climbed onto a stool to face Alex.

'Wine? Or are you driving?'

'Wine, please. I walked again. Still can't find my fob. I'll have to get a replacement unless I want to keep calling the security attendant to open the gates to get my car in and out. I don't know where I lost the thing.'

Maggie lifted a bottle of Pelorus out of an ice bucket, popped the cork and poured small measures into two flutes, letting the bubbles settle before filling each to the rim.

'When we've eaten, we'll talk,' she said, finally. 'You're too thin by half, Alex, and if we talk first you're liable not to eat. So eat!' She gave a pleasant smile.

Half an hour later, deliciously full and beginning to relax from the second glass of sparkling wine, Alex was less inclined to return to the conversation she had started before the meal. If she went home now and didn't think any more about her discovery she was likely to sleep well. She had tomorrow off and she wanted to look fresh for the plan she had in mind. Nathan Bell was going to get a call from her. She had looked at the rota and seen he had the day off as well. Now she just had to persuade him to spend it with her.

'Alex, apart from him saying your name, what else makes you so sure this was real?'

Maggie's voice was gentle, but there was a challenge in her eyes, indicating that she was not ready to accept a simple answer.

'Well, apart from that night, everything else that is happening around me! Amy Abbott died in front of us, Maggie, and I know she was trying to tell us something. Her death was just not normal. You're an obstetrician. Can you honestly believe someone would do that to themselves? My car was left with a message on it for everyone to read. He's phoned me, for God's sake. He's taunting me. That poor woman knocked down in my parking space. She, too, is a part of this. I'm positive he's behind all of it. He's destroying my world and nobody, *nobody* believes me!'

'Alex,' Maggie cried, astonishment in eyes. 'What are you talking about? Who phoned you? What woman in your car park? I haven't a clue what you're talking about!'

Nearly an hour later, after Alex had brought her up to date on everything that was happening, Maggie sat still and silent.

'So, what do you think now?' Alex asked in a tired voice. 'Still all in my head?'

Maggie shook her head. 'I don't know. What I mean is I don't know if it's all related. The call and this message on your car are clearly real. Was anyone with you when the call came?'

'Yes,' Alex sighed heavily. 'Fiona, but she didn't hear what he said.'

'And the police?'

'They haven't got back to me about the call. They think the message on my car was a prank.'

'So that leaves a woman knocked down in your car park, who you found dying?'

Alex nodded. 'Yes. The poor woman died horribly.'

'And you didn't see it happen or the person who did it?'

'No,' Alex replied miserably. 'I drove down the ramp and she was just lying there in my parking space. I didn't see any cars leaving. The gates were open, but no car passed me. I . . . God, Maggie, I'm so stupid!' Her mouth dropped open and her eyes stared into space. 'My fob! My lost fob. The gates were already open when I got home. They're electric and can only be opened with a fob. I didn't lose it! It must have been taken! I need to report this to the police. Not that I think they'll believe me. I think they think I knocked her down.'

Maggie looked worried. 'Christ, Alex, do you need to talk to a lawyer?'

'No!' Alex said sharply. 'I tried to save her!'

Maggie raised her hands in a placating manner. 'OK. So that now leaves Amy Abbott. Well I'm sad to say that yes, I can imagine a woman doing this. Every day women are swallowing potions or inserting pessaries to induce abortion, even in countries where abortion is legal. And they don't always work. Amy Abbott was a qualified nurse and perhaps she felt confident enough in her knowledge to do what she did.'

'Do you really believe that?' Alex said firmly. 'She was telling me something! I know she was, because I was there. On an operating table! Waiting to die!'

'Were you? How were you there? How is it possible you were there?'

'He knocked me out, anaesthetised me. He gagged me with a cloth and knocked me unconscious.'

Maggie let out a deep sigh. She briefly shook her head as if trying to dislodge an annoying thought. 'The old rag anaesthetic trick is a cheesy Hollywood invention,' she said slowly and succinctly. 'You'd need a Schimmelbusch mask at the very least, a long time, some ether, and to be there continually to make it work—'

'He had a Schimmelbusch!'

'Out in the car park, Alex! I'm talking about out in the car park! You'd have been struggling to get away, even if he managed to knock you down. He would have to get you flat on your back, hold the mask over your face, drip ether through it for a long while, and all the time this is going on he would be out in the open for anyone to see.'

Alex's heart was thumping. Maggie was saying things she didn't want to hear. 'You're saying it's impossible?'

'I'm saying it didn't happen that way.'

CHAPTER TWENTY-SIX

Nathan heard the telephone ring just as he covered his face in shaving foam. He considered not answering it – it was the third call he'd received in the last hour and he had no doubt it would be the nursing home again, with more instructions from his mother.

In a carrier bag on his bed he had already packed her ancient button-through dressing gown, a collection of Catherine Cookson audiotapes and her smelling salts. His mother seldom went far without them, and was probably panicking about the small brown bottle. She always carried smelling salts in her cardigan pocket and a cotton hankie tucked up one sleeve.

As a child he had lived with the odour of ammonia on the cotton hankies she used to wipe his face – his eyes had watered when the material touched his face. And he was always left with a guilty feeling because the restorative medicine was only used when he had caused an upset. Smelling salts and her cries of woe were the memories of his childhood. Could he not behave better? Could he not be more thoughtful, be less selfish? What she'd really meant, but was never quite cruel enough to voice, was could he not learn to hide the one side of his face?

The phone stopped ringing, and, relieved by the sudden silence, he quickly shaved and then dressed in preparation for the visit. Today he would sit on her stroke side so that she didn't have to see his face.

Ten minutes later the phone rang again, and, stifling his impatience, he went to answer it. Alex Taylor said hello and for a moment he was lost for words.

'Nathan, can you hear me?' she shouted now.

'Yes. You caught me by surprise. I was expecting someone else.'

'I erm . . . noticed you have the day off.'

Briefly he wondered, and then half-hoped, if she was going to ask him to cover her shift. It would give him a legitimate reason to get out of the visit to his mother.

'Well, I'm off as well and I wondered, if you didn't have plans and were at a loose end, if maybe we could do something together. You know . . . erm . . .' She gave a rushed, girlish laugh. 'I thought we could do something fun.'

Immediately, ideas formed in his mind about how to extricate himself from the visit to his mother. He could ring the nursing home and say he'd been called in to an emergency. 'I, well, that is—'

'I'm meeting Seb Morrisey this afternoon. You know Seb, don't you? I thought perhaps you might like to join us?'

The disappointment was like a slap, and in the mirror above the mantel the pale side of his face flushed. She obviously felt she owed him a favour for supporting her over the last few weeks and was offering to share some of her and Seb's day with him. 'I'm sorry Alex, but I'm not—'

'It'll be fun as long as you can put up with me in the driver's seat.' He sensed a false note and now he cringed. She felt sorry for him. This was why she was calling. She was like all the others, they all just felt sorry for him. He had been hoping for so much more from her. She was different, he had been sure. From the moment he met her he had wanted her to look at him and see him as normal, and now he found himself bitterly disappointed.

'Alex, I'm sorry to be blunt, but why are you calling me?' He sensed her shock and quickly spoke again. 'It's not a good idea. Thank you all the same, but I already have plans for the day.'

Her goodbye was rushed and filled with embarrassment, and he knew he should feel apologetic for his rudeness, but he didn't. Several minutes later he was still standing by the phone, staring bitterly at his reflection in the mirror and wondering, not for the first time, why his mother hadn't suffocated him at birth. He was a freak and it would have been kinder to put him out of his misery. But then if she had done, Cecilia Bell would not have been able to live her life as a martyr – an expression often used by her friends when they rallied round her as she took her smelling salts.

A martyr for keeping him.

CHAPTER TWENTY-SEVEN

Greg could see his eight-year-old son was annoying the people swimming in the fast lane beside them. Joe kept swimming under the rope and interrupting their strokes. The flumes and slides in the children's pool were closed, and the only swimming Joe and he could do was in the lanes. After being in the water for nearly half an hour, Joe was clearly bored. They couldn't even play tag or throw a ball to each other, and Greg was feeling guilty for not checking out the timetable and planning their day more thoroughly. He could see it was time to go, and he would have to think of something else to do to keep a small boy entertained . . .

Perhaps they could check out the Theatre Royal and see if there were any seats left for the afternoon pantomime. *Peter Pan* was on, although he wasn't too sure of the show times, but he'd overheard two female officers raving about it the other day and now thought Joe would probably love it. But he didn't want to scupper any plans or surprises that Sue may already have to take him over the Christmas holiday – she usually had something planned for his first day off school. Maybe they could go to the cinema instead; there was bound to be something on that they could both enjoy.

It would be better than staying here and letting Joe annoy people. Greg had had enough of the water as well. He wasn't much of a swimmer as a rule, preferring a workout at the gym or a game of football.

Still, he decided determinedly, the day was not over yet. There was plenty out there to do. They could play tourists and visit the Pump Rooms and the Roman Baths . . . His son would probably be happy kicking a ball around in a park as long as there was a promise to visit McDonald's afterwards.

Every other Saturday he spent the day with his son. Between his work and Joe now living in Oxford he couldn't commit to more. It didn't bother his ex-wife, Sue; she never moaned at him for not seeing their son more often, nor badgered him about too much else for that matter. She just did what was right by Joe and supported their relationship in any way she could. She was a good woman, and a good mother. Their marriage ended not because she hated her husband, but because he was never there to love, and her feelings for him had simply stopped. Like an unwatered plant, her love had slowly died until it was impossible for it to grow again, and then she had asked him for a divorce.

Greg still loved his ex-wife, but not in the same passionate way he used to. She was more like a close friend, someone he would never hurt and would always help, no matter the situation. He would always love her for being Joe's mum, and that was a fact.

He shivered, realising he was cold, and called over to Joe that they were getting out.

'Can I just jump in once?'

Greg looked around and saw that if Joe was quick enough he could get out and jump in before anyone noticed.

'Go on, then, but make it quick.'

A woman had come out to swim; she had her back towards him as she hung her towel over a rail. She had tawny wavy hair, loosely pinned up to the back of her head, trailing damp tendrils. Her legs were slim from what he could see, ankles finely boned and calves well defined. She slipped off a towelling dressing gown and he saw a long slender back and a small curvy bottom.

Too thin, he thought, maybe even a little skinny, but she was beautifully shaped and her bottom in the olive-green swimsuit was pert and sexy. She turned and he swallowed hard, and felt his face suddenly warm. Alex Taylor was about to step into the pool.

Then Joe let out a blood-curdling scream.

CHAPTER TWENTY-EIGHT

The sight of the blood cleared the pool fast. When he saw his son's bloody face, Greg almost flung people aside in his frantic haste to get to him. There was blood all over his lower face and Greg feared he was going to find something serious.

Alex Taylor took control of the situation by leaning down over the edge of the pool and hoicking Joe out. She immediately wrapped him in her towel and then grabbed someone else's to hold against his face. When she saw Greg hurrying towards her and saw his anxiety she guessed the boy and the man were related.

'Let's get him to the first-aid room,' she calmly instructed. 'I can look at him better there.'

Joe cried all the way to the first-aid room, and Greg was churning with guilt for not seeing what had happened because his eyes had been busy elsewhere.

In the small room, Alex Taylor again took charge. She informed the first aider that came rushing to help that she was a doctor and she would deal with it. She asked for some gauze, a bowl of warm water and some ice.

Patiently and calmly, ignoring Joe's hysterical cries, she wiped his face clean of blood with warm water. Next she pulled his lower lip down and inspected his teeth and gums before giving the same attention to his upper lip. She took a cube of ice out of a plastic container and put it in between Joe's fingers. 'Hold that between your lips as if it's an ice pop. Only don't suck it.'

Amazingly, Joe did as he was asked. She took some more ice and wrapped it in gauze, and then with one hand holding the ice pack to the back of Joe's neck she used her other hand to pinch his nose.

'Well done,' she said encouragingly. 'We'll have you sorted out in no time, and then Daddy can buy you an ice lolly to make your sore lip better.'

She was amazing. In no time the blood flow had ceased and the damage was easy to see. He had bitten into the flesh inside his bottom lip and given himself a nosebleed. 'I hit my head, Daddy, and my nose, and hurt my chin,' Joe said, dribbling melted ice cube down his chin. 'I tried to jump out and fell back in.' Greg imagined he had likely shot up for the ledge, but hadn't cleared it properly and instead crashed his head into it.

He was grateful there was no lasting damage and that he could hand Joe back to his mother with the reassurance that he had been checked over by a doctor.

'Sorry for mucking up your swim,' he said to Alex Taylor.

They were all dressed and standing in the foyer ready to leave. He felt real guilt when he saw the shadows beneath her eyes, and suspected she could have done without the hassle of this emergency. She should have been enjoying a relaxing morning.

'I was only going in for a quick dip. I have to be somewhere else in an hour.'

'What are we going to do now, Daddy?' Joe demanded impatiently.

His nose and lower lip were both slightly puffy and Greg's guilt bit deeper. 'Give me a minute, sport. Let me say thank you to Dr Taylor. She probably saved us a trip to A & E, which, believe me, sunshine, you would not have liked.'

'But what are we going to do?'

'How about the cinema?'

'I'm going to the cinema tomorrow for Matthew's birthday.'

His whingeing tone was making him sound like a spoilt brat and Greg decided that when they were alone he would talk to him about his behaviour.

'Joe, we'll go back home if you're not careful. I've got plenty to keep me busy back there.'

'I don't want to go home. I want to do something fun, and you said we were going to have fun today cos it's nearly Christmas.'

'OK, OK, pipe down. I didn't mean it about going home. We'll do something, just give me a minute to think.'

Alex Taylor was watching the exchange with amused eyes, and Greg took the opportunity to reassess the woman. Could this woman be crazy? She looked sane enough right now.

'Do you want to do something different?' she asked casually.

Greg didn't. He would prefer to go to a pub and get an early lunchtime drink and then find a cinema where Joe could watch something and Greg could sleep. 'What did you have in mind?'

'Are either of you afraid of heights?'

Greg tentatively shook his head.

'Just give me a second,' she said. She moved a short distance away and pulled out her mobile.

After a couple of minutes of conversation she put it back in her coat pocket and rejoined them. 'OK, it looks like you could be doing something different so long as the weather stays good.'

Warily Greg found himself shrugging agreement to something he was still in the dark about. 'What did you have in mind?'

A small smile brightened her tired face. 'A helicopter ride.'

CHAPTER TWENTY-NINE

Saturday was a good day for a guided tour of the hospital. There were fewer heads of department on duty and fewer people about generally.

Laura Best's guide, Harry, a short and stocky man, was one of the longest serving security guards at the hospital and proved to be resourceful at gaining access to off-limits places. With an element of charm and a matter-of-fact manner he had introduced Laura as 'the police', who needed to have a look around.

There was more to the hospital than she had ever imagined. Not just the wards and the operating theatres, but much that patients never saw – changing rooms, training facilities, offices. To begin with Laura was determined to pay attention, but as they proceeded her patience began to wander. Luckily Harry turned out to be a bit of a gossip.

Laura had tuned out the boring bits: the cutbacks, the staff shortages, the closed-down departments and the history of the hospital, her ears pricking up only when the topic was useful to her.

She knew several hospital workers' names now, knew about two affairs that were going on in main theatre, knew of a nurse who had just been suspended for telling a patient to 'fuck off' and of another nurse who recently got his jaw fractured by a patient coming round from an anaesthetic in the recovery room.

It was this last gem that encouraged her to talk to Harry, as he wandered down a short slope to show her yet more of the outdated piping system. 'It sounds like you have as much violence to put up with as we do.'

'Sometimes we do,' Harry agreed, searching through his key chain. 'Especially in A & E. And at night there's only ever two security guards on. We have to ring you lot quite often to come and sort out the troublemakers.'

'It's a wonder more staff don't get attacked.'

'They do if they're not careful. They get given these personal alarms to carry. They press a button and it bleeps the security guards to come running. But as I said, there's only ever two of us.'

'It's a shame Dr Taylor wasn't carrying one a few weeks ago.'

Harry raised his head at this and stared at her strangely, and Laura worded her next comment carefully. 'She could have bleeped for help and been found sooner in the car park instead of lying out there in the cold.'

'Ohh arr,' he agreed, revealing his Somerset accent. 'She could have. It were blowin' all right. For a minute I thought you were thinking she'd been attacked.'

Laura shrugged. 'Well *she* thought she was.'

Harry shook his head. 'It was me that found her, along with her boyfriend. Poor thing was just lying there.'

Laura pressed her advantage. 'So you didn't think she'd been attacked, then?'

He shook his head again. 'No. No reason to. There were bits of tree branches around her, a hell of a wind that night, and her clothes were all in proper order, if you get my drift? She was dressed, in other words. She'd been knocked down, hadn't she? By a tree branch, I mean. I don't know what all that commotion was about afterwards. She must have had a bit of concussion.'

'I heard,' Laura said more quietly, glancing up and down the corridor as if checking they were entirely alone, 'that she had a bit of a strange time last year as well.'

Harry's eyes suddenly bored into hers and she saw what she had missed earlier beneath the charm, the chat and the gossip – the keen intelligence. 'I don't know too much about that. There was something happened, but I don't know what it was about. The young doctor just took a bit of time off. Had about a month away from the place. The only reason I knew something happened was because I saw her with the consultant and Fiona Woods walking along the corridor and Dr Taylor was crying.'

'And you have no idea what it was about?'

'It could have been about anything. I see a lot of staff crying. It's the pressure of the place, especially in A & E. It never lets up. I see a few of them crying when they lose patients . . . They have a hard job, you know, I shouldn't—'

'Don't worry. You've been so helpful, thank you. I think we've seen everything we need?'

Laura Best walked out of the hospital in a positive mood. She had got what she came for. She had met the man who found

Alex that night and heard his take on what had happened. She had established that the doctor was involved in something else last year, and she had learned that Dr Taylor was a liar.

It hadn't happened. Alex Taylor had made it up, and it had something to do with what happened last year.

CHAPTER THIRTY

Wearing black protective earmuffs and a yellow fluorescent jacket with DOCTOR written in green on the back, Alex stood, like her guests, with her back to the helicopter, facing the bushes and wire mesh fence. The blades were still rotating and natural debris – twigs, leaves and even small stones from the ground – could be whipped up and flung into their eyes.

They were standing in the cricket field only yards from the emergency department entrance, separated from the hospital grounds by a simple fence. It was a perfect spot for the airlifting of patients, and the cricket club put up with the occasional interruption without complaint.

The helicopter behind her – privately owned by three of Wiltshire's ambulance pilots – was a Robinson R44, a lightweight four-seater that allowed good visibility to all its passengers.

The tall twin warning lamps in front of her were flashing blue, indicating that the helipad was in use. Alex waited for the engine to be silenced before turning and watching for the 'approach' hand signal to be given.

She could hardly believe what she'd done. This impulsive decision was so out of character. She didn't even like Detective

Inspector Turner; she was well aware he regarded her as some kind of flake. She could only put her behaviour down to her earlier mood and her utter dismay and embarrassment at being rejected by Nathan Bell.

Maybe she was a flake. Her new friend, Maggie, thought so too. She had left Maggie's house the night before vowing silently never to return. She had curled up in the centre of her double bed feeling utterly alone and afraid, and it had only been the thought of seeing Nathan Bell today that stopped her from reaching for the vodka or diazepam to help her through the night.

'Dr Taylor, are you absolutely sure this is OK?' her guest now asked.

His face wasn't a closed book for once, and she saw the questions in his eyes. *Are you sure we can just get on this helicopter and no one will stop us? Is this a wind-up?*

Before she could answer, her name was hollered from across the field. Seb Morrisey had climbed out of the pilot's seat and was walking with an awkward gait towards her.

'Hello, my favourite doctor. It's about time you got yourself back in the driver's seat.' His Australian accent was pleasing and his manner infectious, and she found herself laughing as he swirled her off the ground in a bear hug.

He then noticed her two guests and stepped forward with his hand outstretched. 'You must be Mr Turner,' he said, shaking the man's hand. 'And you must be Joe,' he said to the boy. 'Pleased you could make it. It's going to be a nice flight. Visibility's good for the next few hours or so.'

'You can call me Greg, and thank you for inviting us,' Greg Turner replied. 'It's really good of you.'

'No problem, Greg. Any guest of Alex's is more than welcome. She's a VIP.'

Alex wanted to shut him up before he said any more, but Greg Turner had raised an enquiring eyebrow and Seb Morrisey was happy to give details.

'She saved my life, and I mean literally.'

She cut in before he went too far with the story. 'Shut up, Seb. Mr Turner doesn't need to hear this. And I'm sure Joe is more interested in hearing about the helicopter.'

Seb switched his attention to the small boy. Joe's eyes were fixed on him as if the man were a superhero come to life, which was completely understandable. Wearing a navy flight suit with silver buttons, badges and epaulettes, Seb Morrisey looked like a real-life Action Man. He was six foot two, broad shouldered, had cropped black hair and wind-tanned skin. Alex knew that most of the A & E women, and a couple of the men, swooned whenever Seb flew in with a patient.

'Sorry, Joe,' he said to the worshipping boy. 'You want to know about helicopters?'

Joe nodded silently.

'Good. Well, let me tell you they're very easy to understand. The pilot presses pedals to turn the helicopter left or right, a bit like the pedals you get in a dodgem car. Then he moves a stick, called a cyclic pitch stick, and this tilts the helicopter forward, backwards or sideways. Finally he moves another stick, a collective pitch stick, and this lets the helicopter climb and descend vertically, which means it goes off the ground and straight up without flying anywhere first, and can land the same way.'

Seb used his hands, his arms and his entire body to mime the instruments he mentioned and illustrate the lesson for Joe. 'Didn't I tell you it was simple?' he asked a few minutes later after explaining the full anatomy of the helicopter.

Joe gave another round-eyed look and silent nod.

'So are you up to flying now?'

All three of his audience nodded.

He looked at Alex, before giving her a theatrical bow. 'She's all yours, Doc.'

Greg Turner nearly stumbled on hearing this. 'You mean . . . ? I thought . . . Aren't you flying it?'

'No, the doc is,' was Seb's simple answer.

They flew over the city and Greg took in an aerial view of the Thermae Bath Spa, Britain's only bath fed by natural thermal waters, built on top of an ultra-modern glass building and surrounded by its historic predecessors. The Romans had built the first spas in Bath, and 2,000 years later people were still enjoying them. As he watched the tiny swimmers a thousand feet below, relaxing in the hot waters, he was reminded of Alex Taylor's graceful, slender form.

The view of the architecture was magnificent; the sheer brilliance of the design of Bath – the Circus, the Royal Crescent, Pulteney Bridge – almost brought Greg to tears.

Seb's voice interrupted his daydreaming. 'So Greg, you ready to hear how the young doc saved me?' Greg looked to his son, wary of what he was about to hear. Seb tapped his own head-phones. 'He can't hear unless I switch him on.' Greg nodded to carry on.

'I was one of the victims of the 7/7 London bombings. I was minding my own business, on a day off from work, and I'd just boarded the King's Cross train with no thoughts about anything except the lovely new girlfriend I'd left sleeping in my bed. She had beautiful red hair, and I was sitting there thinking to myself I was a lucky guy.'

'Seb!' Alex Taylor cut in. 'You don't need to tell Mr Turner this now.'

Greg could see a tinge of pink on her right cheek. 'I'm lis-tening, Seb.'

'The noise was horrendous – like a tortured steel animal trying to break free. I thought initially we'd hit another train. Then in the immediate darkness came the screams. I didn't feel anything at first. Yet I had this chunk of steel sticking out of my leg and I knew I was trapped. I kept thinking about stupid stuff like petrol and fire and I could smell rubber burning.

'Well I thought it was over for me, especially when it became silent – I thought this was because people had been rescued. It was only afterwards that I realised why the screaming had stopped.

'After a while I was quite happy to lie there in the dark. I stopped thinking about being afraid and I couldn't feel my leg any more. I don't know how much time passed; it didn't matter any more. The next thing I know is I'm thinking I'm in heaven, I see the lovely doc's face staring down at me. Being as skinny as she is, she got into spaces where others couldn't and she found me.

'She risked her life to save me, Greg. She wasn't even a trained doctor then, just another passenger risking her life for a stranger.'

The pink in Alex's cheek had deepened and Greg felt the story deserved an honest comment. 'Amazing story, Seb. And Dr Taylor, let me say, if ever I face something like Seb, I hope I'm fortunate enough to have someone like you to help me.'

He switched his gaze to the splendid hills surrounding the city, a stunning landscape of deep slopes and rich grasslands in which Bath nestled. This was his home, and Greg felt contentment as he sat with these two people. He would remember this day for a long time.

Later that night Greg was let off the fortnightly ritual of naming every England football player pinned up on Joe's bedroom wall. In the small modern two-bedroom semi he rented, having not given much thought to a permanent place to live since the divorce settlement, Greg had let Joe decorate the spare bedroom how he liked. Posters of various football teams covered the cream-painted wall as Joe hadn't yet chosen a club to support. But tonight the footballers were of little interest to him. He had more exciting heroes occupying his mind.

'Wasn't it just the best day, Daddy?' he said for about the hundredth time. He'd been truly inspired by the day's event and had talked helicopters non-stop since. The cap and badge Seb had given him were on the bedside drawers, as close to him as possible.

'It was a brilliant day, Joe. Maybe we'll do it again sometime.'

'With Alex and Seb?'

'Maybe.'

'Is she his girlfriend?'

'I don't know, Joe. I don't think so.' The pilot had sat beside Alex for the flight, and clearly they were good friends, but Greg didn't pick up on anything more than that. After telling his tale, Seb had spent much of the time speaking through his headset to Joe, pointing out and naming the buildings below. 'I think she goes out with someone else.'

'That's a shame.'

'Why?'

'Because she could go out with you and we could go flying all the time.'

Greg smiled. 'You're a ruthless boy, Joe Turner. I'll have to keep my eye on you.'

When his son was asleep he took a cold bottle of San Miguel, lit a cigarette, and stood by the open patio door to smoke it. He thought about his own star-struck behaviour earlier in the day.

She was incredible and he was a little in awe. She was so capable it was frightening. He wondered how someone so young could have achieved so much. She had handled the helicopter effortlessly, better than he handled a car, and the journey had been smooth all the way. It was a day he would remember for ever, and as Joe rightly said, one of the best.

Alex Taylor just didn't add up. She had all these incredible gifts and yet, only weeks ago he had heard her tell an unbelievable tale. He had seen her bring a hospital department to a standstill, had heard and sensed the concern over her behaviour from some of her colleagues. He had listened to the catalogue of mental illnesses that Laura Best thought she suffered from. When he had made tea in her kitchen to help bring her out of the shock of Lillian Armstrong's death he had seen three empty vodka bottles on the draining board, and while searching for sugar in a cupboard he saw a container of diazepam. Both substances told him she was not coping, and yet he allowed her to fly his son in a helicopter. A possible alcoholic and drug abuser? Maybe he was a bit infatuated, he thought wryly. Or perhaps it was because he had seen evidence of a far stronger person. Today she had taken complete charge and he genuinely hoped she wasn't heading for a major breakdown or suffering some other form of mental illness. He had known other brilliant people to have mental health issues, and it was like watching a rollercoaster ride, only one that got faster and faster until it crashed.

For two pins Greg was tempted to go and see Alex again, when he didn't have Joe for company, and try to get her to have a proper break. Maybe some time off work was what she needed. A bit of time to rebalance herself.

Spending time with her had made him think about his own life. He could do with a bit of rebalancing himself. It was six months since his divorce, and even longer since he had shared his bed with a woman. He discounted that episode with Laura, because it hadn't been making love. It was not too soon to start thinking about that side of his life again, and Joe didn't seem disturbed by the thought of his dad finding a girlfriend. Alex

Taylor had a boyfriend so Joe would have to rethink his matchmaking plans. And anyway, it was a bit of a fanciful notion to think she would be interested in him. He was probably far too pedestrian for the likes of her. Instead of thinking about his love life, maybe he should get a hobby. Maybe he could learn to fly a helicopter . . .

CHAPTER THIRTY-ONE

She should have rung and told him she was coming over to pick up her stuff instead of sneaking in the back way like this. They had broken up, not become arch enemies, and they were adults, not teenagers, and Patrick would probably view this behaviour as very childish. But she simply didn't want to have to face him right now. She didn't want to hear him say one more time that he was there for her. If she hadn't needed her laptop she wouldn't have come at all, but she had a PowerPoint presentation to give to a new batch of house officers and needed the darn thing.

The rain was falling hard, and dripping from her hair into her eyes and beginning to irritate her. She should have turned back and gone in through the front door to his surgery, from where he could have let her into the main part of the house. It would only have meant a minute in his company; he would be too busy to talk, then she could have collected her things and left quickly.

Taking cautious steps up the muddy lane she made it to the gate without falling over. She walked through the garden and passed the kennels where Patrick boarded cats and dogs for extra income. Wendy, his young trainee veterinary nurse, was coming out of the outhouse carrying a metal bucket and bulky sack of dog food.

'Do you want a hand?' Alex asked her.

Wendy shook her head. 'No, you're all right. I can manage.'

She was a strong-looking young woman with muscular thighs and shoulders. With her ruddy cheeks and green wellies she looked like a farm hand. She gave Alex a polite smile and disappeared into the shed beside the kennels.

Alex opened the back door and could see Patrick's shape through the frosted window of the surgery. A dog was yapping and Patrick was speaking loudly over the noise to the owner.

She let herself into a small windowless room, originally the outhouse before the extension for the surgery was built. The floor was concrete and the walls were painted white. It housed a small shower room, a place to hang coats and bags, and a large grey lockable drug cabinet. At the end of the day this was where Patrick shrugged off his white coat and work clothes and washed away the smell of animals.

Alex sometimes wished he was less finicky and more like his father. The retired vet was very different to his son – animal hairs covered whatever jacket he was wearing and he always had bits of food in his pockets.

She let herself into his house, relieved that she was not followed. She took in the familiar surroundings; everywhere looked immaculate as always. The leather couch had a polished shine, no dust had settled on the television screen or any other surface, and on Patrick's desk a computer, a cordless phone and a flat dish of red apples were carefully arranged. Several file boxes, neatly labelled, were on shelves above the desk, and beside the files was a photograph of her.

It had been taken in the summer and she was in white shorts and a lemon-coloured bikini top. They had just eaten ice cream and were sitting on Weymouth's harbour wall. They had gone down for the day and had ended up booking into a B & B because they wanted to make love. When they checked out after only a few hours, the proprietor had given them a knowing look and they had laughed all the way back to the car.

It had been a magical day and she had returned home completely in love with him. Their relationship had grown stronger thereafter and it became normal for them to see each other every day. She had thought she would spend her life with him.

She swallowed hard and turned away from the happy memory.

She made her way up the stairs to his bedroom and saw her laptop on the bedside table on her side of the bed. The bed was made and the pillows plumped. From the drawers she took underwear and socks, a couple of T-shirts, a pair of old jeans, and stuffed them into a carrier bag. From a crystal glass bowl on top of the drawers she retrieved a pair of silver stud earrings and, with relief, her spare key fob for her car park. She'd forgotten she'd given it to Patrick, because he never used it. He always parked outside and buzzed the intercom to be let into the building. She had yet to report her missing fob to the police and give her opinion that it had been taken by whoever ran over Lillian Armstrong. In the bathroom, she gathered her few toiletries. Her things didn't even fill the carrier bag, and she thought it sad that they had been dating a year and there was so little of hers to take away from his home.

He had left even less at hers: two CDs and a jacket. She would post them to him as soon as she could; she didn't want to make this journey again. She took a last look around at the upstairs rooms, her eyes resting on the made bed, filled with a sense of loss. It was finally over. She would not be coming back.

He was sitting at the bottom of the stairs when she went down. He was breaking his own rules by wearing his white work coat in his living quarters. He had his back towards her.

He looked back and up at her as he heard her approach. His blue eyes were confused. 'I really messed up, didn't I?' he quietly said.

'Let's not talk about it any more, Patrick,' she half pleaded.

'I love you, you know, and I really didn't mean to hurt you.'

'So you say.'

'I do,' he said forcefully. 'And I miss you more than I can tell you.'

He caught hold of her hand as she tried to pass and his plea was desperate: 'Don't go. We won't talk about anything. Just stay with me. Stay here with me for the day.'

She shook her head. 'I can't, Patrick. I can't be with someone who doesn't believe me. I can't trust you any more.'

'I've never looked at another woman since being with you!'

'I wasn't speaking of that kind of trust.'

'You mean the kind of trust where you can tell each other everything?'

'Yes.'

'And know you will be safe to tell that person?'

'Yes.'

He let go of her hand and stood up. 'You didn't trust me enough either, it would seem.'

'What do you mean?' she asked, confused.

'You didn't tell me about last year. You didn't tell me about that, did you, Alex? Did you think I wouldn't have understood or that I wouldn't have wanted to go out with you?'

Through trembling lips she tried to speak. 'Who . . . who told you?'

'Fiona. She's worried sick about you. They all are. Even Pamela. She says you had a bit of a breakdown on the day of her wedding. They're all worried about you and they don't know how to help.'

She managed to walk towards his office, one foot blindly in front of the other as she made for the door that would let her back out of his house.

'Let me help you, Alex. Let's tackle this together.'

She stopped as she reached the door, aware he was only a step behind. 'Thank you for letting me collect my things. I need to go to work now.'

'Alex, don't go. You shouldn't be working in this state. We can find someone to help you. Caroline would rather you went off sick and got proper help.'

Dear God, she thought. How many people had he spoken to? How many people were out there analysing her right now?

She felt bile rise in her throat and knew she had to get out fast before she disgraced herself.

'I'm going to be late,' she said woodenly. 'Don't see me out.'

He made one last attempt: 'I'll be here when you need me. Please remember that, Alex.'

She almost flew back along the mud track in her haste to get back to her car. Her hands were shaking as she tried to get the driver's door open. She had parked close to the hedge to allow access for other cars visiting the practice and her clothes were soaking up the wetness as she pressed against them.

Finally, she sat in the driver's seat with the engine off, her clothes wet, her hair dripping again, and the rain pounding the windscreen, making it impossible for her to see out, and it couldn't have come at a better time. Her heartbreaking cries went unheard and the tears joining the rain on her face went unseen.

They were all talking about her, all thinking she had gone mad, and she could bear it no longer.

CHAPTER THIRTY-TWO

The briefing was a fiasco from beginning to end. Greg wanted to wring a few of the officers' necks. Some had turned up late, some hadn't even bothered to turn up at all and the ones that had made it on time had nothing useful to offer. They were all now shifting restlessly in their seats waiting for permission to go. Greg wouldn't give it.

'So to recap: Lillian Armstrong's been dead nearly a week and we still haven't been able to map out her last few remaining hours of life. We haven't been able to locate a single witness. We have yet to discover the name of even one of her punters. And we still haven't located the car or the person who killed her?'

Slow shakes of heads and nonchalant shrugs were given and Greg, furious and unable to stand the lethargy in the room any longer, stood up and banged the table hard.

'A woman is dead! She was thirty-four years old! Wake up to that fact, will you? Someone drove over her and left her to die! Get off your arses and find something. Do something! Talk to her family again. Talk to her friends again. Get her regulars' names! Talk to the people who live in those flats. She had leather boots on, a red mini skirt on that showed her arse, her tits virtually hanging out. Someone must have seen her. She was not fucking invisible.'

The two dozen officers in the room lifted their heads in surprise, the sandwiches and rolls, the coffees and canned drinks in their hands, frozen in mid-air. Their senior investigating officer was angry, and it was rare for them to see him this way.

Greg rarely swore at the officers – there was not often a need to – but this investigation was going nowhere six days on, and he had a horrible feeling that they were slacking because Lillian Armstrong was a prostitute and they felt she didn't merit their full effort.

Peter Spencer had slipped into the room and was making his way to an empty chair. Greg turned on him as well. 'Bit late, aren't you? We're just finished and unless you've got something concrete to contribute there's no point in joining us at all.'

Peter Spencer tapped a finger on a hard-backed envelope. He wasn't the sort of man to play games, and nor was he interested in scoring points. 'She wasn't run over in the parking space where she was found. She was moved into it after she was run over.'

'We know this, Peter,' Greg said, interrupting the forensic officer. 'So, she walked, crawled or was dumped into it?'

'No. Because of what else we found, or rather what we didn't, we have a bit of an anomaly,' Peter Spencer stated.

Everyone in the room was now alert and sitting up straight. They all wanted to know what the senior forensic officer was driving at.

'Here's the thing: we know the cars either side of her were parked there all day. The tyre mark on her jacket has left a good imprint. Yet there is no other impression of that tyre mark leading up to her or driving away from her. It just sits on her chest as if it were painted on. The second thing: there's no blood elsewhere. Her hand was bleeding heavily, so if she was dragged there, there would be a blood trail, but the only blood found is around the body, and because of that and no tyre mark leading up to her, we have to consider that she was knocked down elsewhere and then dumped into that space.'

He had Greg's attention. 'What if a motorbike drove over her? In that space, I mean?'

'But where's the tyre marks, Greg? Like I keep saying, there are none leading up to or away from the body. She might not have been knocked down in that car park.'

'Alex Taylor's tyres should be checked to see if they match the impression found,' Laura Best suddenly said from her end of the table.

Greg felt his throat tighten.

'You think she drove over Lillian Armstrong?' he made himself ask.

She shrugged innocently. 'Could be, guv. She might have moved her into that space after knocking her down, in order to confuse us. When we looked at her car that day she'd had it cleaned. She might have run the woman over, realised she'd left evidence and had her car cleaned.'

'You'd need nerves of steel,' Peter Spencer commented drily.

'She'd know about blood and evidence being left,' Laura pressed on. 'She's a doctor and probably knows more about forensics than any of us lot. It would be simple just to check if the tyres on her Mini match the impression found on Lillian Armstrong.'

'Lillian Armstrong weighed 173 pounds,' Greg said in a voice that managed to convey amazement, and scepticism at the same time. 'Dr Taylor is not Superwoman. You expect us to believe she drove over the woman, then carried her or dragged her into her own parking space. And then what? Pops off to get her car cleaned?'

'Yes,' Laura said confidently. 'And moving a body for a doctor or a nurse wouldn't be difficult. They do it all the time using sheets to drag and roll.'

Greg stood up, gathering his thoughts. 'But how could she risk the woman being found in the meantime? Unless you're suggesting she hid her in her boot while she got the car cleaned. But if that's the case the woman would have died. She'd be dead already when the ambulance got there and there'd be no blood splatter up the wall.'

'All I'm saying is she could have done it. Knocked her down. Wrapped her. Moved her. Taken the wrapping away. The woman then bleeds more and she dies. That leaves Taylor with decisions to make. Leave the body while she gets her car cleaned or else take it with her. But my money's on her leaving the body. Maybe she even wanted it found by somebody else, taking her out of the picture. But as it happens, she arrives back and it's *still* there, so she has to play out her little charade.'

'And what about time of death?' Peter Spencer butted in. 'When the ambulance arrived she'd just died.'

'That's because Dr Taylor said she'd just died!' Laura said excitedly. 'She's a doctor. They're going to accept her stated time of death.'

'But as you say, Dr Taylor had blood all over her. She would have been seen!' Greg objected.

'Not necessarily. It's dark by four. A lot of these car washes are self-service now. You wind down a window, put your money in the slot and drive through. No one need have seen her. Then she comes back and sees an ambulance, so she drives away again or she comes back and finds the woman dead as she left her and she can still carry out her little charade of calling for help.'

Laura was indeed impressive, and Greg felt helpless as she made one argument after the other.

'So why tell us about the tyre mark on the woman's chest? It doesn't add up.'

'She had to tell us. She knew we'd find it. This story is a lot more believable than any of her stories,' Laura answered back. 'Abduction—'

'I'm confused here,' Peter Spencer cut in. 'Why do you think the doctor's involved in the first place?'

Greg answered for Laura: 'DC Best has a theory that Dr Taylor is suffering from some form of Munchausen's. Creating scenarios to gain attention.'

'It's been done before,' Laura argued. 'Back in October, I met Dr Taylor for the first time. She said she had been abducted, taken to a theatre in the hospital and threatened with surgery or rape and then miraculously her colleagues found her in the hospital car park and brought her into A & E. Unharmed, except for a small bump on her head. No sign of a rape or surgery. We were sceptical to say the least. A couple of weeks later Greg gets called into A & E because she says a patient who just died on her was murdered.'

'Who was that?' Peter asked.

'The missing nurse, Amy Abbott,' Greg answered. 'She was brought in by ambulance haemorrhaging, died shortly afterwards. The pathologist said it was a self-induced abortion.'

'It's interesting,' Laura said, 'that we still don't know Amy Abbott's whereabouts while she was missing. No one seems to know where she was. She was alone for five days, with no withdrawals from her account and no reported sightings. Where was she, Greg? Where did that abortion take place? Perhaps Dr Taylor knows.'

'Dr Taylor, and you have checked and confirmed this, was in Barbados when Amy Abbott went missing. Where Amy was in the days leading up to her death we may never know. What we do know is Dr Taylor couldn't have taken her anywhere because she was four thousand miles away. And Laura,' Greg said in a cutting tone, 'in case you haven't realised, Amy Abbott's death is not being investigated.'

'I thought Dr Taylor was out shopping in Bristol and came back to find Lillian Armstrong already injured,' an officer beside Laura piped up.

'So she said,' Laura snapped. 'We haven't checked out her movements or verified her alibi. She says she was in Bristol, but how do we know that?'

'I suppose she could have flown back,' the same officer said, sounding amused.

Laura Best turned to him, and for the second time in the last half hour the officers were shocked by a change in someone's character. Only this time it wasn't the senior officer surprising them – it was the normally self-controlled Laura Best.

'Don't dismiss it,' she said coldly. 'She can fly a fucking helicopter.'

Greg's eyes darted to her face to see if she was looking at him, wondering how she knew this. But the angry woman was concentrating on the officer beside her, leaving Greg in the dark.

He hadn't done anything wrong by going out with Alex that day; she was, after all, only a witness, but that wouldn't stop Laura from trying to cause him trouble. He sensed in her an almost pathological jealousy whenever she mentioned Alex and knew he should tread carefully. He couldn't stop her investigating Alex Taylor, but he didn't have to help her cause by letting slip about the outing.

He directed his final instructions to Peter Spencer. 'Let's get the make of the tyre as soon as possible. As soon as we know that, we can move forward.'

'And Dr Taylor?' Laura asked.

Greg's eyes rested on Laura, his voice firm. 'We do not go near Dr Taylor, unless we find evidence that gives us reason to.'

CHAPTER THIRTY-THREE

Richard Sickert was surprised when she showed up on his doorstep, but was quickly welcoming and reassuring when he saw her distress.

Alex called the department from his sitting room and informed Caroline that she was unwell and couldn't make it in to work. Caroline seemed to be expecting the call and said it didn't matter, that the teaching session assigned to Alex could be rescheduled. The junior doctors could do hands-on practice in the department instead. It was more important for her to get better.

'Take some time off, Alex. You need to get yourself properly better. Patrick is very worried about you,' was her advice, confirming that Patrick had contacted her boss the minute she stepped out of his house. Interfering for her own good, he would no doubt argue. He had made the situation worse by talking to people like Fiona and Pamela. Even if she'd wanted to talk to them herself about it, he'd now made it impossible. They would think the same as him. She needed help. Proper help.

The peppermint tea was easing the tightness in her chest and slowly she was beginning to calm down.

'Thank you for not turning me away. I'm sorry for intruding on your morning,' she said to Richard Sickert.

Today he was wearing jeans and a navy, white and red striped jumper, and on his black and tan golfing shoes she saw bits of grass. He had paperwork out on his desk and a full mug of tea beside it, telling her he had been busy or was about to be before she came.

'I'll go after I've had my tea.'

'There's no rush. I'm having an indecisive day myself. It's too wet to do anything outside, and paperwork . . . well, it will probably rain again tomorrow.'

'I just couldn't think where else to go. Maggie Fielding will get fed up if I keep turning up on her doorstep.'

He smiled at this. 'I'm sure she won't. She doesn't strike me as the Good Samaritan type unless she wishes to be. Friendships are important, and if Dr Fielding is offering, you should feel confident in accepting.'

'She doesn't believe what happened to me.'

'Has she said that?'

Alex nodded. 'Oh yes. She says it's completely impossible.'

'That must be upsetting?'

She didn't answer.

'Have you asked her what else she thinks?'

'The reason I'm here seeing you is because she thinks it could be some kind of post-traumatic thing. Something in my past, or to do with the work I do.'

He gave a slight nod. 'She did say much the same thing to me, but what's important is what you think. Did anything upset you in the days leading up to the event?'

'I lost a baby that morning.' She sighed tiredly. 'A three-month-old baby girl. It was awful. The baby came in blue. Her mum and dad were screaming at anyone and everyone to get their baby breathing again, but she was cold. Ambulance crew should never have brought her in in the first place. It was suspected Sudden Infant Death Syndrome, and the post-mortem findings confirmed that. But once she was with us, the parents thought we could revive her, bring her back to life. Her tiny fingers were already stiffening.' She sighed again. 'So yes, something pretty stressful did happen leading up to that event.'

'And what about other stressful times? Anything else that may have triggered a crisis?'

She stayed mute, unwilling to share the previous year's experience with him. If she told him, he would immediately form the idea that the two events were related, and that her abductor was only in her mind. On the other hand, she couldn't keep avoiding the issue. She had to give him the full facts if this disclosure was to help.

'I was attacked last year.'

His eyes remained calm and his manner unchanged. 'Is that all you wish to tell me?'

Tears flooded her eyes and she had to bite down hard on her lower lip to stay in control. After taking a few calming breaths she was ready to talk.

'He didn't rape me. Just so you know. He didn't rape me.'

Richard Sickert nodded and Alex carried on.

'He was an actor shadowing me for a few days to study for the role of a doctor. He had the main part in this medical thriller. My boss put him with me, partly because she was too busy and partly because he expressed a wish to partner me. He was very pleasant. A charming and intelligent man, who was very courteous to both patients and me. He'd been with me five days and I hadn't found a problem with him at all. If I'm being perfectly honest, he was a delight to have around.'

'Were you attracted to him?' Richard Sickert quietly asked.

She gave a small nod. 'A tiny bit, I suppose. He was a television star. He was familiar right from the beginning, just from seeing him on the TV, and he was modest and seemed genuinely interested in learning. He borrowed loads of medical books off me. Made me explain medical terms until he completely understood. I suppose I admired him for that. He wasn't just going to learn some lines and that was that. He was going to be faithful to the character he was playing. Anyway, as I say, it was day five. It was a hot day. That lovely late summer we had. The department was like a furnace, fans switched on, people guzzling water and desperate to get home so that they could lie out in their gardens.

'I was in the major incident room with him. He wanted me to show him the equipment we used and the suits we have to put on when we're called to a major incident. He had his back towards me while I was trying to struggle into one. Normally, for training purposes, I would have kept my tunic and trousers on underneath the suit, but it was so hot in the room I would have fainted if I'd kept them on.'

'So he turned his back?'

'Yes,' she said quietly. 'I had my back to him as well to give me a bit more privacy. I had the suit hitched to my hips and was trying to get my feet into the heavy-duty boots when suddenly he grabbed me from behind. I couldn't stand up. I was completely bent over and the suit was slipping down round my ankles.'

Her eyes screwed shut as she remembered the moment and her heart began to thump unpleasantly. 'He put his hand down my pants and a hand beneath my bra and then he pressed himself against me. I tried to shove him off, but he leaned his whole weight on my back.' She swallowed hard and could feel her body beginning to shake. 'Shit, I don't want to think about this, I don't want to remember his hands crawling all over me. I could feel him trying to undo his trousers. I was terrified. Then he touched me . . . I could feel him against my skin. He was dragging my pants down. I struggled to get away, shoving backwards and forwards, and then I fell to my knees. My head was shoved in against the bottom shelves and I was thinking it ludicrous that I was looking at all this medical equipment while he was on top of me. I could feel him . . . I knew it was going to happen . . . I . . .'

She gulped for breath and her eyes opened wide, trying to feel safe again. Richard Sickert moved forward in his chair as if to console her. She put a hand up to ward him off. 'I'm all right. I just need a moment.'

'Do you want a glass of water?' he asked.

She shook her head. 'I'm fine.'

'Do you want to carry on?'

'Yes. There's not much more to tell. I managed to grab a boot and I started hitting him blindly on his legs. I must have hit him hard because the next thing he was off me and I was able to turn round. He was bent forward, his trousers undone, his penis exposed. I shouted at him, told him I'd report him. That he wouldn't get away with it. And he . . . he laughed. He said nobody would believe me. They all knew why I'd brought him into that room. They all knew I fancied him. He said, "Let's be honest, Alex, you've been gagging for it all week. Who do you think they'll believe?"'

For the third time that day her face was wet.

Richard Sickert handed her some tissues and she was reminded of the time that Greg Turner had done the same. Her life lately seemed to revolve around people handing her tissues.

The psychoanalyst went and made some more tea while she composed herself, and when he returned, he sat with her quietly for a long time before he eventually said, 'Did you report him?'

She shook her head. 'I couldn't. I was afraid that I wouldn't be believed. Do you think it's only in my mind, what has happened to me recently?'

He gave a small shrug. 'It's possible. This could be your way of dealing with what happened to you last year. I can't tell you if the attack in the car park was real. What I can tell you is that you need to deal with last year. A man nearly raped you and you walked away from that situation feeling that no one would believe you.'

He hesitated, and she could see indecision in his eyes.

'I think you should report this to the police,' he said finally.

Her eyelids were stinging and swollen from the salty tears and her face was tender. Maggie gave her a cold flannel to soothe herself and Alex cooled her tender skin. She then took a gulp of wine and felt herself begin to calm. She was exhausted, but also strangely at peace.

'So I was right? You did suffer a trauma in your past?' Maggie's voice intruded softly.

Alex nodded. 'You know everything now.'

'Richard Sickert's right, Alex. You do need to report him to the police.'

Alex's knees rose up as she tried to curl into a ball and ignore her friend's advice.

'They won't believe me, Maggie,' she cried crossly. 'Not unless I can get him to admit it.'

'So, let's do that.'

Alex looked at her confused.

'Do what?'

'Get him to admit it. I'll help you,' Maggie said determinedly. 'Confront this man, Alex, and then this will be over.'

Laura Best disconnected the call and put away her mobile with a satisfied smile. It was a good start to the day. She had taken the right approach by giving sympathy first, and now she was going to get a result. A meeting place and time had been set up, and by the afternoon she would know what had happened to Dr Taylor last year.

Convinced that it was going to show the doctor in a bad light, she was already planning what to do with the information. By tonight she expected the doctor's car to be impounded and the woman to be brought into the station for questioning.

Greg Turner could then apologise for his less than supportive behaviour and hopefully this apology would take place in front of officers more senior than him.

In the meantime she wanted to check the CCTV at petrol stations that had car washes and find the one Alex Taylor had used. She would drive the route from Bath to Cribbs Causeway in Bristol, where Taylor said she had shopped, and hopefully find not only the petrol station, but also get the time she was there.

The plus side to this fishing expedition was that there were only three shopping days left until Christmas and Laura had yet to buy a single thing for her family and friends. She could kill two birds with one stone by spending the rest of the afternoon this way.

'Planning who to bed next?' Dennis Morgan whispered bitterly in her ear. His eyes were reproachful when she turned to face him.

'Hello, Dennis. I was just thinking about you,' she lied sweetly.

She could see he was not drawn in by the lie, see the disdain in his eyes as he walked away.

Maybe she should just try being honest.

'Dennis,' she called, and he turned around. 'I can't help it. As soon as I feel myself getting close to someone I strike out and hurt them. It stops me getting hurt first.'

His shoulders were less rigid, his arms unfolding. 'I would never hurt you. You're the first woman in ages that I've really liked. I don't sleep around, Laura. I never have.'

'I know that, Dennis,' she said softly.

His manner softened.

'Do you think we could go out sometime? Maybe go to the cinema like a proper date or something?' he asked.

She nodded. 'I'd like that.' Then she smiled at him. 'You can say no, and I'll understand if you're busy, but would you like to come and check out some car washes with me? Then maybe later we could cook dinner together or something?'

'I can't, Laura. DI Turner is sending me to the hospital.'

At the mention of the hospital, Laura sat up straight, her senses on alert. 'Why?' she asked bluntly.

He shrugged. 'No one else available.'

'I mean,' she said, trying to stay patient, 'what are you being sent to the hospital for?'

'Oh,' he laughed. 'Not a lot. Just to take some statement from a doctor who's been involved in an RTA. You can come with me if you want.'

Laura needed no further bidding.

CHAPTER THIRTY-FOUR

Alex kept her eyes off the clock as she walked across the department, calling out a 'sorry' to the coordinator for being late. That had not been part of the plan. She was determined that she was no longer going to be thought of as the one who had 'lost it', and had woken for the first time in ages with a plan to regain control of her life. But here she was, twenty minutes late, without good reason, aside from having taken another blue tablet in the middle of the night. She should have resisted and just come into work tired instead, been more determined and remembered she was no longer alone. She had Maggie's support, and together they would track down this actor and confront him. In the meantime, Alex just needed to stay focused on each day and be good at her job.

'You're here,' Nathan said bluntly as she walked into the doctors' station.

'Sorry, I'll make up for it. What have we got?'

'A situation,' he said. 'Three about to breach if we don't admit or discharge.' 'About to breach' was a commonly used phrase in emergency departments. It meant patients were coming up to the maximum four-hour target time of when they were meant to have been seen, admitted or discharged. 'And Dr Cowan has also just been brought in.'

'With what?' she asked anxiously.

'Whiplash injury. We'll see her first.'

'Do you think we should separate? You can't shadow me with this much work to do. I'll see Caroline and leave you to make a start with the others. It'll be quicker.'

He hesitated and she raised her chin. 'It makes sense, Nathan, and I'm perfectly capable of examining a priority three patient. After all, Dr Cowan is hardly likely to let me misdiagnose her, is she?'

Caroline looked totally vulnerable as she sat with her knees drawn up, a hospital blanket up to her chin, on the examination trolley. Her round pale face was drained of vitality.

It was a shock to see her so badly shaken. She had a bump on her forehead from hitting the steering wheel, and pain in her neck from whiplash. In her present state she was unrecognisable as the consultant who ran this very busy department.

The police were waiting to talk to her, but Alex insisted on making sure she was fit enough first. From what she could ascertain, the accident was a low-speed rear-end car shunt. Caroline's car was stationary, waiting to move out onto a main road. She hadn't lost consciousness, but was dazed; it was the fear of what could have happened that had altered her appearance.

If the car behind had shunted harder, Caroline's Nissan would have gone straight into the path of an oncoming juggernaut.

Alex examined her thoroughly and confirmed the absence of a spinal injury. Completing her final examination, she pocketed her pen torch. Then she reached for the switch on the wall and turned the main overhead light back on. She was satisfied with Caroline's Glasgow Coma score and pupillary reaction. She perched on the edge of the mattress and gently rubbed the back of one of Caroline's hands.

'Everything seems to be fine. I'll sort some analgesic and get you some tea. Are you up to talking to the police?'

Caroline went to nod and then winced. She rested her head gingerly against the pillow. 'I didn't see anything, Alex. It was so quick. There was nothing behind me. I was looking left and right getting ready to pull out when I heard a bang and felt the car move violently. I shot forward, banged my head, and when I looked in the mirror there was no car behind me. The road behind was completely deserted. The driver nearly killed me and then drove off.'

'Unbelievable that someone could just drive off like that?'

Caroline blinked as her eyes watered. 'I know!' She used the bed sheet to wipe them. 'Christ, so many bad things seem to be happening lately. First you end up in a bed in here. Now me! Who's next?'

Alex felt herself stiffen, while her mind leapt to a number of possibilities. Could it be the same man targeting them both? Was he coming after Caroline because of her? Was he hurting people she knew?

'Caroline, do you think this could have anything to do with me?'

'What?' Caroline's tone was sharp, her eyes round with disbelief. 'Just . . . don't!'

Then in a weary voice she said, 'Get someone to bring me in some painkillers.'

'But—'

'I can't talk with this pain,' Caroline said firmly. Then, with a look in her eyes, 'I can't talk to *you*, Alex.'

A half hour later Alex saw Laura Best and a police constable come out from the curtained cubicle. Leaving her place at the desk, she made her way towards it.

Laura Best stepped in her way. 'Leave her be, Dr Taylor. She just wants to rest until her husband picks her up.'

'I beg your pardon?'

Laura Best's voice was firm. 'She doesn't want to be disturbed.'

Alex felt her cheeks flush and she stared at the policewoman resentfully. 'Do you mind? Dr Cowan is my patient! I need to see her before I can discharge her.'

'Dr Bell has already done it,' Laura Best said patiently.

Alex stared through the glass window into the doctors' office. Nathan was in the office studying an X-ray. She wanted to go and ask what was going on, but he had seemed remote all day, unapproachable. She so regretted asking him out. He had gone back to treating her like a work colleague – worse, a nuisance colleague – and she missed his friendship.

Retreating to her seat to carry on reading a patient's notes, she felt Laura Best's eyes follow her. The message couldn't have been clearer. *Stay away from her. She doesn't want to see you.*

Laura sighed with relief when the call ended. Her irate caller was not pleased to have been stood up, and Laura had to promise not to be late or miss the new appointment later. In the wake of seeing Dr Cowan, she had forgotten all about the meeting. She and Dennis had spent the rest of the day trying to find the driver that had gone into the back of Dr Cowan's car. She would not miss this second appointment. This meeting could be important, especially now that Alex Taylor was becoming worrisome.

Her behaviour this morning only confirmed Laura's belief that Alex Taylor had a mental illness. Her concern was that she was still allowed to practice. But not for much longer, Laura imagined. She was on a slippery slope, and she was going to fall very soon.

Laura would make sure she got away in good time to be at the rescheduled meeting. She would text Dennis to cancel their date. While she was pleased that they were back on a friendly footing, a date was not a good enough reason for missing it again. She needed to focus on her job.

She had a few hours spare before the meeting and would spend the time going through the Amy Abbott case files. She would check on anything that may have been missed; any leads that weren't followed up that might have told them her whereabouts while she was missing. Wherever that induced abortion had taken place there would be blood. A lot of it. Amy Abbott had almost exsanguinated before arriving in the emergency department.

It wasn't a murder investigation or even a missing person enquiry any more. Amy Abbott was dead and buried, and to all intents and purposes the case was closed. Greg would tell her she was time-wasting and that she should focus on the Lillian

Armstrong case, but Laura hated loose ends and she couldn't let go of the fact that it was Alex Taylor who had reported the death as suspicious. The post-mortem findings didn't support this – death by misadventure was the coroner's verdict. If it was murder it would be difficult to prove. Alex Taylor was certainly clever enough to murder someone and walk away free.

She was in Barbados when Amy Abbott went missing, but supposing she knew Amy Abbott from before, knew she was pregnant and in a depressed state. Alex Taylor may have given her refuge, let her use her flat while she was away and then returned home and set about causing her death. Amy Abbott was found five days after she went missing, but she died on the night after Taylor returned home from her holiday. Now all Laura had to do was find a connection between the two women. If she could prove Alex Taylor knew the dead nurse, then she would have reason to ask that the case be reopened.

Laura felt excited at the prospect. This could be her ticket to promotion – her path to a new life.

CHAPTER THIRTY-FIVE

She saw the slim cardboard box leaning against her front door as she stepped out of the lift and set down her grocery bags. A scrap of blue paper was taped to the box and Alex saw a message had been left by her next door neighbour: 'Came this afternoon, so I signed for it. Hope that's OK. Trevor.'

She picked up the box and brought it into her apartment. She checked her mailbox and saw Christmas card envelopes. It was nearly Christmas and she still hadn't even sent hers. She had done very little to prepare for the event, except to buy presents, which were still to be wrapped. She had no Christmas tree up and no special drinks or treats bought. Her home looked like it did on any normal day of the week – the leather sofas, glass coffee table and clutter-free floor. There was not even a photograph of her family in the living room to personalise the place. Patrick had said that the framed photographs she had of them needed changing, as they were too old-fashioned. She now realised how wrong he had been; you couldn't create a home simply with furnishings – it needed to be loved and lived in, otherwise coldness crept into the corners.

Now she was alone. All she had was her work and an empty flat to come home to, but even that was compromised. Since this morning, the atmosphere at work had been thick with unspoken words. Everyone seemed to be avoiding her. Fiona seemed to be ever so busy whenever Alex tried to talk to her. Nathan barely spoke to her, unless it was about a patient. Everyone was wary of her. Things were going from bad to worse, and her boss was probably contemplating another meeting, only this time a formal one. She should never have said what she did to Caroline. She should have kept her own counsel, but lately all her actions seemed to be impulsive and, in the eyes of others, irrational. Caroline's accident probably had nothing to do with her situation, and now, in her boss's eyes, she appeared even more of a lunatic.

Inside the box, bubble wrap covered a framed picture. She could feel glass and see colours beneath the plastic. A description to go with the painting had been sent by the gallery, but no note from the sender. She unwrapped the picture and saw an image of a naked woman lying on a bed. The wall behind her was a bright, almost seaside blue. Her face was hidden from view by her arm as she reached out to the retreating figure. Alex loved it and guessed who it was from. She quickly opened her mail and found a Christmas card from Maggie. Her friend hadn't signed it, but she knew the thoughtful message was from her:

'Hope you like it. While I appreciate other versions of this painting, I think in this one Euan Uglow brings the lovely lady into modern times. Remember, Alex, not all men are bastards.'

Alex was astonished by Maggie's thoughtfulness and generosity, and felt a little overwhelmed. Someone liked her. She was not entirely alone.

The knock on her front door startled her. Still wearing her coat and expecting her caller to be her neighbour making sure she got the parcel, she opened the door.

Nathan Bell was standing there, holding a tissue-wrapped bottle of wine. He held it up. 'A small Christmas gift,' he said in a reticent tone, looking awkward, as if unsure whether he was welcome.

'Come in,' she said, utterly amazed that he had called on her, that he even knew where she lived.

'I got your address off Fiona – she said you wouldn't mind.'

'I don't. How is she? She seemed to be too busy to talk to me at work.'

'I think she's a little worried about you. I thought she was seeing you after work. She said she was going to talk to you.'

Alex was puzzled. 'She didn't ask me. But as I say, we didn't talk. She's probably texted me and now thinks I'm ignoring her. Damn, I'll have a look in a minute. But I'm pleased she gave you my address. I'm glad to see you.'

She showed him into her sitting room and was aware he was taking in every detail.

'It's not what I expected,' he said.

'What did you expect?'

'Something more homely. Different. This is a little aseptic,' he answered in his usual blunt fashion.

She didn't take offence, because he was right. It was Patrick's idea of a home, not hers.

'I'll be changing it soon, making it more homely.'

'Good. This room doesn't suit you.'

They stood awkwardly, a silence stretching. She could see he would leave soon if she didn't break the ice and say something more meaningful.

'Would you like a drink?'

He handed her the bottle. 'Only if you are and only if you're able.'

She knew he was asking her if she was capable of having a drink without it leading to a dependency. She didn't know the answer to that, as she hadn't tested herself for a while, but she felt safe enough in his company to try.

'It's nearly Christmas. I'd like to have a drink with a friend.'

He took his black coat off. Wearing a dark grey shirt tucked into black tailored trousers and a silver-grey tie he looked sophisticated and somewhat remote. 'If you fetch a bottle opener I'll do the honours.'

With lightness in her step she quickly fetched glasses and a corkscrew from the kitchen, stopping to check her appearance in the hall mirror on the way. Her face was flushed, framed by wispy tendrils of hair that had come loose from her ponytail, but at least it was clean and she smelled fresh. She discarded her coat and took off her blouse, leaving her wearing only a cream T-shirt and jeans. He was studying the painting when she returned.

'A present?' he asked.

'Yes. It's Potiphar's wife. It's beautiful, isn't it?'

Nathan studied it some more. 'She looks a little desperate to me, hanging on to his clothes like that.'

'She's letting him know she wants him,' Alex explained, without any real knowledge of the painting. She had yet to look up the history of Potiphar's wife.

'Is it a present from your boyfriend?'

She shook her head. 'I don't have a boyfriend. Not any more.'

He raised his eyebrow at this. 'So it did end . . . I wondered after the party that night . . .'

She took a sip of the red wine he handed her and knew she had to say something. 'I wouldn't have asked you out if it hadn't ended.'

'I'm sorry about that,' he quickly said. 'I should have explained. It's difficult . . . I—'

'—have a girlfriend,' she quickly finished for him, not wanting to hear why he had rejected her and feel embarrassed all over again.

'No,' he said quietly. 'That's the bit that's difficult to explain.' He stared around the room at everything but her, and she realised it was he who was embarrassed. Even as she moved closer, he avoided looking at her. It was only when she reached out to touch him that his eyes finally met hers, and there was so much need in their depths it was harrowing.

'I've never had a girlfriend. No girl has ever asked me out before. When I was sixteen I developed a crush on a girl and I knew the only way she would talk to me was if I were in with a group of other lads. I targeted the boys I would become friends with, boys less clever than me, who I hinted to that I could help with their homework. Very quickly I became part of a group, and soon after I got to talk to her.'

He paused, clearly reflecting on that time.

'I couldn't believe my luck. She was actually going to go out with me. Our first date was in a park in the evening when no one was around and we sat on the swings, holding hands for hours. Our second date was on an alley wall, not far from her house, and again we sat for hours chatting.' He smiled, but there was little humour in his eyes. 'You're waiting for the punchline, aren't you? Our third date was in her bed. We got undressed and were lying close to each other. We hadn't kissed yet and I badly wanted to. She suddenly rolled onto her front and said to me, could I do it to her from behind because she couldn't look at my face. After it was over, disgusted with myself, I quickly dressed and scarpered. A few of the lads were at the end of the street sitting on the alley wall. They asked what I'd been up to and I of course said, "Nothing." They laughed and jeered and they said they didn't believe me. They said they knew exactly what I'd been up to because they had paid for it.

'The ironic thing was they thought they were real friends. They knew I liked her and they paid her to have sex with me.'

She put a hand up and gently clasped his blemished cheek, and his head turned sharply away. His voice was heavy with emotion. 'Don't feel sorry for me, Alex. It's more than I can bear.'

She put her glass of wine down and then placed her free hand on his other cheek and turned his face towards her so that he couldn't look away. 'I don't feel sorry for you. I feel sorry for me. I want you . . . and you don't seem to want me back.'

He stared at her for long seconds, staring deeply into her eyes to see if she was telling him the truth, and then with a groan he dragged her into his arms. His first kiss was no slow approach and his arms were confident as they wrapped around her. He may not have had a girlfriend before, but it didn't show in his performance as he hungrily explored her lips and mouth. His strong hands pressed her close against him and it was his lean body she felt. He wasn't as thin as he seemed, but muscular and toned.

She was trembling badly and knew it was only the support of his arms that kept her on her feet.

'Will you let me make love to you?' he whispered fiercely, looking intently into her eyes.

She couldn't speak. She was beyond words. Her answer was in the kiss she gave him. In his safe arms she was carried to her bed and with an unbelievable sensitivity Nathan Bell made love for the first time in his life.

She stood by her bedroom window and gazed at his dark hair and beautifully curved back. His skin was smooth and unblemished. He had been sleeping deeply for several hours, but she was not surprised. The emotions wrung out of him had left him exhausted. It was over in a matter of seconds. She had encouraged him to let go, knowing that he would learn control and be better the second time. And he was. She hoped she pleased him as much as he pleased her.

He was stirring and she saw him slowly become aware that she was not beside him in the bed. His head and shoulders lifted off the pillow as he searched for her, and the heat in his eyes when they fixed on her made her almost dizzy. 'Come back to bed,' he whispered.

She was conscious of smelling slightly musty and feeling

unclean from all the sex, and felt she should wash. 'Let me shower first,' she said softly.

He shook his head from side to side. 'No, you'll wash away your beautiful smell and I'm only just getting to know it.'

Feeling an instant heat buck her insides and a heaviness sweep through her thighs, she slowly walked back to the bed.

CHAPTER THIRTY-SIX

'The tyre impression left on Lillian Armstrong's jacket was a Pirelli 205/45 R17. But as I said, thousands of cars are fitted with these tyres. The chances are, many of the cars in that car park are fitted with these tyres – there are certainly enough sports cars parked in there.'

Greg gazed at Peter Spencer, needing to hear again what the man had said earlier. 'But it does fit a Mini?'

'Yes. I've got the report here.' He held up the sheet of paper and started to read it. 'Pirelli 205/45 R17. It—'

'—and this tyre make is the one that made the impression on Lillian Armstrong's jacket?' Greg said, repeating Peter, as if to cement the fact in his brain.

'Yes.'

Greg's mind was not eased. The likelihood of it being Alex Taylor's car was increasing. 'OK. So let's begin checking all the occupants of the building first.'

Peter Spencer nodded, but his expression was doubtful. 'Do you not think we should start with Dr Taylor's car? At least to eliminate her?'

'So you're buying into DC Best's theory? Dr Taylor ran the woman over to gain attention?'

'I'm not buying into anyone's theory. We haven't proved the tyre came from her car, I haven't even seen what tyres are on her car. She may have Pirellis, she may not. If she has I'll be looking for fresh bitumen. That's what made the impression so clear. Although it may be too late for that, given the doctor had her car cleaned. We really need to just take a look and take her out of the frame. Or . . . I'm letting you know the facts, Greg. Not joining the dots.'

Greg stared around, looking at the spacious CID suite, and saw that even at seven o'clock in the morning the place was busy. Officers were sitting at desks, checking information on their computers or preparing hard copy notes for the morning briefing. Laura Best's desk was still empty, giving him a few minutes' grace. She was late, which was unheard of.

Greg nodded appreciatively. 'Thanks, Peter. Keep at it. We need a location with fresh tar laid. In the meantime let's keep quiet on the tyre information. Laura Best is out to hang the doctor and I do not want any wrongful arrests, especially not of a doctor. The media will have a field day if we're wrong.'

'It's your decision,' Peter Spencer answered. 'I'll do what you want.'

He turned to leave, then stopped. 'It still doesn't make sense to me – why Dr Taylor would run the woman over and then tell you about the tyre mark on her jacket. It all seems a bit strange.'

Greg nodded. 'My sentiments exactly. Which is why we need to check our facts first.'

'Do you think it's possible someone borrowed her car while she was shopping?'

Greg shrugged. He had no answer.

'If Lillian Armstrong was in Dr Taylor's car there *will* be evidence.'

'I'm aware of that,' Greg replied. 'And of the fact that we still have no answers.' He sighed heavily. 'Do it, Peter. But do it discreetly. Check out what tyres her car has. And then we'll know.'

CHAPTER THIRTY-SEVEN

Maria Asif elbowed the door open, taking care not to drop the tray of dirty instruments she carried. It was the final tray she needed to bring into the room. She had piled the others up on the counter so that she could do another quick check and make sure there were no needles or blades among them before they were sent back for sterilisation.

It had been a busy night, especially the last few hours, and an unsuccessful one at that. The body of a young man was still lying on one of the operating tables waiting to be collected by the porters and taken to the mortuary. He was nineteen years old, but looked even younger. He had been brought into A & E with virtually every bone in his body broken after coming off his motorbike at high speed.

There had been little they could do for him, and the attempt to stem bleeding from severed arteries, damaged organs and broken bones had been more of a token gesture. In her opinion it would have been better to have left him to die surrounded by his family, instead of in a cold and sterile operating theatre surrounded by a dozen professionals, desperately wanting to help, but clearly unable to.

Maria Asif had said a prayer for him and had stood with his crying parents as they hugged and kissed him goodbye. It was two days before Christmas and their child had died, and there were no words that could help them. Maria had nothing to say that would lessen their sorrow. She now wanted to get home to her own babies. She wanted to kiss her eldest son while he was still at an age to let her, and hold her two youngest children for the rest of the day.

It was moments like this that made her hate her job. As she checked over all of the instruments that had been used on the dead boy she felt tears run down her face. It was unfair. Sudden death in someone so young was so unfair. There were no answers, only 'what ifs'. With the sleeve of her surgical gown she quickly wiped away the tears.

Moving over to the waist-high dumb waiter she saw blood on the wall beneath the lift. It must have leaked from the lift, and run down the wall.

Staff were continually reminded about the importance of hygiene, the seriousness of cross infection and the out of control MRSA sweeping through most hospitals, and yet a simple thing like cleaning up the mess left by bloody instruments was ignored. Someone had obviously put a tray of dripping instruments into the lift without wrapping them first. She would report this when the day staff came on, because the mess had been left from yesterday, not during the night.

Angry at the state of the lift, which would keep her from her family longer, she raised the outer door. She would send the instruments down to the sterilising unit, bring the lift back up and then clean it. Gripping the inner door, she raised it and saw that the blood was not caused by dripping instruments, but by a body curled up tight, wearing clothes drenched with it.

Maria Asif's screams reached the ears of her colleagues and she stumbled away, backing out of the room and into the corridor, where she vomited.

Greg looked at his watch again. The morning briefing was nearing an end and Laura still hadn't shown up; he was now worried. He had called her on her mobile and tried her home several times and she wasn't answering. It was so unlike her, and as much as he disliked the woman he had a responsibility for her.

Every officer knew the importance of staying in contact. All police officers were targets and knew that at any time in their lives they could find themselves in a situation where they faced danger. Reprisal and revenge from people who felt the police had wronged them, or cornered perpetrators trying to escape a capture, were all a source of potential danger.

Greg had sent an officer over to her home, but she seemed not to be there. When the briefing was over he would get someone to call again and, if necessary, get a doorman to let them in.

He saw Dennis Morgan checking his mobile again and felt irritated by the young officer's rudeness. Walking behind his chair, Greg adopted the manner of a teacher and snatched the mobile out of his hands. 'You need to pay attention when you're in this room, Morgan. You shouldn't be checking up on your love life. Get it back from me at the end of the briefing.'

The tall and newly trained officer reddened. 'Sorry, sir. I was checking on DC Best's whereabouts.'

Greg stared at him with new interest. Had Laura found herself a new playmate, he wondered. He hoped so. He really did. He wanted Laura Best off his back before this year ended.

'And why would you be doing that?'

'Concern, sir. She hasn't shown up.'

'I meant,' Greg said more concisely, 'why you? Why would you take it on yourself to check out her whereabouts?'

'Because I've . . . I've been seeing her lately.'

Greg smiled. 'Seeing, as in . . . romantically seeing?'

Morgan nodded.

'And have you heard from her today?'

'No, sir. She had a meeting yesterday evening with someone. She texted me yesterday to cancel our date and I haven't heard from her since.'

'Were you expecting to hear from her again?'

Another nod. 'After her meeting I thought she might ring me.'

The door to the briefing room opened and Stella Cartwright, a senior civilian support officer, entered the room. 'Sorry to barge in, Greg. We just had a 999 from the hospital. They've got a dead body up there and this one didn't die in a bed.'

Dennis Morgan let out a gasp and Greg quickly looked at him. 'What is it, Dennis?'

His handsome face had turned pale and his eyes gone wide.

'Laura's meeting was at the hospital. That's where she went.'

Laura was not in the best of moods. She was late for work, which was a cardinal sin for her. She had dropped her mobile in the bath this morning and the person she had been meeting had stood her up the night before. Touché, maybe. But enough was enough. So far she had wasted an entire evening and part of her morning.

She was standing in the emergency department trying to speak to the coordinator and get an explanation without a telephone constantly interrupting them, and had so far gleaned that her no-show of last night had no-showed for work as well.

She now needed her mobile number again, as she was unable to access it from her own phone, so that she could get in contact and set up another meeting fast.

As the charge nurse ended yet another call, Laura tried again to speak to him.

His smile was rueful. 'Sorry, it's always like this in the mornings. Just give me a sec and I'll get you the number.' He pulled a red folder towards him and then raised his eyebrows in resignation and sighed loudly as his bleeper went off. He dialled a number on his phone and Laura saw his instant shock as he spoke to the caller. She was about to turn away when she heard him mention the police being called. His face was white when he came off the phone, and she had to ask him twice what the problem was.

His eyes were glazed and blinking fast. 'Theatre. It's up in main theatre. You need to get up there,' he managed to say.

Hurrying through the corridors, she passed others rushing towards the theatres, and when she got to the doors she was barred until she pulled out her ID and informed the orderly that she was a police officer.

Doctors and nurses were gathered in the long corridor, all wearing scrubs and clearly shocked by what had happened, and one woman, an Asian of tiny stature, was crying hysterically.

On the floor outside an open door was a pool of vomit, and Laura began to realise that something very serious had happened.

A man in blue scrubs was comforting the Asian woman, and beside them a second woman, the only person who looked to be remotely in control, was standing quietly by.

Laura approached her. 'My name's Laura Best. I'm with CID. Can you tell me what's going on?'

The woman went to shake hands and then, realising that she was wearing a surgical glove, she let it drop to her side. 'Sandy Bailey. I'm senior theatre sister. We have a very bad situation here. One of the staff nurses has found a body.'

'In that room?' she asked, pointing to the open door by the pool of vomit.

The theatre sister nodded. 'Yes. It's where we send our instruments for sterilisation and collect our new sets. She got a terrible shock when she went in there.'

Aware that she was probably entering a crime scene, Laura told the woman to allow no one to leave the department or let anyone enter unless they were the police. She asked if she could have a pair of plastic shoe covers.

The sister shook her head. 'We don't use them any more. We all wear clogs now.'

'Please don't let anyone in here,' she warned the sister.

Slipping off her jacket she placed it on the floor with her hand-bag, far enough away from the vomit, against the corridor wall.

Her first thought was that the room was small and that it didn't look like a sterilisation area. Her second thought was that there was no body on the floor. Turning impatiently to the sister she saw on the left-hand side of the room an opening in the wall. A woman was curled inside it, her knees and thighs showing, drawn tightly up against her chest. Her right forearm was squashed in across her lap and her long dark hair was hanging loose, hiding her face.

Using a pen from her shirt pocket, Laura lifted the hair up and saw the reason she had been stood up.

Fiona Woods hadn't been able to make it because she was dead.

CHAPTER THIRTY-EIGHT

Maggie's face showed pleasure and curiosity as she let her very happy and flushed visitor into the house. Alex was glowing and her energy was high, making it almost impossible for her to stand still and speak slowly. She thanked her friend for letting her in, thanked her for the beautiful painting and enthused about the beautiful day.

Maggie's eyebrows rose at this, as it was blowing a gale and chucking down rain outside. She eventually managed to squeeze a word in edgeways to ask the cause of this happy change in her new friend.

Alex flushed a deeper red and her eyes brimmed with happy tears. 'Nathan. He came to see me last night.'

'Nathan Bell from A & E?'

'Yes,' said Alex. 'And he's absolutely wonderful.'

'I gather he stayed,' Maggie said drily.

Alex's face scrunched up guiltily, but her lips twitched gleefully.

'Well,' Maggie said, leading the way into her beautiful sitting room. 'He's certainly a fast worker.'

'But he's not,' Alex replied in his defence. 'He's shy and reserved and amazed that any woman could ever want him. He's beautiful, Maggie, and he doesn't know it.'

'If it wasn't so early in the day I would say this is a cause for celebration, but,' and she sighed here, 'you and I have got something else to do. That's if you still want to.'

Alex's happiness diminished a little. Everything was going well for her for the first time in ages, and the thought of what she must do filled her with fear. She could choose to ignore what she should do and go on with her life the way it was now, forgetting the past and even accepting that the terrible night with the psychopath was all in her mind. Richard Sickert had said as much. She could face the man who had attacked her last year by herself at another time.

She could ignore her conscience and make herself believe that no other woman would ever be in danger from him again. She could even let him get away with it.

When it first happened she had been unable to watch television for fear of seeing him, but then gradually she relaxed enough to allow herself to watch the occasional drama without reading the synopsis and checking the cast list. Fortunately, she had not had to suffer his face staring back at her from the screen, and had wondered not so long ago if he'd gone off to Hollywood or was doing theatre instead. She hoped not. She hoped the reason for not seeing him on the telly was because he was out of work and his profile was fading. The thought of actively seeking him out or looking him up on the Internet brought a sickness to her stomach.

There lay her dilemma. He was still terrorising her and still controlling her life.

'Will you help me?'

Maggie nodded firmly. 'You know I will.'

Alex was shaking. 'I can't phone him, Maggie. I need you to sort it out. I'll meet with him, but I can't make the arrangements.'

Maggie moved forward and hugged her. 'I'll do it. But remember, we are doing this together.'

'It was easy,' Maggie said as she came into the kitchen waving sheets of paper in the air. 'I googled him and I've just come off the phone to his agent.'

Alex continued buttering the toasted bagels, stirring the scrambled eggs, pouring water into the teapot. She didn't ask any questions.

'Did you hear me?' Maggie asked.

She nodded.

'He's played bit parts in *Holby City*, *Casualty* and *Lewis*, and is now preparing to play a part in a period drama. Guess where the period drama is set, Alex?' Maggie asked.

'He's in Bath, isn't he?' she said, laying down the wooden spoon and turning to face her.

Maggie nodded. 'He's here right now. His agent has given me his mobile number and I'm going to ring him and set up a meeting for this evening.'

'He might not meet with me.'

'He will,' Maggie said firmly. 'I'll leave him no choice.'

The smell and sight of the food was making Alex nauseous and she moved away from the Aga. She wrung her hands and then folded her arms in agitation. 'I'm not ready. I won't know what to say.'

'Stage it, Alex. Play the part. Take control. If what you went through is all in your mind – the abduction, the rape threat, a death threat – because of what he did to you last year, this could be your way of facing both situations. Face him, Alex. Don't let this man control you any longer. Put yourself back in that car park. Wear the clothes you wore on the night. Look him in the eye and I bet you will quickly realise that he is your real nightmare and what happened to you in the car park several weeks ago only took place in your mind because of what he did to you. He made you vulnerable, Alex, and he made you afraid.'

Alex smiled tearfully. 'The only problem with this is I no longer have the dress. The police do. It hasn't been returned to me yet. I have another dress that's similar, my bridesmaid's dress, but it's still at the drycleaner's. I'm not even sure I know where the ticket is for it. It's been there since my sister got married, because I can't bear to look at it.'

Maggie crossed the floor and hugged her. 'I'll get it back. You don't have to think about it. Go and lie down on my bed and sleep for the rest of the day. Watch telly or finish my crossword for me. I'm stuck on 13 down.'

Alex smiled, looking more in control this time. She picked up the newspaper from the kitchen island and saw most of the cryptic crossword puzzle was filled in. She read number 13. 'Rearing – becoming more incensed (7)'.

'It's an anagram,' she said. 'Rearing makes the word "angrier". It's what I should be. Angry. And then I wouldn't be afraid.'

CHAPTER THIRTY-NINE

The theatres were closed down immediately, operations cancelled and staff taken elsewhere for questioning. Nobody was allowed into the department other than the police.

Greg had toured the area thoroughly, checking there were no other exits and entrances into the theatre suite. The killer had walked through the same door as he had, murdered Fiona Woods, and then exited the same way. He had CCTV footage immediately confiscated so that it could be checked. He'd organised a full-scale murder investigation, talked with numerous officers, met and briefed senior staff, and delegated junior staff tasks – all the while with a heavy heart.

Dr Taylor could not be found, and Peter Spencer could not locate her vehicle; officers headed by Laura Best had been searching for her for the entire morning. Her colleagues and family were being questioned at this very moment. Greg had got a call from one of the officers down in the emergency department with information about a doctor named Nathan Bell who had spent the night with her. His story was being checked and her flat was being searched for any evidence that would direct them to where she was now.

The rumour circulating was that she had gone into hiding after brutally murdering her friend because she had discovered the planned meeting between Laura Best and the dead nurse.

Laura had explained that she was supposed to meet Fiona Woods at the hospital the day before, at seven o'clock in the staff canteen. The nurse hadn't shown, and when Laura checked with her colleagues she was told she'd gone off duty in the early evening and was due back on this morning. Laura was certain that Fiona Woods was going to tell her something important about Dr Taylor, relating to something that had happened to her a year ago. Fiona Woods had told Laura that the doctor was beginning to worry her. Their consultant, Caroline Cowan, had been brought into A & E yesterday after a car collision and Alex Taylor was trying to get the consultant to believe that the person who drove into the back of her car was the same person who abducted Alex from the car park. The driver in question had in fact reported the accident yesterday evening; his lame excuse for leaving the scene was that he had a meeting.

Greg didn't know what to think. He certainly couldn't think of her as a murderer yet. More than anything he was worried about her, the warm and caring woman he had briefly got to know; he was concerned for her safety. If she was involved, and he prayed she was not, would she do something stupid to herself?

Only two other officers were in the room when he arrived back at the crime scene – Peter Spencer and the police photographer. Fiona Woods was still wedged inside the lift, as the pathologist had not yet given permission to move the body. He was out in the corridor on his phone and had made a preliminary examination while the body was still in situ. He would be back in shortly.

Before she was moved from the lift he wanted every bit of the room and the body photographed and videoed.

The cause of death hadn't been determined yet, but Greg had lifted her hair and seen the scalpel embedded in the right side of her throat. He was pretty sure from the massive amount of blood loss that she'd had a main artery severed. She was twenty-eight, unmarried with no children. She was an incredibly talented nurse, and someone had ended her life.

His day out with Alex was still fresh in his mind, her laughter, when Seb Morrisey picked her up off the ground and swung her around, still sounding in his ears. He remembered her kindness and patience with Joe as he sat screaming and bleeding while she attended him, and the small, uncertain smile on her face when she invited him and Joe on the helicopter flight. He liked Alex Taylor. He wished he could be certain she was innocent.

Slowing down to a walking pace, Alex stared up at the black clouds above. They were heavy and low with a promise of more rain. The barges moored along the river were closed up, their owners inside in the warm. The bright colours – reds, blues and greens – were dulled and the wood on a few of them looked sodden and spongy. Bicycles and plastic chairs and small tables lay abandoned on the decks, and large sheets of brown tarpaulin covered the roofs of some of the barges.

She normally saw a dog or two sprawled out on the decks or standing with stiff fur, barking at her as she walked or ran by, but today the owners were taking pity on them and had let them into the dry.

Unclipping her water bottle, she took a long drink and then looked at her watch to check the time. She had four more hours before she met with him. The meeting place and time was set, and all she had to do was wait. She had decided the best way to spend the time was out running, the exercise distracting her from the evening ahead. It wasn't working. Her mind could only focus on one thing. Of how she would be when she met him. Would she have the courage to face him? Sweat had wet the waistband of her running shorts and she was beginning to shiver as her skin cooled in the cold air.

She had parked her car at Weston Lock on the western outskirts of Bath and had run as far as Saltford and back, an eight-mile route of grassy banks and shady trees that in the summer sheltered you from the sun and in winter, the rain. She was familiar with this route and had used it often to run when she lived on site at the hospital. She didn't want to be near home today and use the running path on her doorstep, otherwise she might bottle out. In a short while she would head back to Maggie's and start preparing for the evening. She had no intention of going near her own home until after the job was done.

By the time she returned there later tonight, he would have been dealt with and her home would be a place where she no longer thought of him. She would find the courage to face him somehow, and if she had to call the police and get him arrested she would do so. She intended that her life from now on would be positive and free of him. Even if she wasn't believed she would be satisfied that she had done her best to bring this man to justice.

She wished for the umpteenth time that she had her mobile with her. She couldn't find it this morning and was beginning to think she must have left it at work. She wanted to hear Nathan's voice. She wanted to tell him she couldn't see him tonight and hoped he would understand. They had made love again before he left for work and she had never felt more adored than she did in his arms.

Alex had seen the anguish in his eyes as he told her of his painful experience, and knew there and then that she would always love his face. Nathan, she believed, was a man who wanted to be loved for who he was, not for what he looked like.

She would hate for him to think she was rejecting him by not being in contact.

It was probably a good thing that she didn't have her phone. She couldn't call him. Today was something she had to deal with alone – a grubby, dirty situation which she didn't want anywhere near her new life. She would tell Nathan about it at a later date, when there was no chance of it tarnishing what they had just begun.

Filling her mind with only him – his voice, his image and his touch – she began the half-mile walk back to her car.

Greg stared at the tall, thin man and tried to keep his eyes from fixing on the birthmark covering the left side of his face. A part of his forehead, an eyelid, the side of the nose and cheek and a corner of his mouth was a deep purple. This was the man Alex had slept with last night. He was not the boyfriend. Laura had taken a statement from a man named Patrick Ford.

Nathan Bell was a rare man; there was a humility and dignity in his manner. Greg sensed the challenges the man faced each day. His eyes were filled with a quiet despair at the thought of Alex being in trouble. Greg could give him no words of comfort.

Officers found clear evidence that a man had spent the night at Dr Taylor's flat, and Greg believed it was him. He also believed the times he said he arrived and left. None of it helped Alex Taylor, though. Fiona Woods's death occurred before the time he had spent with Alex Taylor; the nurse was captured on CCTV on a corridor leaving A & E at 18.05 and the glass on her wristwatch had been broken at 18.35.

Peter Spencer and the pathologist had worked out a theory that it got broken when the lift door was shut on her wrist. The tissue damage on her arm showed two parallel lines, which suggested the inner plate of the door had hit flesh as well as the watch. The killer then probably raised the lift door again and pushed her arm in properly.

Nathan Bell could offer no alibi for Alex Taylor.

What perplexed Greg was the time of the death. The theatres would still have been busy, and that lift could have been used at any time. Someone very confident had killed the woman. The pathologist thought that the nurse was still alive when she was bundled into the lift. The blood pattern on the lift's ceiling and walls showed spurting. She would not have been alive for long, but she may have been conscious and aware that she was dying as she sat imprisoned in the steel box. Someone very confident had walked away from the murder scene, someone who perhaps knew it didn't matter if they were seen, he reasoned, wearing theatre clothing, paper cap and mask.

'She didn't do this,' Nathan Bell said for the second time since Greg had entered the office. 'She isn't a killer.'

'Has she been in touch with you today?'

'No, not since I left her this morning.'

'And have you tried to contact her since you found out?'

'Yes. I wanted to warn her, but her mobile is switched off, so I just left a message asking her to contact me. I want to be with her when she hears about Fiona.'

'What did she say to you this morning?'

'Nothing. We kissed goodbye. I expected to see her this evening.'

'Did you make plans?'

'No. I thought we'd talk later.'

'When you went to her flat yesterday, you said she still had her coat on.'

'Yes.'

'And this was just gone half seven.'

'Yes.'

'Dr Taylor finished her shift at five thirty. Do you know what she was doing after that time?'

'No. I have no idea.'

The interview had ended there and the doctor had gone miserably back to his department. Greg sympathised. Neither of them wanted Alex Taylor to be in trouble. Every member of staff had been questioned, some of them at length, and the worrying thing was that although they were shocked by the death of Fiona

Woods, none of them showed surprise that the police were asking questions about Alex Taylor's whereabouts. There were several who volunteered information about the doctor, telling officers that they had been concerned about her for a while, that she hadn't been herself lately.

Greg had two home interviews to do which he wanted to conduct himself. The first with Alex's ex-boyfriend – he was assuming he was an ex if she was in another relationship – and the other with her boss, Caroline Cowan. These two knew her well and he hoped one of them could verify her whereabouts and her well-being.

Tom Collins was walking along the main corridor when Greg saw him. He waved and caught up with the tall forensic medical examiner. The man looked tired and Greg guessed he'd been on the night shift.

'Bad business, hey, Tom?' Greg said, making conversation.

'Shocking. Fiona Woods was a nice lady. Last time we talked she asked about working in New Zealand. She'd have got snapped up. It's a real tragedy.'

'What are your thoughts on Dr Taylor being the killer?' Greg asked.

Tom Collins stopped walking and his shoulders slumped a bit. 'Be a shame if it was her. Another very talented lady.'

'You were there the night she was brought into A & E. What did you make of that business?'

Tom shook his head. 'I don't know. Difficult to say. She was definitely shook up, and initially I believed we had a rape case, but nothing added up. She had all her clothes on, no signs of any tears in them, and nothing was found in the examination, just a bit of a bump on her head.'

Greg wanted to take the man into his confidence and share with him Laura Best's thoughts. He wanted the opinion of someone neutral. 'One of my officers has an idea that she made it up, that she could be suffering from some form of Munchausen's by proxy.'

The forensic medical examiner's eyes widened at the thought, and Greg could see his scepticism. 'That's a bit of a stretch. Not the first thing I would have concluded. There would normally be a pattern of behaviour on which to base that diagnosis.'

'What if there was?' Greg suggested, and told the man about Alex Taylor's connection with the deaths of Amy Abbott and Lillian Armstrong, the drug error she made, the anonymous call and the message left on her car.

Tom Collins frowned. 'With this mental disorder the idea is to make a person sick, not kill them. This sounds closer to 'Mercy Killings' rather than Munchausen. And even then, it's still a stretch.'

They carried on walking while Greg talked and they neared the hospital exit. Tom Collins's final comments gave Greg no answers and no comfort. 'First case, she was right to call in the police and it did prove suspicious, didn't it? The woman did an illegal abortion on herself. Second case: can happen to anyone. Drug errors are made, not often – especially given the amount of drugs they give in A & E – but it happens. Third case: your hit and run, sounds like Lunchtime Lilly got herself into a bad situation with a whacko punter. And the anonymous phone call and message left on Dr Taylor's car I'd say were malicious pranks.'

Tom stretched his shoulders back and rolled his neck. 'Christ, I'm tired.' Then he focused back on Greg. 'The thing is, Greg, everything you've told me would be scoffed at by the CPS. You don't have any evidence.'

'What about Fiona Woods?'

Tom grimaced. 'Whoever killed her, Greg, as far as I'm concerned, is a cold-blooded psychopath. Long time since I saw such a brutal murder. Goes without saying that I hope you're wrong about Dr Taylor. I don't envy you one bit going down that avenue.' As Tom exited the glass doors he gave a casual salute. 'Be seeing you soon, no doubt.'

Greg wished he could go home to a warm bed too. He could then bury himself under the blankets and not be the one who had to investigate Alex Taylor.

CHAPTER FORTY

The sky was getting darker and heavy clouds were shutting out the moon. A cold breeze was making her shiver and her thigh and calf muscles were stiffening.

She was alone on the path, and watched the leaves on the trees shake with each gust of wind while she steadied her breathing and let her heart slow down. There was nothing here to disturb her, and she leaned against a tree and tried to relax.

During the last couple of miles, thoughts of the evening ahead had almost buckled her legs with fear. She wasn't ready to face him again and her biggest fear was that Richard Sickert and Maggie had got it wrong. She had begun to allow herself to believe they were right, to believe that her abduction from the car park was only in her imagination. But supposing they were wrong and she really had been abducted, not by some unknown psychopath that she had made up, but by the same man she was meeting tonight. It might have been him who abducted her from the car park. He was an actor. He would know all about disguises. He had learned the role of a doctor with her help. She had been unable to recognise the voice of the man who attacked her, but what if it was him all along?

He could be getting back at her for rejecting him. In his sick mind he might think she deserved to be raped last year and was now targeting her again. If so, then maybe he was involved in the death of Amy Abbott. He may also have killed Lillian Armstrong. But why would he? Why would he target them as well? What was the connection between these other women and herself? Amy Abbott had been a nurse. Was it possible he met her in the hospital during the time he was shadowing Alex? Over three and a half thousand people worked at the hospital and Alex had only met her because she became a patient. And Lillian Armstrong had been a prostitute. Could he also have known her? Could he have stolen Alex's fob key and lured the woman to where Alex lived?

Alex was terrified that she could be right, and that the man who attacked her last year could in fact be a serial killer and a rapist.

She needed to get back to Maggie's and discuss it with her. She did not want to put either of them at risk if there was the slightest chance that she was right.

There was a sound in the bushes behind her and she was sure it wasn't leaves rustling in the wind. She tensed and waited for someone to come hurtling out at her and felt fresh sweat break out on her skin. A minute or more passed and the bushes stayed still. Releasing an unsteady breath she pushed away from the tree and headed up the slippery embankment, towards her car.

The senior consultant of the emergency department had the beginnings of a black eye and an obvious bump on her forehead, but it didn't hamper her as she hurled fresh bales of hay into a row of stables. Her husband had pointed Greg in the direction of the yard and told him the stables were to the left. He promised to bring out tea shortly, leaving Greg to find Dr Cowan by himself.

The doctor was well muscled, dressed in a checked shirt and jeans tucked into wellingtons. He couldn't imagine her dealing with intricate situations, having to use fine motor skills to suture or cut into flesh. She looked like a farmer's wife, very at home with a pitchfork.

She was not surprised by his visit and said that after she finished in the stables she had planned on going to the hospital to talk to her staff. Some of them might need counselling. She had already rung Fiona Woods's parents and offered her condolences and she had spoken to the chief executive several times since the morning. Her cheeks were puffy and Greg wondered if the cause was her recent injury or from crying. Her eyes had welled up at the mention of Fiona Woods.

'I just can't believe she's dead,' she now said, stopping work and leaning on the pitchfork. 'I can't believe I'm never going to see her again.' She rubbed her eyes with the back of her hand.

'And when was the last time you saw her?' Greg asked.

'Yesterday,' she sighed heavily. 'It seems a lifetime ago.'

'Did she say anything to you about anything troubling her?'

'Only about Alex. That's all we seemed to talk about lately. How worried we were about her. *Her!* And now poor Fiona is dead!' She closed her eyes and shook her head in despair. 'I blame myself! I should have forced Alex to take leave when I first felt she was having a breakdown. This is my fault – mine entirely. She's been screaming out for help for a long time now and I should have done something about it. She's been drinking. I suspect she's been taking other substances. I should have done it yesterday, after this.' She pointed at the bump on her head. 'Alex attended me and after checking me over she asked me if I thought my car accident was connected to *her*.' She sighed heavily. 'As you're probably aware, the driver who drove into the back of me has owned up. I should have put her on sick leave immediately. I've got a young woman's death on my conscience now because I didn't deal with it when I should have.'

Greg was shocked by how ready she was to condemn Alex Taylor. Everything she said was damning.

'You seem positive that it's Alex who killed Fiona Woods. I thought they were best friends?'

'They were,' she said. 'But who else could have done this? Alex has been falling apart for weeks. I've had colleagues ring me up with their concerns, which I should have listened to more carefully. I had to get another doctor to shadow her in case she made any more errors. You'll probably – if you haven't already – hear about it, but she nearly gave a drug to a man that would have killed him.'

'Would it be an easy mistake to make?'

She shook her head. 'Most definitely not. She'd been drinking; that's the only reason, and Fiona Woods was trying to cover it up.'

Greg's heart picked up speed at this information. He hadn't known that Fiona Woods was a witness to the drug error. She may have been covering for Alex because it wasn't an error, but a deliberate mistake.

He shook his head hard, trying to dislodge the uncomfortable thought. He felt treacherous for thinking it.

'Fiona Woods was meant to have met with one of my officers yesterday evening. She didn't show up for that meeting. The officer believes she was going to give her information about something that happened to Dr Taylor last year.'

'She was attacked,' Caroline Cowan blurted out.

Again he felt shock. 'By whom?'

'An actor we had in the department. He was playing the role of doctor in a TV drama and was shadowing Alex.'

'And she reported this to the police?'

'No. We tried to get her to, but she wouldn't.' Caroline Cowan raised a hand and gingerly touched the bump on her forehead. She seemed weary and sad at the same time. 'The thing is,' she said in a subdued and careful tone, 'I never really pushed her that hard to report it.'

'Why not?'

'Because I couldn't be sure it happened. She was tearful and very uncomfortable talking about it and there was no evidence.' She looked at him earnestly. 'I couldn't be sure. You see, after she reported him to me, he telephoned me and said that he understood my ringing his agent requesting he no longer come to the department, but it was a shame I didn't speak with him first. He told me he had been planning to come and see me. He was concerned that Alex was becoming a little attached to him. Making excuses to see him. He thought her a very nice woman, and was grateful for the help she gave him, but he felt a little uncomfortable because he had to rebuff her.'

Greg felt the interview was coming to an end and stood silently for a moment. In the longest time since he could remember, he was faced with a situation where he wanted to be wrong. He wanted Alex Taylor to be innocent. And now after what this woman just said he was beginning to feel angry that no one had made her feel supported. He was overcome with the thought that he couldn't save her and he shivered as the first real doubts crept into his mind. She could be guilty. She could be a cold-blooded killer.

'Forgive me for saying so,' he said harshly, 'but I think it was your duty to report that incident. Whether you believed it or not is irrelevant. You have a duty of care to your staff first and foremost, and you should have rung the police yourself.' He turned away angrily and breathed heavily for a moment. She had tears in her eyes when he faced her again. 'How do you know it didn't set this whole thing off? How do you know she wasn't attacked and that this is now the price she's paying – having a major breakdown and destroying not only her life, but others' lives as well. How do you know he hasn't done this before? That he hasn't attacked another woman since then? I want his name, because I most definitely will be paying him a visit.'

'His name is Oliver Ryan,' she said in a drained voice.

The name meant nothing to him.

'Is he famous? A movie star? Television, Hollywood or what?'

She shook her head. 'No. He's one of those actors you would immediately recognise but can't remember what he's been in, and you don't know their name. He's been in lots of things . . . He was the diver, the main character in *Black*

Waters, the one about Loch Ness, who goes down in a sub and discovers a woman's body and tries to prove the history of the Loch Ness monster was an invention to cover up a murder that took place in the 1930s.' She paused and then said, 'It wasn't that good, really.'

Greg hadn't heard of the film. He would google both it and the man's name when he got back to the station.

He turned to leave, but she stopped him. Her eyes were filled with regret. 'I really am sorry. I don't know what else to say. I care a lot about Alex Taylor, you must believe that.'

He softened his expression as best he could and acknowledged what she had said. 'She's going to need someone strong and supportive when we find her, Dr Cowan. She's going to need people who care.'

CHAPTER FORTY-ONE

The paper bag was inflating and deflating like a bellows and Alex's eyes were round with fear as she fought to slow down her breathing. Maggie was standing behind her, gently massaging her tense shoulders and offering words of encouragement. 'All the way in and all the way out. Breathe nice and slowly. There's no rush.'

It was days since she'd had a panic attack, and this one had come out of the blue while she was drying herself in Maggie's bedroom. She'd shut the door and then seen her bridesmaid's dress hanging on the back of it. It was identical in colour to the one she'd worn on that fateful night. Her mind had filled with the terrible memory of lying on that operating table and suddenly she was unable to breathe.

Feeling air fill and leave her lungs more easily, she removed the bag from her mouth. 'I'm sorry,' she said wearily.

Maggie squeezed her shoulders comfortingly. 'We can call it off . . . ? I've thought over what you said, and even though I still believe you couldn't have been anaesthetised in the way you say it happened, I now believe you, Alex. I'm sorry for everything you've gone through, and I'm sorry for ever doubting you.'

Alex shook with relief; her heart was pounding and quickly she turned her head and buried it against Maggie's breast. 'Thank you, Maggie. Thank you so much.'

'I'm going to the police with you. I'm going to make them listen to what you have to say, and they better do something about it.'

'They won't believe me,' Alex said. She raised her head, her eyes full of conviction. 'They won't, Maggie. The only way to prove this is to confront this man and get him to admit what he did. I want to do it. I want this over with. This man is not taking over any more of my life. It ends tonight.'

Maggie's eyes were worried, but finally she nodded. 'Well, I'll be with you, don't you forget that,' she said. 'We're in this together.'

For the next hour Alex concentrated on getting ready and keeping calm. In a couple of hours she would meet Oliver Ryan again and she needed to be brave.

Greg didn't like the ex-boyfriend. His righteous tone was getting right up his nose. The man seemed to be patting himself on the back for being right about Alex needing help. Greg had listened to Patrick Ford's opinion for the last ten minutes and was still waiting for him to say something positive about Alex Taylor, but the best he got was how sorry he was not to have spotted her downward spiral sooner.

'It's so hard to watch someone you love behave this way. I tried to believe her. I truly did, but in the end you have to go with sanity.'

Greg would rather the man argued a case for Alex Taylor, stood by her side, insisting she be believed, until the bitter end, when truth prevailed. But he was just a normal man, Greg suspected, who perhaps could be a bit weak. Still, he'd like to wipe the satisfied look off his handsome face just the same.

Patrick Ford may well be an educated and professional man, and no doubt doing a sterling job helping sick animals, but he was a prat.

He made it sound like he was bestowing a great honour by inviting Greg into the treatment room while he examined a dog, explaining he needed to finish his surgery first, and if Greg could wait a short while he would then talk to him at length about Alex.

Greg leaned against a wall, gazing at anatomical posters of cats, rabbits and dogs, waiting while the man showered. His behaviour was odd. Greg had come to see him on urgent police business wanting to know if he had any information on Alex Taylor's whereabouts, and the bloke was having a shower before they could carry on their talk.

Greg stared at the array of drugs on display in an open cabinet and wondered if he could get him on some law concerning keeping drug cupboards locked. The ketamine on view was surely a no-no; any member of the public could slip in here and help themselves to an ampoule.

The door opened and a sturdy young woman in a green tunic and trousers came in. She briefly studied him and then reached for a grey quilted jacket that was hung on a coat peg. She put it on, zipped it up and then banged on the door to the shower room.

'You left the drug cupboard unlocked, Patrick. I'll see you in the morning.'

Then, without saying a word to Greg, she left by the door she came through.

They were an odd pair, and Greg had wasted enough time in the place. He wanted to be back at the station in case any new information came in. He now banged on the shower room door. 'Mr Ford, do you know where Alex is?'

The door opened and the man popped his dripping head out. 'No, but when she comes here, be assured I will call you.'

Greg eyed him carefully. 'What makes you so sure she'll come here?'

'We're an item, Inspector. Alex knows she'll be safe here. She'll come to me for help.'

Greg really felt like punching the man on the nose. His arrogance was astounding. Then he relaxed as he realised he had an easier and more effective way to punish him.

'Do I take it that Dr Taylor is still your girlfriend then, sir?'

Patrick Ford's eyes shot open and his head jerked back as if punched, and Greg almost crowed. *That made you think, didn't it?* he wanted to say.

'Why would you think differently?' he asked in a tight voice.

Greg shrugged. 'No reason. Just checking. We'll need your DNA for testing against bed linen and such things.'

The man's face had turned red, and not from the heat of the water he'd just showered in.

'Are you suggesting someone other than Dr Taylor has slept in her bed?'

Greg shrugged again, his manner feigning apology, as if trying to retract what he'd just let out. He turned to leave. 'I'm sure it will be your DNA, sir. I shouldn't worry about it.'

With a satisfied smile of his own, he left Patrick Ford less cocksure and arrogant than when he arrived.

'You look beautiful,' Maggie said as Alex came into the sitting room. 'It's a shame we're not going to a Christmas party.'

Alex had lost weight since Pamela's wedding and the bridesmaid's dress was loose, but the colour suited her tawny hair and her still lightly tanned skin.

Maggie was dressed in a black tracksuit and black trainers so that she wouldn't be seen in the dark.

'You'd have to wear something a bit dressier if we were,' Alex replied with a smile on her face. It was Christmas Eve tomorrow; maybe they could dress up and go somewhere special, and spend the evening forgetting about tonight and just enjoying themselves.

Maggie handed her some champagne; she had given her a smaller measure earlier to calm her nerves. They moved to the centre of the room and clinked glasses. 'Together,' Maggie firmly said.

Alex drained her glass and then gazed around the room. Maggie had decorated the mantelpiece with greenery and a magnificent red and gold flower display. A Christmas tree twice as tall as her was decorated with white fairy lights, large muted gold balls and ruby-red teardrops. It was a fine tree, tall and strong and now elegantly dressed, and it reminded her of Maggie Fielding.

'Together,' Alex said, borrowing some of her friend's confidence.

CHAPTER FORTY-TWO

The shoes Maggie had lent her were slightly too big and were pushing her off balance. She'd been standing for five or ten minutes alone in the dark and her body was rigid with tension. If she didn't move soon she would fall over. The reassurance of Maggie being parked close by was less comforting than she had imagined. It would be impossible for Maggie to rescue her if he decided to knock her down with his car.

She could feel a throbbing in her temple and the slight headache that started earlier was now worse, making her feel nauseous. Too much champagne and not enough food, she realised.

She heard the drone of an engine in the distance and looked over the hospital car park searching for oncoming headlights. A car was turning past a row of parked cars and she was paralysed with fear as she waited for it to get closer.

The sting in her left buttock barely registered, until the same sensation nipped her thigh. The heaviness in her limbs was almost immediate, and a feeling of being punch-drunk whooshed through her. She was seriously lightheaded and felt disconnected from her body.

'Maggie,' she cried feebly, desperately feeling for whatever had stung her skin. She had to let her friend know what was happening. Then her understanding of her other night here in this car park became painfully clear. All the sensations that she remembered happening to her: the wave of dizziness buckling her legs and her knees slamming to the ground, a pain to the crook of her neck, a pressure on her mouth, no air, gagging and then . . . nothing, were all that she had previously remembered until now. Until this small sting in her leg. She had felt the same sensation on that night as she was trying to exit the department. A scratch against her thigh and the fleeting thought that something had snagged her dress, which she hoped hadn't pulled a thread in the delicate material. She finally knew how he had abducted her. 'You were right, Maggie,' she drunkenly mumbled. Her arm dropped to her side, and then she crumpled to the ground.

Her eyes were still open and her mind still working, but she was unable to call out. She could feel the gravelly ground against her cheek and hear it lightly crunching as footsteps approached. The toe of a dark shoe stopped an inch from her eyes, making it impossible for her to focus on it clearly. She wondered if he would draw back the foot and kick her in the face.

You only pretended to gag me, to confuse my senses, she said bitterly in her mind to the man beside her.

You knew I wouldn't be believed.

The sting she'd felt in her buttock and thigh told her she was right. *He injected me instead, Maggie. He injected me. Oh fuck, please help me.*

CHAPTER FORTY-THREE

The incident room was milling with people, still busily making calls and still on a motivated high. On the first day of a murder investigation every effort was made to get a result. Greg glanced at the evidence boards and thought they showed very little results for the work that had been put in that day. But then there wasn't a lot of information to gather. Merely a suspect to catch.

Alex's photograph was on the board; a head and shoulders snap that the hospital had given them. She looked incredibly young, and he felt deeply saddened every time he looked over at it.

Officers were still out searching for her; airports, railways and coach stations were alerted. Her car's description and registration plate were being watched for on the motorways, and of course her photograph had been emailed to every police station in the country.

Laura Best had officers hunting for her throughout the hospital, in case she was hiding there, and any reputation the doctor had left was being eroded fast.

Greg half hoped she was across the Atlantic by now, escaping all these people wanting to catch her. He would like to see Laura bested by her. He would like to see her fly a helicopter again one day. He sighed deeply and wished he were any other place but here.

Moving over to one of the computers to do the job he'd meant to do when he first came into the room, he logged onto the Internet and googled the name Oliver Ryan. There were several hits. He saw the words 'Black Waters' and 'actor' in one of them and clicked it open.

His mobile rang, and, pulling it out of his jacket pocket, he saw Joe's name on the screen. He inwardly groaned, realising it had gone ten and he hadn't rung him as promised. He moved away from the computer, out of earshot of the others, and said hello to his son.

'You not in bed yet?' he asked in a surprised voice.

'I wanted to say goodnight and make sure you're coming tomorrow.'

'What's happening tomorrow?' Greg asked, deliberately pretending he'd forgotten what day it was.

'It's Christmas Eve, Dad!'

Dad? This was new. Joe was losing his babyish language. 'Is it? Are you sure it's not the day after? I reckon you're a day ahead, Joe.'

'Stop messing, Dad – you know it's Christmas Eve.'

Greg smiled. He had bought Joe a present that he knew he would love. A remote control helicopter that could hover at twenty feet. He couldn't wait to see his face when he opened it, and hoped to get over to Oxford the next day to give it to him.

'Joe,' he said, turning more serious. 'I'm not going to promise you, because I can't, but if it is possible, I *will* be there.'

There was silence on the end of the line.

'Do you believe me, Joe?'

'Yes, Dad.' His voice had gone quiet and Greg felt riddled with guilt.

'Good. Now get some sleep, buddy, you've got a big day tomorrow. I want you up bright and early to give your mum a hand so that she can put her feet up tomorrow evening.'

'She's going out.'

'Is she?' Greg asked, very surprised. Sue never went out on Christmas Eve; she stayed at home getting ready for the big day.

He couldn't help asking where she was going.

'Out with Tony.'

A knot in his throat stopped him from swallowing. It had to happen sometime. She was a lovely woman and there would be plenty of men out there wanting to date her. He felt an ache somewhere in the region of his chest. His first real love, his wife of ten years, was moving on.

'You could go out with Alex now,' his son said, as if somehow this was the right thing to do. His mum was OK, so now his dad could be too.

But only fairytales had happy endings. They weren't for murderers or the policemen who chased them.

He realised he'd just thought of her as a murderer for the first time and felt a coldness go right through him. Was it possible she had killed Fiona Woods? He closed his eyes tightly as he saw the dead nurse in his mind and hoped she was unconscious when she was squashed and stuffed into that steel box. She had been left to die in the darkness in a space not big enough to even raise her head, and she may have felt or even heard the hiss of her own blood spurting on the walls enclosing her. It was a cold and heartless death, and only a ruthless killer could end someone's life that way.

Was it possible Alex Taylor was such a person?

Alex opened her eyes and had to quickly shut them again because the overhead lights were blindingly bright. Her head was pounding and the slight movement she made was making her feel sick. A strap across her forehead prevented her from turning her head sideways and she was afraid to vomit in case she choked.

Where are you, Maggie? Please be here to save me.

Risking the glare again, she squinted up at the light, made out the circular outline and knew she was back in the same theatre as before. She took no comfort in having it confirmed that it never was just in her mind. She had been to this place before, where she thought she was going to die, only to awaken later as if nothing had happened. But now she knew who it was that had abducted her. Oliver Ryan.

Steeling herself, she focused down on her chest and saw the green theatre drapes covering her. Her breath caught in her throat as she saw the shape of her raised bent legs. She was in the lithotomy position again – her calves supported on knee troughs and her ankles held in stirrups – and from the cool air touching her skin beneath the drapes she knew she was naked.

In the background she could hear the sounds of instruments –

steel being placed against steel – and the urge to vomit was imminent as she shook with fear. He was close by, getting ready to deal with her.

Holding her breath and grinding her teeth until her jaw went rigid, she tried to quell the rising terror. She had to be strong and think of a way out of this situation. She had to believe she could be saved.

Trying to keep as still as possible and not alert him to her being awake, she tried to work out how tightly tied down she was. If he had secured her with only Velcro straps there was a chance that she could work them loose and get free.

Her arms were resting on supports, but she couldn't see what banded them because the drapes covered them as well. She moved both arms at the same time and felt no give whatsoever.

A monitor close to her ear suddenly started beeping and her terror escalated as she heard the sound of her own panicked heartbeat. It was thumping loud and fast, which panicked her even more because this would tell him she was awake. He had obviously switched it on for this reason and was now toying with her.

Please, God, make it go slower. Make him not realise I'm awake.

It was a pathetic prayer, but ironically her heart did slow; her teeth bit right through her lower lip as he suddenly leaned over her. His head and shoulders were out of view, but the blue surgical gown and the purple gloved hands were right in front of her face. He reached across her and hung a bag of fluid on a drip stand.

'Please don't hurt me, Oliver,' she pleaded through chattering teeth. 'I beg you.'

He didn't answer. Instead he moved away from the operating table and a second later she heard him at a metal cupboard. Drugs. He was getting out drugs.

Her bladder emptied and hot wetness gushed between her buttocks.

Her enraged screams filled the room, and for a few precious seconds she felt in control. Someone would hear her. Someone would come running. They would hear her screams out in the corridors. A doctor or a nurse, a porter or even a visitor passing by would hear her. She wouldn't, *wouldn't* give in to him this time. Tasting the blood in her mouth she spat in the direction of where she thought he was standing. 'You fuckhead. You coward. You piece of shit. I'll kill you, you fuckhead.'

An uncontrollable rage consumed her, sweat bathed her face and chest and the desperate need to fight back gave her strength. She heaved her body up as high as she could go; her chest and abdomen lifting several inches off the table. Her head strained against the unyielding strap. Pain shot up her thighs and into her groin as the stirrup straps tightened and metal dug into her ankle bones. Her wrists and forearms were burning as she wrenched and rubbed against the restraints, trying to break free. She was using every muscle in her body, every ounce of energy, twisting and turning in the hope of something loosening or breaking and setting her free, but it wasn't happening.

Finally, exhausted and panting, she had to admit defeat. The band across her forehead was as secure as ever, her arms and legs still trapped in the supports and stirrups.

It was hopeless. She was as helpless as a baby and he could do to her what he liked. Nobody would come running.

Oh, Maggie, please don't be dead, she pleaded in her mind. *Please come quickly and don't be dead.*

CHAPTER FORTY-FOUR

Greg sipped the strong black coffee, his mind trying to catalogue all the events over the last few weeks that Alex Taylor had been involved in: her allegation that someone had abducted her, her presence at the death of Amy Abbott, her presence at the death of Lillian Armstrong, her presence when a near-fatal drug error was made.

Alex Taylor was present for all of it. Was Laura Best correct in her thinking that Alex Taylor was the only person responsible?

And now Fiona Woods lay brutally murdered and she too had been connected to Alex. She was Alex Taylor's best friend and she had been present, according to Caroline Cowan, when Alex Taylor had made a serious drug error. Was she dead because of what she knew? Had she known incriminating things about her best friend? Had Greg badly judged the situation through wilful blindness and was he now partly to blame for Fiona Woods's death? He sighed deeply. Where was Alex Taylor? Where or to whom would she run? Patrick Ford seemed to think it would be him. He was cocksure about his place in her life. He didn't question or doubt her next move.

In fact, Greg suddenly realised, he didn't question anything. He didn't even ask why the police were looking for her. That surely wasn't normal? Maybe he had judged Patrick Ford wrong. He may have already given Alex Taylor a place to hide.

His thoughts were interrupted by the officers around him as chairs scraped on the floor and voices asked questions. Laura had stepped into the incident room and Greg observed how some of the officers were surrounding her as if greeting a hero back from a war. Their voices were rich with admiration and he could see she was basking in the glory. She was wearing a well-tailored navy suit and cerise blouse, and guessed the get-up was in preparation for meeting the top brass.

She was obviously hoping, or assuming, that they would come to the station if an arrest was made, and she was probably right. Announcements to the press would have to be made, and an officer interviewed by reporters for the local news. *He* wouldn't be chosen for the job. He wasn't wearing the right shirt or suit and he still hadn't got around to getting a haircut, so the chance of her being in the limelight was high.

Why, he wondered, had she come back? Last he heard she was staking out the hospital. She looked incredibly excited about something. Her eyes were bright, her top teeth exposed as she bit her lower lip. He didn't have to wait long to find out.

'I've secured the scene. *You* need to get up there fast,' she said, talking only to him, but making sure the others were listening.

Her tone was officious, as if she were the boss and not the other way round.

He took a slow sip of his coffee, his manner completely unrushed. 'What scene and where?' he calmly asked, not giving her the satisfaction of seeing him jump to attention.

'She's left her car abandoned at the north side of the hospital, unlocked and driver door open. It has to have been left in the last hour or so, because it wasn't there earlier. She can't be far away, and my bet is she's in that hospital somewhere.'

'Who,' he asked, 'can't be far away?'

'Alex Taylor, of course,' she said back impatiently, as if it was obvious.

He walked slowly across the room towards her; he wanted to be standing very close to her when he told her to take the sarcasm out of her voice, when he told her if she disrespected him one more time she'd be up on report.

Two things got in the way of what he was about to say: the smug grin on Laura Best's face and the Internet site he'd opened earlier. Joe's phone call had interrupted him before he got a chance to view it, and since then he'd forgotten about it.

The small inset photograph showed a handsome fair-haired man who looked well groomed, and appeared to be someone used to the finer things. Greg vaguely recognised him. His name and a date were beside the photo: Oliver Ryan 1979–2016.

The man he needed to speak to was dead.

Her eyes were closed against the glare of the lights. They stung from the tears she had cried, and the only way to soothe them was by keeping them closed. Her heart was beating loudly, but not as fast as before. It had settled into a rhythm that was more bearable.

It was quite conceivable that she could have a heart attack, even as young and fit as she was, if she was terrorised sufficiently. She almost relished the thought. It would be a quick death and he would have no more control over her.

When he next came to her she wouldn't fight her fear; she wouldn't try to block out what was happening to her and what he was about to do. She would let him into her mind, and then hopefully her heart would betray her and she would die.

She held her breath as she felt his presence, and then she made herself open her eyes.

Joy of great magnitude instantly filled her and more tears flooded her eyes. She couldn't speak for the tightness in her throat. Her prayers had finally been answered. Maggie's face stared down at her.

She couldn't think fast enough to ask when and how she had got there because already she was thinking they had to get out fast. He was close by, and if he caught Maggie then she too would be in danger.

'Get me up,' she whispered urgently. 'Hurry before he comes back.'

Maggie looked over her shoulder and then down at her friend. 'He's not here.'

'He's not far, then,' Alex answered fiercely. 'Hurry, Maggie! He'll come back any second. Undo my arms.'

Maggie raised the green drape and dropped it back in place. 'You're naked.'

'Forget that!' Alex hissed. 'Just get me off this fucking table.'

Maggie bit her lip and for a moment looked as if she was about to cry. 'He's left all these things out,' she whispered. Her hands lifted surgical instruments, wasting precious seconds. 'I told you it couldn't have happened the way you said it did.'

'Maggie, we haven't got time!' Alex whispered urgently. 'Please, he'll kill us both.'

Maggie raised something in her hand, her voice excited. 'Look, Alex! Look what I found!' A small black rubber disc was held between her fingers, a thin wire dangling from it. 'You know what this is, don't you?' She moved things noisily on the metal tray, clanking instruments, urgently searching for something.

'Leave it!' Alex desperately hissed. 'Please, Maggie!'

'I can't! Do you realise what this means?' She moved away from the head of the bed and Alex could hear her frantically searching. 'It's here somewhere. I know it is!' She crossed back over to Alex, quickly patting the space around Alex's head and then she heaved a sigh of relief. 'God it was so . . .' She held up something square, silver and no bigger than a matchbox. She deftly attached the two things she'd found together. She sighed again. 'It was just so damn . . .'

She placed the black rubber disk close to her mouth and spoke: 'Easy to fool you.'

Alex bucked violently as if electrocuted, her eyes stretched in horror. The voice! His voice! Coming from Maggie's mouth! Sweet Jesus, it couldn't be true? *Maggie*, the person she had come to trust, the one who believed in her, helped her . . .

Maggie laughed cruelly, her male voice terrifying Alex. It had never occurred to her that it was a woman speaking.

A simple little voice changer, the gadget hidden behind a surgical mask, confusing her into thinking that it was a man speaking to her. When all the time it was Maggie beside her wearing a mask, a gown, a pair of purple gloves, creating a work of make-believe. With the operating lights blinding her and her arms strapped down, she had even believed that cannulas had been inserted in her veins, when in reality no needles punctured her skin. Just a bit of tape holding the cannula against the skin like they would do in a medical drama; she was, as Maggie said, easy to fool.

Maggie moved the gadget away from her lips. She sighed, and smiled down at Alex. 'Are you comfortable?'

Both sides of the road were cordoned off, and behind the blue and white tape two police cars were parked. Very little traffic had passed this way and Greg understood why. The exit from the north side of the hospital was closed at night, so all traffic into and out of the hospital used the main entrance. It cut down on noise for the neighbouring houses.

The hospital security guard was stamping his feet with the cold. He was here when Greg got to the scene, having been stationed here from the start by Laura Best. Greg realised the poor man was probably perishing.

'You,' he called out, and the man gazed over. 'Go and warm up, get a hot drink.'

The man's shoulders shrugged stiffly. 'Cheers. You want me to send my colleague in my place?'

Greg shook his head. 'No. There'll be more police officers swarming round the place soon enough. You could let the site manager know what's going on. We haven't informed anyone in the hospital yet.'

'Right you are. I'll get on to it,' the guard answered.

As he trotted away on cold, stiff limbs, Greg donned a pair of latex gloves as he prepared to examine the vehicle. He stepped carefully so as not to disturb possible evidence and peered through the windows. Empty; she wasn't hiding inside it. He knelt down by the driver's seat and located the catch to pop open the boot. Pulling out a pencil torch from his jacket he switched it on and prepared to look inside. Images of Fiona Woods crowded his mind and he realised he was fearful of finding another body.

He relaxed as his eyes took in the contents of the boot, which thankfully didn't contain a body. A Fitness First logo on a sports bag, which he unzipped to find gym clothes, toiletries and a towel. A pair of green wellingtons, an open pack of six 500ml bottles of water, one missing. A cardboard box of medical equipment, dressings, bandages and various sealed needles and intravenous tubing. He placed the box to one side and saw that it had been resting on clothing, and his heart skipped a beat as he identified a large dark hooded top.

He lifted it up to reveal a bundle of blue plastic hospital drapes, the type used in operations. From the way they had been folded, they had already been used. He unravelled an edge slightly so that he could separate the layers, and by the light of the torch he saw dark red stains. His hand trembled and he let the layers fall back into place. He moved the drapes to one side and there beneath everything else was a spare tyre. A Pirelli.

Aiming the torch along the rubber grooves he saw bits of embedded black grit. He touched his finger in a groove and the tip of his blue rubber glove came away slightly tacky. Tarmac. Now he knew why Laura had been so excited. She'd already seen inside the boot. She already knew what he would find, but instead of staying with the car she had hurried back to the station so that he would be the one to find the evidence, and she would be the one standing with all their colleagues when he had to tell them what he found. She would then bask in the glow of being proved right. No doubt she'd be of the opinion that if they'd searched her car sooner, then the murder of Fiona Woods could have been prevented. He could have stopped her death from happening.

Hearing the sound of a diesel engine he glanced up the narrow road and saw the forensics van coming towards them. He waved at the unseen driver, indicating to him to keep coming.

Greg felt sick to the core. Each time he resisted believing in Alex Taylor's guilt something else showed up to prove him wrong. And that something, right now, was overwhelming. Everything in the car indicated that she had killed Lillian Armstrong.

'Sir?'

'What?'

The police constable who had driven him to the scene was shining a torch inside the Mini.

Greg walked over to him.

'There's empty pill packets on the passenger seat.'

The man shone the torch through the driver's door and Greg saw three empty blister packets. He reached in and picked one up and made out the word through the torn bits of foil: diazepam.

Shit. Fucking hell, he thought. She's taken an overdose.

CHAPTER FORTY-FIVE

Alex was still reeling with the shock of being deceived by her friend. Maggie's eyes that told her it was true. They were full of hatred, raging with a malevolent need.

She had yet to feel fear, because at the moment, mixed in with the shock, was grief at the loss of someone she had come to like so much.

Through pale dry lips she managed to ask, 'What have I done? I don't understand, Maggie. What did I do?'

The spit on her face felt as shocking as any physical assault. The vile action was almost impossible to believe. Yet the wet sliding down her cheek was testimony to what Maggie thought of her.

Maggie leaned very close so that their faces were only inches apart. Her breath was hot against Alex's cheek as she spoke: 'Have you ever watched someone die?'

Alex briefly closed her eyes in the face of so much hatred.

'Of course you have,' Maggie said in the same icy whisper. 'You see it every day . . . but it's not the same when it's someone you love. I watched Oliver die. It wasn't pleasant. The rope . . . His face . . . His black tongue . . . I live with that image in my head.

'I blamed them, Alex. I blame every one of them. And I was right to. There are women out there . . . tarts, prostitutes, sluts, who parade their goods and then say no. And then there are the clever ones who entice and tease. Women like you, who think they have the right to lead a man on. A good man.'

The heart monitor beside her betrayed Alex; it was beeping as her heartbeat went over the safe limit. She relived the morning, saw Maggie standing in the kitchen waving the sheets of paper she'd printed off the Internet. Oliver Ryan was appearing in a period drama in Bath. He couldn't be dead . . . unless Maggie had lied. Which of course she had. It was a set-up, staged so that Alex would believe she was meeting him.

The realisation that it had all been planned terrified her more. Maggie had wanted to hurt her very badly for a very long time.

'I never enticed him, Maggie. He attacked me.'

The cloth suddenly pressing into her mouth nearly drove her teeth backwards. The pain in her jaw was passing into her neck. Maggie's full weight was behind the hand.

'Shut your filthy mouth. Oliver would never attack any woman. He would never defile himself with a woman like you.'

Maggie shifted the cloth so that it covered her nostrils as well and Alex could no longer breathe. She tried inching her head up, moving her nose out of the way, desperate to draw air.

She gasped as the cloth was lifted off her face.

'I nearly gave in and killed you quickly,' Maggie said, breathing hard. 'I expect that's what you're hoping for. But we have a long night ahead of us, Alex. Plenty of time to do what I plan. You need to rest. I want you fit for what I intend. But you better keep quiet.'

She held up the staple gun for Alex to see.

Despite her fear, Alex was not yet ready to give in to it. She had resolved not to fight it, but instead to let it in in the hope that she would literally be frightened to death, then this could finally be over. But she couldn't. She had to believe she still had a chance.

'You won't get away with it, Maggie. When they find me, they'll come looking for you. They'll find a connection that will lead them to you. Oliver will lead them to you. They'll find out he was your boyfriend.'

Maggie laughed but the sound was false. 'Oliver was an actor. His private life was his own. No one will connect me to him. He loved me and wanted to protect me, so he kept me a secret.'

Alex wanted to hurt and shock her; anything to bring her out of her present mindset. 'He didn't love you! He was probably using you. You have money, Maggie. A house worth a fortune. You told me yourself he only came to your house to use your parents' studio. He was using you! And the only reason he kept you secret was so that he could try it on with other women.'

The sharp click of the staple gun sucked the newly drawn breath back out of her lungs. Maggie slammed it against her skull and fired it again and again.

'You slut. You lying little slut. If you don't shut your mouth, I'll staple it shut.'

Tears drenched Alex's eyes and through them she blurrily saw Maggie's face. Bravely she fought to carry on taunting her. She would rather rile her and take the chance of being killed in an instant than put up with this slow wait for death. 'Richard Sickert will connect me to you. He'll tell the police you sent me to him. He'll lead them to you, Maggie.'

This time Maggie's laugh sounded genuine. 'You fool. Why wouldn't I send you to get professional help? Everybody knows you've been falling apart. Dr Sickert will only confirm what everyone already believes. That you're mad.' Her grin looked manic and she spoke in a high, sickly-girly voice: 'Oh Maggie, I'm so scared. Help me, Maggie. Help me.' She prodded Alex's forehead with a hard finger. 'Why Oliver ever wasted his time with you I don't know. You really are quite stupid. But none of that matters any more. He's dead, and by tomorrow you will be too. Now, I have a lot to prepare. I want you to lie here and rest. You'll need all your strength.'

She smiled pleasantly. 'Did I tell you what I have planned?'

All Alex could do was stare. Maggie had to be mad to behave like this. Her hatred was completely out of control.

She realised now that the disintegration of her life had been engineered. Maggie Fielding had deliberately entered her life to destroy her.

'They'll come looking for you, Maggie.'

'No, they won't. You told them I was a man.'

In the hospital canteen, which had been opened by the site manager especially for this meeting, a large number of police officers were gathered. Greg brought them to attention.

'Settle down and listen up,' he said loudly.

Laura Best was at the front, still looking wide awake and immaculate. She was fuelled with adrenaline at the prospect of the hunt.

The site manager had urgently summoned the chief executive, and architectural plans of the hospital had been obtained.

The chief fire officer of the city was also in attendance as he knew the grounds of the hospital better than most.

He had commandeered a canteen table to lay out the drawings. When he was ready he would speak to the officers about the layout and then Greg would sort them into groups to begin the search. He had finally accepted that Laura Best was right, that Alex Taylor probably was hiding somewhere on site. She had the advantage of knowing where to hide. The hospital grounds and buildings made for a difficult search. The place was like a small town.

Before going into the canteen, his mobile rang and Greg was surprised to hear Seb Morrisey's voice and the clear thrum of helicopter blades rotating.

'What are you doing, Seb? You can't get in the way here. What are you doing up there flying?'

'We got a floater,' he answered coldly.

Greg's breath caught in this throat. 'Is it Alex?'

'No,' Seb answered, less hostile. 'Male, middle-aged – they just retrieved his body from the river. Said he's wearing military dog tags, so you should get an ID.'

Greg was relieved it wasn't her.

'But I'm staying up here now to help search for her.'

'You still can't get in the way, Seb. This is police business.'

'You're wrong, Turner.' The anger in the pilot's voice was clear. 'Alex wouldn't harm a fly. You've got this so wrong if even for one minute you let yourself believe she's your killer. Fiona Woods was like a sister to her, and her killer has got Alex.'

'We have to find her, Seb. We need to question her,' Greg said calmly. 'And if you hear from her you need to let me know.'

'I judged you wrong, Turner. I thought you were a sound bloke, I thought you had a bit of vision. I'm staying up here and don't try and stop me. Alex is in danger and you're too stupid to realise it.'

The man's opinion – not the personal stuff, but his thoughts on what was happening – shook Greg. Supposing he was right and Alex Taylor was not hiding, but was trapped by the real killer. The empty pill packets found in her car could have been planted. She could be dead, and everyone who believed her guilty could be wrong. Uncertainty and indecision weighed heavily on him. But he couldn't afford to blind himself with emotion, or hide from the truth any longer.

He had watched yesterday afternoon's CCTV footage again, and had nearly overlooked the porter pushing a trolley along the corridor. He had spoken to the man not long ago and been told the loaded trolley was carrying dirty instruments and laundry bags. It was normal practice at that time of the day to use a large cage trolley to take the load away; the dumb waiter was only used when in need of a quick return, usually for a particular or specialised type of equipment. The porter was filmed at just gone six and Fiona Woods was seen on the first floor near main theatres at twenty past. Alex Taylor may have known of this practice and could have taken the chance, guessing it might not be used for a while, to use the dumb waiter to hide Fiona Woods's body. According to Nathan Bell, she was still in her coat when he called on her in her flat later that evening. Maybe the purpose of the coat was to hide Fiona Woods's blood.

But the most damning piece of evidence of all was the one Peter Spencer handed him a half hour ago. Found in Alex Taylor's locker was her mobile.

The last message was sent to Fiona: 'Meet me in theatre. I found the operating room. Tell no one.' It was sent at two minutes after six.

With this last crucial piece of evidence he could no longer ignore the truth.

The faces of the officers before him were attentive. They were waiting for him to begin.

'Remember that there are sick people in these buildings and they still need looking after. Do not alarm any of the staff unnecessarily. Do each search thoroughly so that it doesn't have to be repeated, and then move on to the next place. All the exits are blocked so if she is here there can be no escape. In a moment, the chief fire officer is going to explain the layout of the hospital and the grounds. Listen carefully so that nowhere gets missed.'

He drew breath and avoided clashing eyes with Laura Best. 'Lastly, be cautious if you do find her. She may be armed and dangerous. Do not – I repeat – do not put yourself in danger. As soon as you have a sighting, call for back-up.'

'Are you bringing in armed officers?' Laura Best asked.

He shook his head. 'No.'

'You just said she could be armed and dangerous,' she argued with an edge of steel in her voice. 'I think you should reconsider, sir.'

Greg had had enough of her insolence and her 'I can say and do what I like attitude'. He wanted to shrug the nasty little cow off his back once and for all, even if it cost him.

'DC Best, when I want your opinion, I'll ask for it. Please do not think, because we had an indiscreet five minute romp, that it gives you the right to lord it over me and the rest of the officers.' Greg pointedly looked at Dennis Morgan, who had gone bright red with shock. 'You will take orders like the rest of them and carry them out as instructed. Do I make myself clear?'

The silence in the room was deafening, and Greg knew he had just damaged his career, but it was worth it. He could see many of the officers looking at him in shock, and then looking at her with dismissive shakes of their heads. It was definitely worth it, if only to put a stop to the power she'd had over him.

CHAPTER FORTY-SIX

Alex shivered with the cold; the sheet she had wet earlier was damp beneath her lower back and bottom. She was shivering and she was thirsty. The infusion bag of fluid hanging above her head was still full and she could only conclude that Maggie had either deliberately not started it, or else the intravenous tubing connected to it was not connected to her; that beneath the theatre drape her arms were free of needles. And if that were so, maybe the rest of it was a scam too. She would wake up later and find it had all been a mind fuck again. No needle marks, no evidence to prove what had happened to her.

How clever Maggie had been. The first abduction had been the perfect set-up to make sure she was never believed. Alex would look deranged as she tried to get the police, her colleagues and Patrick to believe her. But how could they, when apart from being put to sleep nothing else had happened to her?

She had been alone for a long while now, maybe an hour or so, and had no idea of the time. The room she lay in was silent; the monitor had been switched off and the lights turned out. There had been no warning. Maggie had simply turned everything off and left her in the dark.

The thought that kept trying to creep into her mind and settle firmly was that Maggie had left her here for good. She was going to leave her to die slowly from thirst or the cold. Her organs would slowly pack up, her heart would become weak, her skin pale and cold. She would become lethargic, irritable and then confused, and her kidneys would cease to function until finally her body gave up completely.

Alex thought of all the people she loved and would leave behind. She wondered how soon they would raise the alarm.

Her mother – by tomorrow, for sure. It was Christmas Eve and she would wonder why Alex hadn't rung about Christmas Day arrangements. Caroline would also be alerted. Alex was meant to be on an early in the morning. Fiona was also on the early; Alex had checked because she intended to give her the present she'd bought. Fiona liked pretty things, and when Alex saw the pearl-grey satin pyjamas she got them without hesitation, knowing they were just right for her friend.

Nathan might miss her sooner, though. He might even call wanting to wish her goodnight. He might think she was with Patrick if she didn't return his call. She hoped not, because if she didn't survive this, she didn't want him left with any lasting guilt.

He had made love to her in a way she had never experienced before, not even with Patrick at the beginning of their relationship. Patrick had never touched her just out of the need to touch her. Nathan had kissed her and touched her because he had seemed desperate to. Even as he slept he had held her close against his side.

The sudden loud clapping jolted her entire being. Maggie was back, standing somewhere in the dark. Alex trembled with fear. Had she been standing there the whole time, just waiting to begin?

The clapping stopped and Alex blinked as the lights came back on. The glare was as punishing as ever.

Maggie's face momentarily blocked the light as she leaned over the operating table. 'Wakey-wakey,' she said pleasantly.

Alex heard her moving behind the head of the bed. An alarm beeped as a machine was turned on and a chugging sound began, and Alex instantly recognised what it was: a ventilator starting up.

It was finally happening. The waiting was over. This time Maggie Fielding would put her to sleep and do things to her which she would not survive. Alex felt real physical pain in anticipation of what her body was about to go through. It could be cut wide open or even cut up, depending on how creative Maggie intended to be.

She whimpered with fear as the end drew near.

And then, cutting through some of the fear, she saw her mother's face. She was smiling – a gentle, peaceful smile – and Alex took comfort. It would be over soon and she would know nothing more about it. Clinging on to her mother's image, her crying ceased.

The ventilator chugged on, imitating the rhythm of normal respiration. Alex could hear gas cylinders releasing pressure as they were turned on. There were high-pitched whistles and beeps as the safety checks were carried out.

Maggie's face came back into view. Over the blue scrubs she wore a surgical gown, on her head a blue disposable cap and on her hands purple rubber gloves. She was ready to operate.

Strangely, instead of terrifying her, the familiar garb offered some comfort, and Alex realised she could turn her fear around. Maggie Fielding was a doctor and she was in safe hands. She repeated the sentence like a mantra, focusing on the words and washing them through her mind.

Maggie Fielding is a doctor and I'm in safe hands.

'I never did get round to telling you my plans,' Maggie interrupted.

Maggie Fielding is a doctor and I'm in safe hands.

'You remember the rudiments of anaesthesia, don't you, Alex? Of course you do. I'm being patronising, but in case you've forgotten: anaesthesia is sleep without sensation and pain.'

Maggie Fielding is a doctor and I'm in safe hands.

She was now screaming the words inside her head.

'Imagine what would happen if you only received a muscle relaxant. You would have to be ventilated of course, because you wouldn't be able to breathe. You would be awake, but unable to move. And pain . . . well, you would feel pain. You would be able to feel everything being done to you.'

Maggie held up a syringe full of fluid. 'It's a good plan, isn't it, Alex?'

They were nearing the end of the second hour of the search and Laura Best's immaculate appearance was somewhat altered. Her hair was drenched from the rain and some of her mascara had run. The right sleeve of her suit jacket had a small rip in it from getting caught on a sharp edge in one of the bin sheds. She was getting sweaty and her high heels were pinching her feet.

She was tired and thirsty and very, very angry with Greg Turner. How dare he embarrass her like that in front of the others? She had heard one female officer behind her snigger and vowed she would find a way to make her pay. As for Greg, if he thought by bringing their affair into the open he could walk away scot-free, he had another think coming. She would tell her side of the story – how difficult it was to refuse him, especially as he was her senior officer. He was not going to get away with treating her like this.

Coming up to the next shed, she held back and let Dennis go ahead of her. Her suit was damaged enough. Dennis unlocked the door and shone his torch inside.

'You need to get in there properly, pull the bins out and look inside them.' She shouted into the shed: 'You might be hiding in one of them, mightn't you, Dr Taylor?'

Dennis stayed by the door, going no further. He then shone the torch in Laura's face. 'You want the bins moved, you move them. I am not your slave.'

Astonished for a second, she could only gape. 'What the hell! How dare you talk to me like that!'

'You've been having it off with boss! And now you're with a lowly plod. So what am I, Laura – the poor sap you used to spite him?'

Laura stamped her feet. 'I'll have you up on report, Dennis Morgan. How dare you refuse an order.'

He shone the torch at himself so that she could see his response. With a smile on his face he gave her a two-fingered salute.

Greg could hear the thrum of the helicopter's rotor blades through the walls of the canteen. Seb had been circling and spotlighting the grounds of the hospital for the last half hour, and the blue warning lights were switched on outside the A & E department like a beacon for when he was ready to land. His mobile suddenly vibrated against his chest, jolting him, and spookily he realised it was the man in his thoughts calling.

'What do you want, Seb?'

'Just to see if you've come to your senses yet?'

Greg moved over to a window so that he could watch the helicopter; he doubted Seb could see him, though.

'I'm just doing my job, Seb.'

'Man, you are so wrong about her. Alex would never take a life. I told you how she saved me.'

'Seb—'

'I know. You don't need to hear. You're just doing your job. Well, you've labelled her a murderer and you don't even know her.'

Greg sighed. 'People can change, Seb – something unscrews inside them and they do things that they would never nor- mally do.'

'You mean like murder their best friend?' Seb answered heatedly.

Greg heard his sharp intake of breath, then Seb spoke again. 'Alex didn't do this, and you better hurry up and believe it, or it will be her you find dead.'

CHAPTER FORTY-SEVEN

'Please, Maggie, tell me why you killed them. At least let me understand why.'

Maggie's eyes glinted at her over the facemask. 'You won't stop me doing this, Alex. You'll merely delay the inevitable.'

'Surely you want me to understand. Why did you let me live the first time? Why did you kill Amy Abbott?'

Maggie eased her mask down so that it settled under her chin.

'You think you're clever, Alex. You think you'll get me talking and I'll end up forgiving you. My life ended the day Oliver met you. You led him on. And then you accused him!'

The words were quietly spoken, not in anger, but Alex wasn't fooled into thinking that her mood had mellowed.

'He was trying to rape me!'

'Rape?' she said in a scornful tone. 'He didn't have to force himself on any woman.'

'No, of course he didn't.' Alex jeered. 'He just had to pay for it! Is that why you killed Lillian Armstrong? Because your precious Oliver paid her for sex?'

Maggie's lips pulled back as she bared her teeth. 'She looked like a fat Barbie doll standing there waiting for her no-show client.

I offered her a lift home, told her I was only parking for a minute so I could fetch something from my apartment. I used your key fob to open the gates and drove to your space and asked her if she'd mind backing me in – you know how big my car is.

'She was delighted to help. Standing there waving her hand at me. The first bump merely knocked her to the ground, and I of course rushed to her aid.

'She looked up at me, like a fat fool. Her exposed thighs, sagging breasts and garish make-up and I wanted to so badly tell her she was going to die.

'Instead, I bent down and positioned her comfortably. "Stay still," I said. "I'm a doctor. I need to check you over." What I should have said is, I need to run you over.'

Alex was sickened. 'I don't want to hear it.'

'But you wanted me to talk,' Maggie taunted. 'You need to know the best bit. While you were doing your life-saving bit, I got to watch you. You nearly caught me, Alex. I heard you arrive and quickly parked my car. I sat there and watched, and you really are good, Alex, and I would have liked to stay to hear you explain another death, but that would have been risky. So I simply got out of my car, left it in your car park and walked away.'

'You're a monster, Maggie. And you will be caught. You're not as clever as you think you are. You left your tyre mark across her chest!'

Maggie smiled. 'Ooops! Wrong again, Alex. Your tyre. Your spare wheel. I rolled it in some tarmac at the hospital and then rolled it across her chest. It's back in your car now, though, so not to worry about getting a new one.'

Tears of frustration dripped down Alex's face. 'And Amy?'

Maggie shook her head. 'No more questions, Alex. It's time . . .'

In the canteen Nathan Bell joined Greg at one of the tables. He brought with him two mugs of strong coffee. He was wearing his A & E tunic and trousers and Greg was surprised. 'You were working this morning. I mean, yesterday morning,' he amended, catching sight of the time on his wristwatch. It was past 2 a.m.

'They're short-staffed. I took a few hours off earlier to rest. Anyway, it helps to keep busy.'

Greg lifted one of the mugs and took a grateful sip of the coffee.

'We need to find her fast. She could be unconscious. How much longer are you going to search the hospital? Surely you would have found her by now if she was here?'

Greg shrugged. He was beginning to think the same thing himself. They had covered nearly every inch of the place and he'd sent most of the officers back to the station. Only a few were still out there searching, Laura Best among them, doggedly holding fast to her belief that the doctor was in the hospital somewhere. Greg let her get on with it. As long as she stayed out of his hair he didn't care. Since his outburst earlier he was more at peace than he'd been in a long time. He didn't care that tomorrow he'd probably have to face the superintendent, that he could be suspended. If that happened he'd go and see Joe. Spend the day with his son.

Tiredness, he knew, was making him a little too relaxed about the whole thing, but he'd gained a real satisfaction from standing up to her. A few of the officers had patted him on the back and more than one had let slip a comment. 'Well done', and 'Good on you, mate', had been said a couple of times. They said it in a tone that implied he'd done a good thing. But Greg knew they were wrong. He was not blameless. He'd had sex with a junior officer and had given no thought to the consequences. He'd behaved shabbily and should have faced up to what he did before.

'You're still convinced she's the perpetrator,' Nathan Bell said, breaking into his reverie. It was said as more of a statement than a question.

Greg answered tactically. 'Everything points to her being guilty.'

The frustration and anxiety in the doctor's eyes was plain to see, and Greg wanted to offer him some comfort.

'When this is all over she'll need people like you to support her. She's lucky to have you, Dr Bell. There aren't many that would stick by someone in a situation like this.'

Nathan Bell swiftly shook his head and made a sound of demurral. 'Lucky? I'm the one who was lucky. I've grown up a lonely man because I had an ignorant mother. From an early age she drummed into me that vanity was a sin, and I should accept how I was born. I learned to not look at my face and be reminded of why others turned away.'

He pointed at the birthmark on his face. 'I stayed lonely until I met Alex. She's not a killer, Inspector. It's unthinkable.'

Greg didn't want to have to remind the man that he was emotionally involved and therefore not the best judge. He stayed silent instead.

'So how much longer will you be looking for her?' the doctor again asked.

'Probably another half hour. There are only a few places left to check. First, second and third floors have been done. They're trying to find keys to unlock the doors to the underground of the hospital. The fire officer says it's been out of bounds for years, but we need to rule it out.'

'And then what? You give up? Call it a day? Her life could be in danger for all you know.'

Greg felt his chest grow heavy at the thought.

His phone vibrated again, this time against the table. It was Seb again; his voice sounded echoey, but his words were clear enough. 'I found her. She's in the west wing car park. She's on the ground, Greg, and she's not moving.'

CHAPTER FORTY-EIGHT

Resus was standing by. Caroline Cowan, her black eye even more obvious under the harsh lights, along with another doctor and two senior nurses, was preparing to receive the patient. An air ambulance crew and Nathan Bell had gone out into the car park and would be bringing her in very soon. Caroline had no clinical information on Alex's status, only a report of a possible overdose, and was therefore preparing for every eventuality.

She had got switchboard to fast-bleep the trauma team, including obs and gynae, and couldn't care less if it proved to be a waste of their time. She wanted them in here waiting for Alex just in case. She was, after all, one of their own.

She had put from her mind what Alex had done and would treat her as best she could. Her job was to help the sick, and Alex was more ill than most. She'd had the feeling all day that Alex would do something stupid and had been in contact with Nathan earlier to have him page her if he heard anything. When he called to say the police thought she'd taken an overdose, she instantly dismissed any thought of sleep or staying at home. She had driven all the way to the hospital over the speed limit and had been flashed twice by speed cameras.

They had found Alex ten minutes ago, soon after Caroline arrived at work, and she was glad for Nathan's sake that she had made the decision to come in.

She guessed Nathan was involved with her, and as good a doctor as he was, he couldn't be allowed to lead this care. And if Alex was in a critical condition she wanted him out of resus fast. She had been burned once already with a doctor not being able to cope. She didn't wish to repeat the mistake.

The outer double doors in the corridor suddenly banged open and the two nurses quickly moved over to the resus doors and opened them for the oncoming trolley.

She was collared and was lying on a spinal board. Her eyes were open and she was awake. An oxygen mask was attached to her face and she was clearly in an agitated state.

She was pulling at the collar around her neck, twisting her shoulders, thrashing her legs, desperately trying to get off the trolley, and she was spitting and shouting at the two men: Nathan Bell and Seb Morrisey. 'Get away from me, you fuckers. I'll kill you! You come near me, I'll take your fucking head off.'

Caroline silenced the beeping monitors to lessen the noise, and on her count of three she and the two men transferred Alex to the resus trolley. Alex suddenly swiped her hand out and dug her nails into Caroline's wrist and Seb Morrisey had to unbend her fingers to release the grip on the consultant. 'Easy does it, Doc. You're in safe hands,' he said kindly.

Her teeth bared, her intention to sink them into any part of him she could bite was clear. It was only the head blocks and straps pinning her head to the trolley that saved Seb from injury.

'Draw up some lorazepam, we need to get her calm,' Caroline instructed the nearest nurse.

Nathan Bell put a hand up to stop the nurse hurrying away. Beneath the trolley they'd just transferred Alex from he retrieved a black handbag. 'We need to check what she's already taken.' His face was pale and his eyes filled with anguish. 'She's got diazepam and ketamine in her bag. Syringes and needles as well.' He pressed the bag against his chest and his breathing came fast with his delayed reaction. 'This is my fault. I knew she was taking something. I should have stopped her. I should have told you,' he said to Caroline.

The consultant quickly came to his side. 'None of this is your fault, Nathan. None of it. If anyone's to blame, it's me. Now I want you to leave here – let us help Alex.'

The distraught doctor shook his head. 'I need to help.'

Caroline gripped his shoulder. 'I need you to be strong, Nathan. I need someone I can trust out in the department looking after all the other patients. You need to be out there while I look after her in here.'

Caroline knew there were enough other doctors to do what she'd just asked Nathan to do, but his presence was a distraction and Alex had to come first. Seb stepped in and took the bag out of Nathan's grip and then, placing his arm lightly around Nathan's shoulders, he led him away.

Caroline took a deep breath and turned back to the remaining people: the trauma doctors, the obs and gynae doctor, the A & E registrar, the two nurses and Greg Turner. She thought the senior police officer looked nearly as shaken up as Nathan Bell, and was surprised. Her patient was still spitting and shouting obscenities; the pink dress she was wearing was rising above her thighs, showing her underwear. She needed to be cared for and examined thoroughly.

She looked in the direction of the trauma team and other specialists she had called, all waiting with their backpacks on their shoulders full of emergency equipment, and smiled at them apologetically. They were not needed and could now go. To the nurse she'd just spoken to, she said, 'Call security and have them come down. If she starts kicking off we'll need more than just us to hold her down.' And to the other A & E doctor and nurse: 'We need full obs, ECG and bloods. Check the contents of her handbag and ascertain, if possible, how much she's taken and of what. Ring path lab and ask them to be ready to do paracetamol and salicylate levels. We need to know exactly what she's overdosed on.'

To Greg Turner she said, 'This could take a while; you might want to take a seat somewhere. I'll keep you posted. And if you haven't already, I'd be grateful if you could ring the family and let them know she's here.'

It was several hours later when Caroline finally stepped into the relatives' room and spoke to Greg Turner. He'd been waiting for an update for most of the night and she was grateful that he'd stayed because he'd been there when Alex's parents and sister had arrived. Caroline briefly spoke to them and let them know Alex was stable, but the rest of it, the horrific crimes she was suspected of, she had left to Greg Turner to explain. The three of them had gone back to their homes with their worlds turned upside down.

His eyes were closed and she saw they were bloodshot when he opened them. He rolled his neck and blinked a few times as he became more awake, and then he was quickly alert.

'What's the story?'

Caroline sat down in the chair facing him. 'She's sleeping at the moment, but she's now lucid. She's aware of where she is and is just sleeping off the effects of what she's taken.'

'Any lasting damage?'

Caroline shook her head. 'No. I thought she might have taken other substances, but paracetamol levels are normal. She's had a hefty dose of diazepam and taken ketamine too, which is why she's sleeping now, and also accounts for her behaviour when they brought her in.'

Caroline arched her neck tiredly. 'When she's more awake the psychiatrist will come and do an assessment.'

Greg remembered seeing the ketamine in Patrick Ford's surgery and wondered if she'd stolen it from there, but the consultant admitted the most obvious source: 'I meant what I said earlier. If anyone's to blame, it's me. I was sure she was taking something else, apart from alcohol, and I should have checked stock levels ages ago. She's been falling apart before my very eyes and I ignored it.'

She closed her eyes and sighed despondently, before focusing on him again. 'What's going to happen now?'

'That will depend on the psychiatric review. If she's deemed unfit for questioning I won't arrest her. While she's here I'll keep an officer stationed. What medical treatment does she need?'

'Repeat bloods and observations. And wait for the psychiatric review.' She sighed. 'I just wish I'd been more observant and noticed her breakdown.'

He raised an eyebrow. 'I'd say it's a little more than a breakdown. She's suspected of killing two people – possibly a third, if Amy Abbott was also a victim.'

The consultant briefly shut her eyes in despair. 'Dear God. Has this all happened because of that actor?'

He undid the top button of his shirt and loosed the slightly grubby tie. Then he said: 'Which reminds me, can I use one of the computers? I googled your actor from last year and it seems that I'll not be able to question him, because he's dead.'

Caroline was shocked. 'How?'

Greg shrugged. 'That's what I want to find out.'

There was a light tap on the door and a nurse popped her head into the room. She smiled politely. 'Sorry for disturbing you, but she's asking for you, Caroline.'

Caroline stood up and Greg Turner did the same. 'Do you mind if I come in and listen? I'll stay in the background so as not to alarm her.'

Caroline nodded. She was glad the officer would be in the room. As a senior consultant she should be able to deal with any situation brought into the department; she had had dealt with many criminals, but she had never treated someone she knew who was also a suspected murderer. She had no past experience to draw on and no way to know how this would proceed.

Alex smiled tearfully and gratefully at the people surrounding her. They all looked shell-shocked and exhausted by their efforts to save her. This was the second time Caroline Cowan had cared for her, and she could only imagine how hard this had been for her. Her poor bruised face was haggard. Seb and Nathan were standing on either side of her bed, like bodyguards, looking equally shattered; Alex would for ever more be grateful to these two men in her life. They had searched for her and found her and now finally she could put this whole nightmare into the hands of the police and begin to heal. They would finally believe her.

'Oh, Caroline, thank you for being here. I thought I was going to die.'

Caroline gazed at her and smiled kindly. 'You're safe now, Alex, and you're not going to die.'

'Thank you, Seb, for finding me,' Alex said to her friend through teary eyes. 'And you, Nathan,' she added, reaching for his hand. 'Thank you all for looking for me.'

Seb Morrisey kissed her on the forehead. 'Just returning the favour, Doc. You're my VIP, remember.'

Nathan didn't comment; he simply squeezed her hand.

Alex switched her attention back to Caroline. 'I'm scared to ask, but how bad am I?'

Caroline's expression was light, and her voice calm. 'So far so good. Blood pressure up a little, heart a little fast. Temperature a little low. Otherwise you're in pretty good working order.'

'And what about physically?'

'Nothing.'

Alex smiled bitterly. 'So a mind fuck again.' She raised an arm over her head and touched her scalp, and after a second said, 'So they weren't actually put in?'

Caroline frowned. 'What weren't?'

Alex's voice raised a decibel. 'Staples!' She bit her lip before continuing. 'Sorry, I don't mean to shout. I thought my head was covered with them. I heard the click-clunk of the stapler. I felt it against my head.'

Caroline slowly leaned over her patient's head and carefully searched her scalp. 'You've got a couple of scratches,' she said. 'But there are no staples in your head.'

Alex sighed. 'So all of it was playacting? So very clever.' Her eyes widened as if remembering something. 'But my bottom and thigh were injected! It must have been done with a dart gun or even a blowgun. I want them photographed. To be checked thoroughly. I obviously wasn't anaesthetised for long and I don't know exactly what I was given, but it wasn't just a muscle relaxant as threatened, otherwise I would remember.' She paused to take a shaky breath. 'I assume the police are checking the theatres?'

'The police are here,' Caroline answered.

'And Maggie Fielding? Have they got her yet?'

Caroline stared at her, perplexed, her eyes cagey. 'Why would they want Dr Fielding? Has something happened to her?'

Alex stared at Caroline, looking right into her eyes, beseeching her to understand. She felt the wail begin somewhere in her chest, twisting its way past the tightness in her throat until it became a shrill. 'Don't do this to me again! Maggie Fielding is the fuckhead who did this to me! She abducted me because that actor who attacked me last year was her boyfriend and he killed himself. She did all this to me to get back at me. And these other women – Amy Abbott, Lillian Armstrong, the drug error I made – she did it all. She killed them. You have to get the police to arrest her before it's too fucking late and she gets away.'

'Alex, you need to listen.'

'There's no time, Caroline! Maggie Fielding is a very dangerous woman. She'll kill again!'

'Shut up, Alex, just shut up.' The softly spoken command held a warning.

Alex switched her gaze to Seb and Nathan. 'Seb! Nathan! You need to find her. You need—'

'SHUT UP!' The words ricocheted off the walls and the room silenced. Her eyes pinned Alex to the bed and Caroline took the last few steps towards her.

'I want you to listen to me carefully, Alex. In your car the police found empty packets of diazepam. In your handbag we found diazepam and ketamine. You have taken an overdose and you came in here very confused. You have no other injuries. No staples in your scalp.'

Alex raised her head in fury and Seb swiftly positioned himself closer. Alex stared at him, dismayed. Surely he didn't think she was a danger? Her eyes almost popping with anger, she swiftly denied the allegation. 'I never took any overdose! How dare you suggest it? It's what she gave me.'

Caroline leaned forward, almost touching Alex, and for the first time her voice and eyes held real anger. 'Are you trying to tell me that you haven't been taking drugs and that you haven't been hitting the bottle?'

Alex shook her head fast and her eyes squeezed shut as she desperately yelled: 'Diazepam! That's all I've been taking. I haven't touched alcohol for weeks.'

Alex saw Nathan quickly lower his eyes. She saw Caroline witness his action and knew she had to make them understand. 'I haven't depended on the stuff, that's what I'm trying to say.'

Alex closed her eyes, trying to block out the accusations. She needed to calm down and breathe before this situation imploded. Otherwise she would be labelled an alcoholic with mental problems. They clearly didn't accept what she said had happened to her, which meant Maggie had covered her tracks again. She had to get them to believe her before it was too late and Maggie escaped. Caroline stepped back from the trolley, giving Alex some space. Her voice was now calm.

' You need to listen to me, Alex.'

Alex opened her eyes and lay back against the pillow, exhausted. Her gaze locked on Caroline.

Caroline gave a sad smile. 'When you were rushed in here late last night I had switchboard fast-bleep the trauma team in case it was needed. I also got them to bleep obs and gynae. Maggie Fielding couldn't come, so one of her colleagues came instead. She couldn't come because she was still tied up in theatre. She was in the middle of an operation, doing a section, delivering twins. Maggie Fielding did not do this to you, Alex. And you now need to admit that you need help.'

Alex stared frantically at the people around her. 'None of you believe me. You're all going to let her get away with it. Maggie Fielding killed those women and you think it was me. She set this whole thing up. She's taken revenge on me and anyone else that had anything to do with her boyfriend!'

Caroline could no longer control herself and her voice shook with emotion. 'And what about Fiona, Alex? Did she kill her too?'

CHAPTER FORTY-NINE

Greg walked along the empty corridor towards the obstetric theatres. As he passed some of the wards he heard the sound of rattling china and guessed that patients were having their first cups of tea of the day.

He had always quite liked hospitals and had never felt the dread of them that a lot of people experienced. He felt comforted at the thought of people being looked after.

At the end of the corridor he turned right and walked up to the locked doors. He pressed the intercom and, after identifying himself, he was buzzed through. He needed to meet Dr Fielding and assess the situation for himself.

Alex Taylor's accusations, regardless of how insane they sounded, had to be followed up. Greg had heard similar rationalisations, mainly from men, who, when arrested said they were innocent and that someone else had done it, or blamed the voices they heard or the apparitions they saw. When he made DS, he was called to the home of a dead fourteen-year-old girl. Her body had been painted with her own blood and she was covered in parrot feathers. Her father was sitting in an armchair with the bald bird in his lap stroking its pale flesh, and his excuse for cutting his daughter's throat was that his pet parrot had told him to.

Alex Taylor had told everyone it was a man impersonating a doctor who had abducted her, and then said it was the same man who was killing these women. Then last night, back in the A & E department after trying to get them to believe she had been taken to a theatre again and been subjected to muscle relaxants and anaesthetics and staples fired into her skull, she throws this other doctor's name at them.

It was too far-fetched to be true.

He was directed by a nurse to an open door and found the doctor sitting in an office at a desk with a pen gripped between her teeth as she read notes. She had dark hair and was attractive, and she was obviously busy. She barely looked up when he introduced himself.

She wore theatre clothing and a paper facemask hanging loosely around her neck. He watched her face closely as he revealed why he wished to speak to her. Her head quickly lifted and shock was clear in her features, especially when he mentioned that Dr Taylor believed her to be the real killer.

She swallowed hard, and her face turned pale.

'Why would she say that? I don't even know her. Not personally, that is. Why has she said these things? This is unbelievable . . . I feel like I'm going to cry.'

Clearly distressed, she reached for the glass of water beside her and took a shaky sip. The pen disappeared briefly between her lips again; Greg saw it was a habit, as he spied a second one chewed up on the desk.

'Why would she say these things?' she said again. 'Why me? I don't understand. Do I have to make some sort of statement? Prove that I didn't do this?'

Greg nodded. 'Yes. We'll ask you where you were at particular dates and times.'

'My God. You're serious. I actually have to do this? What has she said I've done?'

He kept his eyes on her and his voice was calm. 'She stated that you abducted and attempted to murder her, have murdered two other women, and that last night you attempted to murder her again.'

Her eyes instantly glazed over and he could see her trying to swallow. Her voice was strained as she spoke. 'Last night . . . last night I was here. I started my shift at 9 p.m., and as you can see I'm still here now. We've had a very busy night. Three caesareans, one of which involved delivering twins, and a woman with a post-partum haemorrhage. She died . . . It's been an awful night . . . and now this.'

'And you've been here all night?'

'Yes,' she said firmly. 'I've been here. In this office. In the operating room. I've been up to intensive care to check on my patient. Do you want me to gather all the staff who have seen me tonight?'

'No, not right now. If Dr Taylor continues with this allegation, we will then have to take statements.'

Tears hung on her lashes and she quickly reached for a tissue.

He gave her a second to compose herself, and then said, 'Dr Cowan tells me you're the doctor who examined Dr Taylor when she was brought into A & E a couple of months ago?'

'That's right,' she said, taking the pen from her mouth and sounding and looking a bit calmer. 'Tom Collins was in attendance as well. It was a . . . strange situation.'

'And have you seen her since?'

Her nod was firm, but her voice sounded husky again. 'Here, of course, but also at my house. She turned up out of the blue, some weeks ago. How she got my address I don't even know, but I suppose she felt she could come and see me. I'd left a recorded message of her results on her answer machine – the results of her examination – and I told her if she needed to talk she could call me. I never expected her to turn up at my house, though. And she didn't really want to talk about the results anyway – she wanted me to help her catch the man who abducted her. I felt terribly sorry for her.'

Maggie Fielding rubbed her face hard. 'I suggested she get in touch with someone I know, a therapist. I've used him in the past for some of my patients and they found him very helpful. Richard Sickert. I can give you his number if it helps? After she left, I immediately contacted Dr Cowan, because I was con-cerned. Dr Cowan said she would deal with it. I have to say, I found it very upsetting.'

'Because she wanted your help?' Greg asked bluntly. He was getting tired of hearing of the number of people who had turned her away.

'No!' she vehemently denied. 'I was more than happy to help. But the stuff she was saying went beyond my abilities to help. A dead woman in her car park. Phone calls she got, her car . . . I wasn't about to help her find someone who didn't exist.'

Greg accepted her explanation. He could only imagine how he would react if a colleague of his presented with a tall story like this. He too would have sent them to get professional help. He felt she was telling the truth, and knew it wasn't her fault that all this had happened; he was just looking to share the blame. His chest had become increasingly heavy as he stood, unseen, in the bay beside Alex, and it had almost broken him to hear her unravel.

'I just have a couple more questions,' he said. 'The first: Have you ever been out with a man called Oliver Ryan?'

She shook her head.

'He was an actor, and he was here in this hospital for a short while last year. Not sure what date.'

Again she shook her head. 'I started here in August. I wasn't here last year. But even so, I don't know this man.'

Greg's expression was candid. 'Dr Taylor said he was your boyfriend.'

'What! This is truly unbelievable. Why would she make up such a story?'

He shrugged. 'We don't know yet. The other question I want to ask is did you ever meet Amy Abbott? She was a nurse here and your paths may have crossed.'

Her head tilted slightly and she gave a little sigh of despair. 'The one and only time I met her was on the day she died. Our paths never crossed before. Again, I've only been here since August. We probably would have met eventually. And the fact that you're asking questions about her is telling me that *you are* suspicious about her death?'

Greg stood up. He would let her carry on with her work. 'I'm sorry to have upset you.'

'You have upset me – not only with what Dr Taylor said, but also hearing how in trouble she is. She is a fine doctor. I wish now I hadn't been so hasty in calling Dr Cowan and instead found the time to talk to Dr Taylor properly myself.'

As Greg wandered back along the corridor, making his way to the exit, he found himself wishing that they'd all taken the time to talk to her properly. She had been crying out for their help, and each in their own way had not listened. He counted himself and Laura Best among the people who turned her away. Patrick Ford, Caroline Cowan and even Maggie Fielding; they each were accountable in some measure for letting this happen.

The sky outside was still black, but the morning had arrived. The day shift workers would be arriving soon and care would continue uninterrupted. He would have to come back later and formally arrest Alex Taylor, and he was not looking forward to it. He had a mountain of paperwork to fill in before then, but it could all wait.

When he got in his car he had no intention of going back to the station. He would make one stop at home and then head for Oxford to see his son.

Maggie cast her eyes carefully over the floor and was reassured that nothing had been left behind. The place was as she found it: dark, dank and desolate. It was Oliver who had told her about the underground. He'd been shown it as a part of his tour around the hospital and thought it was a great place to do a horror story; another *Silence of the Lambs* as he called it, with him taking the starring role.

This would be her third trip back to the room in the last hour and also her last. The police were still roaming the place and she didn't want to chance being seen. She had no more use for the room and had returned the keys and various pieces of equipment she'd borrowed back to their rightful places. The plastic sheeting which had covered the floor for Amy Abbott's visit had been rolled up carefully after the blood had dried and, if not still in the boot of Alex's car, was now being forensically examined by the police. She would have to get rid of the Schimmelbusch mask; as much as she would like to keep it as a keepsake, it was safer to destroy it.

The playacting of knocking Alex to the ground and holding a vaporous cloth to her mouth had been risky, but Maggie wanted Alex to believe she'd been rendered unconscious in this way so that when she told her story it would be an unbelievable one.

Dressed for a windy night, her hair beneath a woollen hat, a scarf wrapped halfway round her face, Maggie had simply waited and watched for Alex leaving the department. With a loaded syringe of ketamine, all she had to do was make a small jab as she passed, then follow her to the car park and perform a mock knockout, confident that there would be little struggle because the drug in Alex's system was already working. The theatrics had greatly appealed to Maggie. In fact the last several weeks had, on the whole, been amusing. To watch and wait for the right opportunities to manipulate the story that was unfolding. To take the risks and get to watch what she'd done. So much of it had been effortless.

The simple switching of the wrong drug left waiting to be found. The spraying of the message on Alex's car while she wandered off into the night without a witness to testify she hadn't sprayed it herself. Those were merely teasers, like the phone call. But each moment had then lent an opportunity to fuel the belief that Alex Taylor was falling apart. What Maggie hadn't banked on was the gift Alex would bring to the play. The beauty of it was that Maggie had to do so little. If Alex hadn't been drinking she would have been more easily believed. She had destroyed her own credibility so easily.

And the gifts just kept coming.

Leaving her handbag at the doctors' party had been one. A simple search and Maggie was given the setting for the next killing. However, leaving her own car parked near the scene of the crime had not been part of the plan, and she had theorised what she would say if the police had come knocking wanting to know why her car was there. A visit to her troubled colleague would have been her pretext, but finding her not at home she went back to her car only to find it wouldn't start. If asked how she got into the car park, she'd say the gates were open. But they hadn't come knocking because they weren't interested in vehicles with fat tyres.

Still, it was now immaterial. She had given a good performance to that police officer and he still believed Alex was guilty. That was all that mattered. Alex had finally shown she was a murderer by killing her best friend.

She would get rid of the tranquilliser gun – a very useful tool that she couldn't imagine ever needing again – which she had used on both occasions to incapacitate Alex. She would also destroy the audio tapes – real recordings of the sounds in an operating room, created especially for Alex. To make her believe that what she heard was really real.

Last night was the end of a make-believe friendship. Alex would have assumed that after she met Oliver and confronted him she and Maggie would drive back to Maggie's house for a late supper. But of course that was never to be. How could they eat together when Maggie would be at the hospital on a night shift and Alex would be under arrest for murder? And no matter how much she protested, her car would be full of incriminating evidence. Her car, which Maggie had suggested they use.

She tapped grit from the soles of the shoes she had lent Alex. She'd not bothered with putting them back on Alex's feet. Why give anyone the chance to question why they were too big for her? Better for them to think that Alex had lost her shoes instead. She cast another look around the room. Maggie listened to the cold silence and shivered. It was time to go. She had a life to live.

CHAPTER FIFTY

Alex ached with grief for her friend. She'd drifted in and out of sleep for most of the day, partly from all the drugs she'd been given and partly from exhaustion. The psychiatrist had visited a short while ago, and no matter how hard Alex insisted she wasn't in need of an assessment, he had been equally persistent in staying and assessing her.

Most of the day she lay in the bed numb, refusing to eat or drink and afraid to talk in case she made things worse for herself. She desperately wanted to see her parents and sister; they might be able to help, but the psychiatrist had said they'd already been in while she was asleep and it really was for the best that everyone just try and stay calm for the rest of the day.

Alex wondered if her mother or Pamela had become hysterical on their visit and had been told to keep away. She could imagine her mother crying and Pamela yelling, wanting to know what was going on. Her dad would have been more restrained. He would have wrung his hands and walked up and down, quietly waiting to be told what was going on. Her poor parents must be out of their minds with worry, she realised, and she so badly wanted to reassure them, but she didn't know how. Maggie Fielding had covered all the bases. Even down to her being in an operating theatre during the time she was with Alex. She had a perfect alibi, and Alex now realised why she had been left alone in the dark for so long. Maggie hadn't been waiting with her; she'd been carrying on as normal – delivering twins.

She felt the fresh sting of tears. This had been happening frequently in the last few hours. She would suddenly find her cheeks wet and one side of the pillow damp from where she lay curled on her side. The tears now, though, were for Fiona. Her dear, sweet friend. No one would tell her how she had died, believing that she already knew, and she could only imagine the situation her friend had faced and the fear she had felt. Maggie Fielding was a very resourceful woman when it came to thinking up deaths, and Alex prayed it had been quick for Fiona and she hadn't suffered too long.

The reason Maggie had let Alex live was now obvious. She never did intend for her to die, merely that she be destroyed. She would be blamed for all the deaths, including Fiona's, and Maggie would have made sure there was no way she could prove her innocence. She would eventually be declared sane, or not, depending on how she handled this situation; either way, she would be locked away for ever.

Her only hope now was the one person she hoped would visit – Greg Turner. He was a good man and he was adept at recognising when people told lies. He would know she was telling the truth.

Her heart lifted at the prospect and then quickly, like most of her hope that day, it was instantly crushed, leaving her feeling distraught. Greg Turner was an ordinary man dealing with an extraordinary killer. There was no way he could set her free.

CHAPTER FIFTY-ONE

Joe's face beamed at him through the car window as Greg waved goodbye. Clad in Spider-Man pyjamas, cheeks flushed and hair still sleep-tousled, he held on for dear life to the bright yellow toy helicopter he had been given. It had been a wonderful morning and now, guilt-free, Greg set the car in motion back to Bath.

At midday, as he drove through the outskirts of the city his mobile rang, and, pulling over into a lay-by, he took the call. The man's secretary had come up trumps. Greg had spoken to her while he was at his ex-wife's house and she had said she would do her best to get a hold of Robert Fitzgerald.

Robert Fitzgerald had an American accent and his voice was loud in Greg's ear. 'So what can I do for you, Inspector? My secretary said it was urgent.'

Greg held the mobile further away from his ear. 'It concerns Oliver Ryan. You represented him.'

'That's right, I did.'

'Could you tell me exactly when he died, and how?' All Greg had managed to find from his Internet search were the years for when the actor was born and had died.

'It happened in July. And it came as a complete shock,' Robert Fitzgerald answered. 'Oliver Ryan was a narcissist, and not someone I would ever have believed would do this. They didn't find any drugs in him at the autopsy, only alcohol. The only thing that I can think of is that it was a prank that went wrong. The coroner didn't buy it, though.'

'What did he do?'

'Hanged himself.'

'And why do you think this happened?'

'I dropped him. Told him that I didn't wish to represent him any more.'

'When was this?'

'The day before he killed himself.'

'Why did you drop him?'

'In a nutshell? The man was a loose cannon. I gave him a second chance last year after a bit of trouble he got himself into. Got him a few parts on prime time television in several dramas, kept him busy and in the eye of Joe Public. Then in July I was negotiating a lead part for him with a film producer, a sure winner, and what does he go and do? – gets himself in another jam. Only this time, there's no walking away from it. The woman rings me up, crying, wanting to know where Oliver is. She's pregnant, and lover boy has scarpered.

'Well, that was it. I saw red. I could see the road he was going down and knew that wherever he went scandal would follow. Put him in a big movie and it would just give him licence to create havoc. So we had a little chat and he walked out of my office as arrogant as when he walked in, threatening to sue me.'

Greg was mildly surprised. He would have thought it unlikely that an agent would dump someone over a bit of scandal, especially if they were about to get a big part. Maybe Robert Fitzgerald was a principled man.

He had been doing the maths in his head as soon as heard the word pregnant, and now wanted to know who the woman was.

'So this all happened in July? The negotiation for a new part and a woman ringing you to tell you she's pregnant?'

'All happened the same day, July 30. I'd spent most of the morning on the phone to the producer and his secretary discussing contract details. It gets to lunchtime and I'm about to ring Oliver to give him the good news. Only I get this other call from this pregnant woman.'

'Did she give her name?'

'No, and I didn't ask, but I reckon she was from Bath. She asked if I knew when he was coming back. I reckon she was either a nurse or a policewoman, because she asked me to tell Oliver she was on duty and could he call her workplace. The fool got into trouble with another woman there last year, and then goes back to the same place for more. Anyway, as I said, I saw red. I invited him over for a chat and gave it to him straight. Told him about the big part he was no longer getting and told him he was off my books for good. The problem with Oliver is he couldn't keep his pants zipped for five minutes.'

It had to be Amy Abbott he got pregnant, Greg thought. She was admitted to A & E in mid-November, and, according to the post-mortem, she was sixteen weeks pregnant.

He had used his ex-wife's computer to look up the actor and had gathered a brief history of his career. He would have to get more information on the man from other sources, and he would also have to re-examine Amy Abbott's and Lillian Armstrong's case files. Alex Taylor claimed that both women were killed by Maggie Fielding, but the reality was she had probably killed them herself. Laura Best was therefore right – Alex did have some form of Munchausen's, or else she had killed them in cold blood for having some involvement with Oliver Ryan. Maybe, as Caroline Cowan suggested, Alex got too involved and became obsessed by him.

'The woman from last year, what was that about?'

The American agent sighed. 'She was a doctor. Oliver was in her hospital learning the role of a doctor. Her boss rings me up after he's only been there a few days and requests that he doesn't come any more. She said there'd been a situation, that one of her doctors had been sexually assaulted. Oliver denied it, of course, and the doctor who made the complaint didn't go to the police, so nothing came of it.' The man paused. 'I didn't believe him for a minute. He was a danger where women were concerned.'

'Was there anyone special in his life?' Greg asked, and then decided to throw another woman's name into the equation. 'You ever hear of a Maggie Fielding?'

'No, never heard of her. But yes, there was someone special.'

Greg's chest momentarily tightened.

'Oliver Ryan. That was the only special someone in his life. There was no room for anyone else.'

His mood more sombre, Greg carried on driving, the conversation with the American playing in his mind. Fitzgerald didn't believe the actor had intentionally killed himself, but that it was an accident. Greg wondered if it was neither suicide nor accident. He would have to speak to the police who investigated the death. A vague memory of the man's face kept prodding him. He knew the memory could be from the TV, but somehow he didn't think so. He had a feeling he had met Oliver Ryan, but couldn't recall where.

Alex Taylor's apartment was still being searched, and he would head that way now and give them some help with what they should be looking for – links to Oliver Ryan, Amy Abbott and Lillian Armstrong. Even the old man she had nearly killed in the emergency department. They would run his name into the police computer on the chance that he was somehow connected.

If they proved that she had in fact killed all of these people, including Fiona Woods, her name would go down in history along with all the other notorious serial killers. And he would become known as the lead detective of the biggest murder case to ever hit Bath.

He felt no joy at the prospect. In the short time he'd known Alex Taylor she had wormed her way under his skin. Maybe the answer was to walk away. When this was over he could ask for a transfer to Oxford so that he could put it all behind him and be nearer his son. He could then see him more often, instead of trying to fit everything in on these quick visits. These last weeks had taught him one thing: going after someone you liked was the hardest thing.

A PC was in the process of shutting the front door, a roll of yellow police tape in his hand, ready to use. Greg asked him for the log book. He flicked through and saw that his team had vacated the flat at 12.15, an hour ago. He asked the officer if he knew why.

'I don't think they found much in there, sir. They were in there a few hours, took away a computer and a load of paper-work, but that's about it. With it being Christmas tomorrow I think they were hoping to get that lot sorted out back at the station. I'm just about to tape the door.'

Greg suspected that the team had chosen the easy option. He knew he should be annoyed with them, knew they would have searched the flat for obvious signs of the crime – blood-stained clothes, the blood of Fiona Woods – but in the short time they were in the place there was surely no way they could have searched it thoroughly. He suspected they had all knocked off early so that they could get to the pub and begin their Christmas celebrations.

He asked the constable to hold off putting the tape over the front door until he'd had a look. He pulled on shoe covers and gloved his hands. The lift behind him dinged as the doors opened and a man stepped out into the carpeted corridor. John Taylor was slim, grey haired and dressed in jeans and blue fisherman's jumper.

Greg could see a resemblance between him and his daughter in his cheekbones and the shape of his mouth. The man looked haunted, and Greg went to speak to him.

'Good afternoon, Mr Taylor. May I ask what you're doing here?'

He nodded at the front door. 'Probably the same as you – searching for answers. Only I'm looking for ones to prove her innocence.'

Greg nodded sympathetically. 'I can't let you in there, sir. I'm sure you realise why.'

The man looked down at the box marked 'major incident' set against the wall. It held white zip-up Tyvek suits, slipover plastic shoes, paper masks and gloves, so that whoever traipsed in and out of the place didn't leave any traces behind, or take trace evidence away with them. 'What about if I put that lot on?' Taylor said.

Greg shook his head and John Taylor sighed.

'My daughter is accused of a double murder. Now that may not mean much to you, you being a police officer, but she's my daughter and I know she's innocent, and so while you carry on trying to prove otherwise all I need is a few moments sitting in her place. They had her sedated up at the hospital, so I couldn't talk to her . . . I just need to feel near her.'

The anguish in the man's eyes grew and Greg made a decision. He might as well be hanged for a sheep as a lamb. He was already expecting a call from the superintendent over his misconduct with Laura. He pulled out a second pair of shoe covers and handed him a pair of gloves. 'Don't touch anything, and stay in my sight.'

The two men stepped into the flat and took in the quiet and ordered surroundings. It was nearly as immaculate as the last time Greg had visited. Not a shoe on the floor, or a newspaper discarded on the table, or a cushion out of place. If the other rooms were like this it was no wonder the officers had come and gone so quickly. It would have been an easy search.

The only thing marring the tidiness was the large painting partially unwrapped and resting on bubble wrap on one of the leather sofas. A slim cardboard box was leaning next to it. The painting showed a naked woman lying in a bed, her breasts bare and her hands tugging a red scarf, which was held in the hand of the man exiting the room, as if to pull him back to her. The colours were big and bold and bright. Alex's father hunched down and inspected it closely. Then he spoke: 'It is no new thing for the best of men to be falsely accused of the worst crime, by those who themselves are the worst of criminals.'

Greg didn't have a clue what he was on about. 'Meaning?'

'Genesis, chapter 39.'

Greg was surprised. 'Are you a religious man, Mr Taylor?'

'No. Merely interested in art. This is a modern version of *Potiphar's Wife*. There are several versions, but they all tell the same story.'

'Which is?'

'A powerful woman accuses her slave of rape. Joseph was a loyal slave and his master's wife tried to entice him into her bed. When he refused she told her husband that he had raped her and Joseph was put in prison.'

Greg stared at the painting some more, and then acting on instinct, he called Nathan Bell. He was in luck when the receptionist said he'd just come on duty. As soon as the man said hello, Greg cut in. 'Nathan. It's Greg Turner. The night you came to see Alex, was there a painting on one of the sofas?'

The doctor sounded remote, but his answer was immediate. 'Yes, she'd just received it, by the look of things. It was half unwrapped. Why?'

'Did she say if she'd bought it or where she got it from?'

'No, she didn't. Why? Is it important?'

Greg didn't know. All he knew was the story behind the painting was making him uneasy. Why would she buy herself a painting like this, especially in view of what she had accused Oliver Ryan of?

He heard an intake of breath on the end of the line and then Nathan Bell spoke again. 'It was a present! I asked her if it was from her old boyfriend and she said no. But it was a present – she told me it was.'

Alex Taylor's father was staring at him with hope in his eyes, but Greg wasn't yet ready to give him any. Aware that the man was listening, he spoke carefully to Nathan Bell. 'You remember the hospital underground we didn't get to explore?'

'Yes, of course.'

'Will you meet me there?'

'Yes. Give me an hour to sort out some cover and then meet me here.'

Greg turned to Alex Taylor's father. 'I must ask you to leave now as I have to head back to the station.'

The man nodded. 'I don't care where you're going as long as you're going in the right direction.'

Greg didn't know if he was. This could just be a blind alley and he could be building up hope only to have it suddenly come crashing down again. There was probably not the slightest chance of finding anything, but he had to try.

On the way out of the flat he gave instructions to the PC to ring the art gallery who sent the painting and find out who had purchased it, and then to contact him immediately.

CHAPTER FIFTY-TWO

It was while Maggie was cooking that she realised her mistake. The thought of Christmas Day and the presents she had bought triggered the memory. She had left evidence that could tie her to Alex Taylor. If they searched Alex's home and found the Christmas card she sent, even though she hadn't signed it, they might deduce that the written message was about the painting.

Simple mistakes like this could trip her up.

Especially in view of how much she'd accomplished. The killing of Amy Abbott had been no easy feat. When she'd woken strapped down on a theatre table the idea to kill her there and then was put on hold as a new idea began to form. To keep her alive would set in motion another way to destroy Alex Taylor. Keeping her alive for several days had been the real challenge. When her screams got too loud, Maggie had taped her mouth. Not for fear of her being heard, but the noise had been driving her mad.

In the end she'd become delirious, and with death imminent it had been easy to dispose of her in the hospital grounds. In her wildest dreams Maggie could not have foreseen that the nurse would still be able to talk. When she whispered, 'You said you'd help me,' she had of course been directing those last words to Maggie.

Now this memory was spoiled, the outcome no longer satisfying. She had ruined it by trying to be too clever. She had wanted Alex to live, to be destroyed. Now she had to change the ending.

The tomato sauce in the large pan began to bubble and she quickly lowered the heat. The pasta was ready, but she couldn't eat it now. Her appetite had gone with the thought of what she must do. The fragrant red liquid bubbling away was too red and too thin to look like blood, but she thought of it as blood as she imagined Alex Taylor dead.

Maggie wrung her hands in rage and frustration. Giving her the painting had been a mistake. She had wanted Alex to one day learn the meaning of the present, but now realised she had given the police evidence to question *her*.

She could say Dr Taylor had fallen in love with her version and had all but begged Maggie to get her one. She had taken pity on the woman and had agreed. She had not mentioned it when questioned, because she saw no point. But it was a chance she was not prepared to take. Once they started looking into her, they would start questioning staff about her movements that night, and her alibi would start to unravel. Like the fact that she had taken over midway through an operation to deliver twins, because her junior registrar was unable to cope. When she was bleeped by switchboard to attend the emergency department, she had said she couldn't, because she was in the middle of an operation. What she didn't want known was that her whereabouts were unaccounted for during the first part of the operation. She had to act quickly before Alex Taylor was set free.

Dylan moved close to the covered plate of pasta, chancing his luck to steal an exposed strand poking out from under the lid. Maggie watched the rat as its naked hands and long teeth gripped hold of the strand and dragged it away. Its round black eyes looked at her innocently, and while her feelings of hatred for Alex Taylor grew like a giant fist inside, she forgot that she quite loved the brown rat. Without hesitation she picked up the large pot of boiling red liquid and poured it all over him.

The rat squealed and shook itself violently to shake off the burning liquid. Its bulbous eyes turned white, and blindly and in agony it could find no relief as it skidded repeatedly on the wet surface. Maggie's heart was beating faster and the rat was squealing louder, and unable to think over the noise or turn away from the desperate creature she snatched it up and flung it hard against the kitchen wall. The rat fell to the floor and twitched for a few pitiful seconds, and then lay still.

For the first time since Oliver died Maggie Fielding cried.

'It's all their fault, Maggs,' he'd said, naming each of them. 'All their fault that I lost the part.'

He had taken her out to dinner and told her that his agent had dropped him and that he had lost the best part he was ever likely to have. None of it was his fault, he explained. These women targeted him.

Under the influence of alcohol and the reassurances she gave that he was not to blame, he told her about Alex Taylor. He told how the woman led him on all day and then rejected him. 'I'm a man, Maggs, not a saint. What was I to do? It was her fault that I went with a stupid tart. If she hadn't got me all fired up I wouldn't have needed to. It was only a release, Maggs. I just needed a release.'

Maggie refrained from asking him why he had gone back to Bath six months ago to seek release with yet another woman, this time leaving his seed behind. She'd found out about the nurse from the text messages he'd received. It was easy enough to track her down once Maggie moved to Bath.

She also refrained from telling him that she had been aware for some time of his need for other women – the pink business card she'd found, *Unwind with Lillian*, advertising the woman selling her wares.

'It was all their fault, Maggs,' he repeated again and again throughout the evening, and Maggie had wanted to believe him, until she went back to his place. Until he told her of his plans.

Nathan Bell wore a tailored jacket over his green A & E tunic and trousers. He and Greg both carried torches because the overhead fluorescent strip lights along the hundred-foot corridor were dim, their encasements coated with dirt, and barely lit the way.

They were standing roughly beneath the main theatre block, and Nathan pointed out the old disused lift shaft that used to carry staff and equipment down to the underground area. On the first and second floor above them the lift shaft had been walled up, and most people had no knowledge of its existence behind the plaster.

They looked in the lift and saw it was stacked with old bedside lockers, a couple of geriatric armchairs and a dismantled, old-style hospital bed with a brown rubber mattress. The disused lift had been used as a dumping site.

Miles of cable and pipes were attached to the low ceiling. Batting aside cobwebs and passing more abandoned equipment, they continued their search. The fragile hope Greg had felt earlier upon entering the underground area was diminishing fast. They hadn't found anywhere so far that resembled a theatre, and he wished he'd thought to ask Nathan to bring the floor plans.

At the end of the second corridor they reached a junction. Greg gave a nod to Nathan indicating that he would take the left. Ten minutes later they had returned to the junction and slowly and despondently headed back the way they had come. Their search was over, and unsuccessful.

'You know, if Alex is telling the truth, the real killer would have had to know about these underground corridors. And if Maggie Fielding is the killer, she must have had an accomplice. There's no way she could have carried Alex down here by herself,' Nathan commented.

'I was thinking nearly the same,' Greg answered, trying to imagine a woman carrying another person this far by herself. He suspected that it was highly unlikely that he and Nathan would come across this mysterious theatre, and that maybe there was no such place to be found.

Greg wondered about the painting. Could it have come from Oliver Ryan? He was dead. It was possible of course that before he died he'd arranged for it to be sent to her as a Christmas present.

A taunt, perhaps? Or maybe it was one of the dead women who had sent it? Maybe these women were dead because Alex Taylor had been in love with Oliver Ryan. Oliver Ryan—

He stopped dead. He remembered where he'd met Oliver Ryan before. He remembered the restaurant manager apologising to him for allowing the woman to disturb him. He remembered him trying to hide behind a menu, and at the time thought it was because he was embarrassed. But Oliver Ryan had been trying to hide his face because he thought he would be recognised, because his unwelcome visitor had been Lillian Armstrong – a woman that, in public, he clearly didn't want to be associated with. Especially as Lillian Armstrong – while telling everyone to piss off – had said she'd been invited.

At the time Greg hadn't believed her, but now he thought that maybe she *had* been invited. Maybe Oliver Ryan hadn't actually invited her into the hotel's restaurant, maybe it was only to his bedroom.

'We need to find proof that Dr Fielding was involved,' Nathan said.

Greg shook his head. 'We need to find proof that Alex is innocent. Otherwise it's game over.'

It was by sheer chance that he saw the outline of a door behind an upright bed base. His torch had glanced off it and he saw a metal plate on the wall. On closer inspection he saw the metal plate was attached to a door, a place where once a handle had been secured. Putting down his torch he moved the bed base to one side, and then prised the door open using his fingertips.

CHAPTER FIFTY-THREE

Jakie Jackson, as he was known to everyone, including his wife, was standing up to stretch his legs when the fire alarm went off. The sound box was on the wall outside the cubicle, and the whooping sound was deafening. His prisoner shot bolt upright, clearly terrified, and was trying to throw the blankets off and get out of bed.

Jakie saw how small and defenceless she was and felt sorry for her. He hadn't liked sitting in the room for most of the day. It felt strange to be guarding a doctor, and the truth of it was that to his experienced eyes she just didn't look like a killer. He knew he was being daft. There was no blueprint of a killer's face in any book. The stereotype of close-set-eyes and eyebrows that joined in the middle was just nonsense. A killer only looked like a killer when you knew they were one, and that's where he had a problem. This slip of a girl didn't look like one, even though he knew she was.

Over the screeching alarm he shouted to be heard. 'I'm just going to check if it's for real.' He held up a pair of handcuffs.

'Don't! Please! I'll stay here,' Alex shouted back.

Jakie Jackson hesitated. The doctor had yet to be officially arrested. His job was to guard her until DI Turner returned to do the deed. 'It'll only be for a minute.'

'Please, it could be real and you may not be able to get back to me. Please. I'll stay here. I'll wait for you. But don't leave me chained up.'

'Just let me check. It won't be real, and then I'll be back.'

The door burst open and a nurse frantically waved her hand at the police officer. 'Can I grab you? I need help quickly. The fire's real and I've got a patient trapped in a bathroom. Bloody door's jammed.'

Jakie Jackson did something he had never done in his thirty-four years on the force. He left his charge unguarded. 'I'll be back in a jiff.'

From along the corridor Maggie watched the people darting past her, nurses and porters pushing patients to safety on trolleys and in wheelchairs. Doctors were still trying to give treatments along the way. On Christmas Eve the place was packed with people rushed in from accidents, fights and illnesses, and then there were the ones who were there because they had been unable to get appointments with GPs and just wanted to be better for the big day tomorrow.

The tall burly police officer stood head and shoulders above most of them.

It was Nathan who spotted it, but he didn't need to explain what it was to Greg. Greg had seen plenty of needle caps on the ground before, in alleyways and on the floors of public toilets. The white plastic sheath was a protective cover for an injection needle.

Like an experienced detective, Nathan retrieved a rubber glove from his pocket. 'New. I haven't worn it,' he said of the glove. He wrapped the sheath in the glove and handed it to Greg.

'I'll bet you anything we won't lift a print. It's too small, and the killer would certainly have worn gloves as well.'

Nathan Bell gave a rare smile. 'You've never seen Maggie Fielding with a syringe in her hand. She always bites the cap off and keeps it like a matchstick in her mouth. You'll have DNA, Greg – even better than a fingerprint.'

With the fire alarm still screaming, Alex couldn't hear what was going on outside the room. She didn't want to risk bumping into the policeman, but knew that this would be her only chance of escape. Carefully she inched open the door and peered out. There was no sign of the police officer, or anyone else for that matter. She had been left behind while everyone else was hurrying out of the building. She could hear them down the corridor, their voices raised with excitement. She could smell smoke and suspected it was a rubbish bin set alight by someone – a patient, visitor or even staff – having a crafty cigarette in one of the cubicles.

Risking opening the door another few inches she saw the corridor was still empty. If she was going to escape she had to do it now, because there wouldn't be another opportunity. It was the first time she had been left entirely alone since being brought in last night. She must seize the moment to try and undo all the damage Maggie had done and somehow find a way to prove she was innocent. If she could contact Seb she would ask for his help. She needed time and a place where she could think. Out of everyone she knew he was the only one with the means to help her escape.

Before she could change her mind she quickly moved along the corridor; she could see the throng of people gathering outside through the windows. As she passed the staff room she slipped inside, and a couple of minutes later emerged dressed in a white doctor's coat and green tunic trousers. Her feet were bare, but there was nobody around to notice.

She would pass through the crowd. With all the commotion, she expected it to be easy. She stopped dead as she spotted the policeman outside and decided against this escape route. She would head to the north side of the hospital instead and leave that way. His back was towards her, and not wasting the opportunity she rushed past the windows, keeping her head down, and walked fast along the south corridor, taking quick checks over her shoulder to see if she was being chased. It was less noisy here; quiet enough to hear her own unsteady breathing. She heaved a jagged breath as she planned her next move. She needed to get to a phone, call Seb, and decide what to do. She needed clothes, money and proof that Maggie was guilty. She would find Oliver Ryan's agent, find out how he died, and find someone who knew he was involved with Maggie, someone who had seen them together.

Almost running now, she reached the end of the corridor, turned a sharp left, and then almost collapsed in fear as Maggie

Fielding gripped her by the neck and stuck something sharp into her skin.

'One word and I will cut your throat,' Maggie said in a vicious voice. Her face was white with hatred, and Alex could feel Maggie's hand shaking badly as she held the blade against her neck.

Keeping perfectly still, Alex tried to review her options. Fight Maggie off and risk being killed? Cooperate and face the threat of something worse? She thought of everything that had already happened to her and everything waiting to happen. She saw the ending clearly, like a film in her head, and then she made up her mind. She was tired of running and being afraid. She was tired of it all. She spread her feet apart, making sure she was properly balanced, and then swiftly, without hesitation she jerked her head to the side so that the blade sliced right across her neck. Her blood immediately began to flow and Maggie looked at her as if she had gone mad.

'You stupid woman, you've barely nicked the skin. I'm not going to kill you here, Alex, no matter how much you try to make me.'

Grabbing a handful of Alex's hair, Maggie jerked her head hard and pushed the blade into her side, piercing clothes and then flesh. Alex sucked in breath at the pain as the blade penetrated her body.

'Just enough pain to keep you in check,' Maggie growled into her ear. 'Now walk, and don't make me stab you harder.'

CHAPTER FIFTY-FOUR

Jakie Jackson scanned the empty room in the hope that Alex Taylor would somehow materialise. He was becoming frantic. He had already looked under the bed and checked the en suite shower room, and even gone back outside the department where everybody was gathering, but had seen no sign of her.

Taking out his mobile he called the station and asked for more officers to be sent so that a search for the missing doctor could be made. Then he ran back down the corridor to start the search alone. He felt relief when he saw his boss coming towards him. He didn't care about being in trouble. He only cared about the safety of the young woman left in his charge.

'Where is she?' Greg Turner asked, already guessing the situation.

Jakie didn't waste too much time explaining or wondering how his boss had got there so quickly. 'The fire alarm went off. I left her while I checked it out, and when I returned she was gone.'

'You let her escape?' Greg Turner yelled above the still shrilling fire alarm.

'Yes, and I've got a bad feeling about it, sir.'

Greg's phone vibrated against his chest. He pulled it out of his shirt pocket and stabbed a finger in one ear as he put the phone to the other. He was shouting down the phone when the fire alarm suddenly ceased. 'Who is it and what do you want?' he continued to shout in frustration.

'It's me, sir,' a voice came back. 'PC Norman. I got that information you wanted. On the painting.'

Greg's heart beat a little faster as he waited for a name to be given. The name of the killer, perhaps? For one awful moment he wondered if he would be given the name Alex Taylor. That it was she who sent the painting to herself. The name slipped off the young officer's lips and Greg was both shocked and relieved. Alex had been telling the truth, and he had thought it too far-fetched to be true.

'A Margaret Fielding. She paid by Visa and had it sent to the address I'm guarding.'

Greg thanked him and hung up. Then he faced Nathan Bell and Jakie Jackson. 'Let's find her.'

Her side was burning and Alex suspected the wound would require stitches – if she lived that long. For the third time in as many months Maggie had her strapped down on an operating table. Only this time she knew exactly which one she was lying on: the trauma theatre table. She had Velcroed her arms down and then bound them with bandages to secure them even tighter. She had used a sheet to bind her legs to the trolley and now stood over her with a scalpel in her hand.

'You get your wish, Alex. No more messing. We end it right here. They find you dead and pronounce it suicide.'

'Suicide?' Alex stared at her in disbelief. 'You stabbed me in the side and my neck is sliced. No one will believe it.'

Maggie gave no answer, but Alex didn't care. She felt no fear any more; her mind had grown immune to it. Her thoughts were now only of her mother, her father, Pamela and her dear friend.

'Why did you kill her, Maggie? Why Fiona?'

Maggie shook her head.

'Please . . .'

Maggie finally stared at her, and for the first time Alex thought she was looking at the real Maggie Fielding. A woman troubled by her conscience. Her chest heaved and then she looked away from Alex. 'She found me with your phone, and I tried to brush her off. She said she'd texted you, but that you hadn't replied. I said you'd just called your phone, that you'd realised you'd left it at work. Fiona didn't believe me. I said I was going to meet you and she could ask you herself. I told her where I was going and she marched away.' Maggie paused. The silence stretching. She seemed to be making up her mind about something. Then she locked eyes with Alex. 'If she hadn't looked back, I wouldn't have followed, but she did and she said, I don't believe you. What was I to do, Alex? Except to let it be thought that you had done something serious . . . like murder your best friend.'

'You'll go to hell for this, Maggie.'

In an instant the blade flashed in front of her eyes and she felt agonising pain as it sliced deep into her right wrist. Her blood spurted high and fast. Alex watched it splash the theatre lights above.

'I liked you, Maggie. I really did.'

The blade swiftly moved again, this time slicing through her left wrist. The pain was worse because she was expecting it. She felt her hand become quickly wet and her fingers were warm and slippery.

She was dying. Within a few minutes her heart would stop. Her birthday was next month, but she would never reach the age of twenty-nine. She breathed in deeply and felt the thud of her heart beneath her breastbone.

'Hold my hand, Maggie,' she whispered. 'Don't let me die alone.'

There was no response, because Maggie had moved away from the table, but Alex knew she was still there. She was waiting for her to die. Then she would undo the straps and leave the blade beside her so that whoever found her would think she had taken her own life. Her other wounds might be considered previous attempts. Maggie was going to win in the end, and everyone who had ever known or loved Alex would think she had died a murderer.

Her mouth was dry and her body felt cold. She could no longer see the arc of her blood nor feel the pound of her heart. She was floating, and a gentle buzzing rang in her ears.

Then her eyes fluttered closed.

They were following the regular pattern of blood along the corridor, each man silent, each worrying about what they would find. But the blood that led them to the operating theatre in no way prepared them for the sight they were presented with. It was on the floor on each side of the operating table. All three men stood still at the theatre doorway. There was too much of it. Pints of the stuff had been spilled; it had settled thick and red and had spread as far as it could go. Alex lay on an operating table with her arms strapped down and her head to one side.

Nathan was the first to rush forward, throwing out commands to the other two as he ran to her side. 'Ring 333. Tell them it's in trauma theatre. Pull that emergency red button on the wall behind me and grab any cloths you can and cover this floor. Greg, get over here and help me.'

Jakie Jackson went to the phone and Greg, careful not to slip in the blood, went and joined the doctor.

'Take off your tie and tie it hard around her wrist and then raise her arm above her head.'

While Greg did as he was told, Nathan attached a blood pressure cuff around her other wrist and pressed a switch on a machine so that the cuff quickly inflated and acted as a tourniquet. He then took a regular tourniquet and pulled it tight around Greg's tie. He pressed a foot pedal and the head of the operating table lowered. Then he rushed to a drawer and pulled out orange cannulas. 'Lift her chin and put your ear to her mouth and check if she's breathing.'

Greg again did as he was told while Nathan got two large intravenous needles into her arms. He grabbed two bags of fluids and within seconds had them attached to drip lines and had fluid pouring into Alex's veins. 'Can you feel her breathing?'

Greg raised desperate eyes and shook his head. Nathan took his place at the head of the table and at the same time placed two fingers against her throat. 'She's got a pulse, but she's not breathing. Breathe into her mouth, Greg, until I get the oxygen on and bag her. Pinch her nostrils, tilt her chin and cover her mouth with your own.'

Her lips were cool against his lips and Greg felt his insides quiver in panic. *You mustn't die*, he prayed. *You're too young. Fight, Alex. Please, please fight.*

He was grateful as Nathan took over the job with an inflated bag and mask. He took a gulp of air and tried to calm himself and then he saw her chest rise. 'Is she breathing?'

'Not on her own yet. She's too weak. Greg, I want you to bag her. I want you to do exactly what I'm doing. I need to get more fluids into her ASAP. And I need to get blood fast.'

Over the next few minutes several people arrived, and twenty minutes later the place was swarming with activity. Two bags of blood had already replaced some of what Alex had lost, and a third and fourth were hung ready to flow through a blood warmer.

Greg was leaning against a wall out of the way of everyone. Jakie Jackson was against another, looking shell-shocked. He had rung the station and alerted them to arrest Maggie Fielding on sight. Greg didn't care about the capture of the other woman; he could only think about Alex. He could tell that she wasn't out of the woods yet. He could hear them talking about clotting factors and about the fact that she had lost so much blood that the new blood was unable to clot. He imagined her blood being too thin, less sticky, like watered-down tomato sauce. His eyes were fixed on her chalky face and he found himself praying like he had never prayed before.

A trio of miniscule tubes were inserted into her neck. Cannulas were in both her arms. Another cannula was placed in her groin artery so that her blood pressure could be monitored accurately, and a urinary catheter had been positioned into her bladder so that they could watch her output. Several pieces of complicated equipment surrounded her. She was on a ventilator and her body was covered with the thinnest lightweight plastic, which looked like it would easily tear. They were waiting until she was stable before they could move her to intensive care. He heard someone mention that she had a sixty to seventy per cent blood loss, and from the strain on Nathan Bell's face she was clearly critical.

A couple of times nurses had looked at Greg pointedly, clearly indicating they thought he shouldn't be in the theatre, but he had no intention of leaving either Alex or Nathan Bell. If the outlook was bleak he wanted to be there for both of them.

A surgeon was suturing the arteries in her wrists and an anaesthetist was monitoring her airway. There was tension in the air, as the crisis was clearly not over.

CHAPTER FIFTY-SIX

It was Laura Best who brought the news to Greg. Maggie Fielding had been declared dead outside the hospital after being hit by an ambulance and a bus. Both drivers were being treated for injuries in A & E. The second crew member in the ambulance had also been admitted with a suspected heart attack. And a baby was delivered at the scene as its mother died.

Greg felt the news like a depression. She had taken another life, and two were still in the balance. Alex's condition was still critical, which was why he was still at the hospital.

Laura Best held a clipboard in her hands as if she were doing a tour of inspection. Her chocolate suit and cream shirt were of good quality. Her hair shone and her skin and make-up were immaculate. She would one day reach the higher ranks, if only because she looked good.

'Is Alex Taylor up to talking?' she asked.

He raised his eyebrows. 'What do you think?'

She tapped her pen on the clipboard impatiently. 'I'm asking you, Greg.'

He snatched the pen out of her hand and snapped it in two. 'You will address me as Inspector, DC Best. Why do you want to speak to Dr Taylor?'

Her face flushed and her eyes immediately sparkled with temper. 'Because I want to clear up this mess and all the rubbish I'm now hearing about her being innocent.'

Before Laura Best knew what was happening or could utter a word of protest, Greg dragged her halfway down the theatre corridor. He shoved her through the double doors and let her see the place where Alex Taylor almost died. The blood-soaked cloths and towels still lay on the floor, the equipment used to save her life left abandoned. They had only just moved her down to ITU, and no one had yet had a chance to clean up.

'That blood you see is Alex Taylor's blood. She is fighting for her life, you stupid woman!'

Laura's face had now gone white. 'Well, she tried to kill herself, didn't she? Jakie Jackson let her escape. She was bound to try and commit suicide.'

Greg clamped his hands around her shoulders and dragged her over to the operating table. He pointed at the blood-stained arm-rests. 'Alex Taylor was strapped to this table, her arms pinned, her legs bound, unable to defend herself, and Maggie Fielding slit her wrists and left her here to die. Everything Alex Taylor told us was true. All of it. Maggie Fielding abducted her and put her through unimaginable torture. She killed Amy Abbott, Lillian Armstrong, Fiona Woods, and tonight she attempted to murder Alex Taylor.

'You were wrong, DC Best, and so was I. But guess what? I'll probably get a promotion for collaring Maggie Fielding, while you, Laura Best, all the time you're working for me, will stay a DC. So you might want to think about a transfer, far away from me, where you can dig your spurs into some other fool's back.'

There was a brief silence after she left the theatre suite before Nathan took her place. 'I take it that was personal?'

Greg shook his head. His voice was firm. 'No, not any more. That was professional.'

Nathan gave a faint smile. 'Alex is stable. She's going to make it.'

Then Nathan suddenly doubled over and vomited. Greg grabbed the only clean cloth he could find, discarded swabs from the suture tray, and handed them to him.

He felt the depression inside lift as hope took its place. 'That's great news, Nathan. You're a bloody good doctor.'

Nathan shrugged, spitting hard before wiping his mouth. 'I had a good assistant.'

Greg remembered her cold bloodless lips beneath his own and knew that it had been a close call. He looked at the two clocks on the far wall – one counting minutes and the other simply telling the time – and was shocked to see it had just gone midnight. 'What time do you knock off?'

'Four hours ago,' Nathan replied.

'You want a Christmas drink?'

Nathan nodded. 'Yeah. A big one. A hell of a big one.'

They walked back along the corridor, seeing Alex's blood still on the floor. It had dried now and would soon be washed away. Greg kept his eyes on the trail all the way down the corridor, and then suddenly he realised: Alex had let them know where she was being taken. She had led them to her. He didn't know how she did it, but he was sure she had somehow let herself get cut so that she could leave them this trail.

His admiration grew stronger. She was the bravest person he knew – in the face of no one believing her, she still coped.

Alex opened her eyes and knew she was safe. She could hear ventilators and monitors beeping and the noise of colleagues working. Nathan was the first face she had seen when she opened her eyes earlier, and he had quickly reassured her that everyone knew she was innocent and that the police were now out looking for Maggie Fielding. He had also spoken to Patrick and let him know that she was safe. Patrick, he said, had cried. Nathan said it in a way that would allow her to forgive Patrick. Allow her to walk away from Nathan.

She had seen the greyness in his face and the strain in his eyes and, separated from all other emotion, standing alone, she saw his uncertainty. Questioning his right to be in her life? They had only just begun the first step on this new path. It was a beginning. When he placed his hand against her cheek she had leaned into its warmth.

Maybe one day she would tell him how she had tried to kill herself. The clear decision she had made as Maggie Fielding abducted her in the corridor. She had so badly wanted to die there and then, and put an end to her fear. It hadn't mattered to her in that second as she sliced her neck along the blade that she would die – only that it would be over.

Maybe one day she would tell him when she was brave again. When she accepted that she was Alex Taylor, a doctor who saved people's lives, who had faced things that most people can't even imagine . . .

ACKNOWLEDGMENTS

This book would not have been possible without the support and encouragement from my husband, Mike, our three children, Lorcan, Katherine, and Alexandra, and daughter-in-law, Harriet. You guys inspire me daily with your utter selflessness and determination to be good people. Thank you for allowing me time to finally finish!

Thank you also to my six brothers and five sisters, especially to Sue, Bernie, and brother-in-law, Kevin, for reading the earlier drafts—how lucky are we to have shared so much, especially our incredible parents.

A very special thank-you to Dr Monica Baird, consultant anaesthetist, and Dr Peter Forster, MBBS, FRCA, for their generous time and expertise. Thank you both so very much. Any mistakes are of course mine!

Thank you to Martyn Folkes for always keeping opinions honest!

Last but not least, thank you to Joel Richardson, editor and publisher extraordinaire. Thanks to you and the amazing team at Twenty7 for making this book the very best it could be.

Without working in the medical profession, I would not have been able to draw on past experiences (I promise no nasty stuff ever happened, bar eating patients' leftover cold toast), and I would not be able to give true praise to the medical and police professionals out there fighting the good fight to make all our lives better. There are no finer people.

For you, Mum—who I miss sharing books with.

And for Darcie—who I love reading to.

ABOUT THE AUTHOR

Born in Chatham, England, and partly raised in Dublin, Ireland, Liz Lawler is one of fourteen children and grew up sharing socks, pants, stuffed bras, and a table space to eat at. Liz spent more than twenty years working as a nurse, and has since worked as a flight attendant and as the general manager of a five-star hotel. She now lives in Bath with her husband. *Don't Wake Up* is her first novel.